Leslie Halliwell was born in Bolton. He buys most of the feature films and series screened by the ITV network and goes twice a year to Hollywood in search of them; he has been an enthusiast for the mediums since childhood. He has managed several Rank Organisation and specialist cinemas and is a member of two National Film Archive committees.

Ghost stories are a new departure for the indefatigable author of *Halliwell's Filmgoer's Companion, Halliwell's Film Guide* and *Halliwell's Hundred*. Yes, there *is* a haunted cinema in *The Ghost of Sherlock Holmes*: but only in the preface.

G000150885

By the same author

Halliwell's Filmgoer's Companion
Halliwell's Film Guide
Halliwell's Hundred
The Filmgoer's Book of Quotes
The Clapperboard Book of the Cinema (co-author)
Mountain of Dreams
Halliwell's Teleguide

LESLIE HALLIWELL

The Ghost of Sherlock Holmes

Seventeen Supernatural Stories

PANTHER
Granada Publishing

Panther Books
Granada Publishing Ltd
8 Grafton Street, London W1X 3LA

Published by Panther Books 1984
A Panther Book Original

Copyright © Leslie Halliwell 1984

ISBN 0-586-05995-4

Printed and bound in Great Britain by
Collins, Glasgow

Set in Baskerville

These stories are dedicated to
STANLEY LEATHERBARROW
who introduced me to M. R. James
and is no mean ghost writer himself

Contents

Preface

Some of these tales are written in the first person singular, but the 'I' is seldom the same person, and almost never me. All are fancies, though I willingly admit that one is based on an extremely vivid dream of my youth, and that two others are elaborations of apparently supernatural moments from my waking experience. Most of the rest spring from a feeling for places I have visited, though oddly enough none are based in Hollywood, where business takes me so regularly, and only one in California. Perhaps that west coast civilization is too new and too sunny to attract the other world, even to San José's Winchester House of Mystery, which was built to a deliberately eccentric design for the specific purpose of baffling any evil spirits which might happen along, with doors that lead into brick walls and stairs rising only into the ceiling.

The nearest I came to being scared by a monstrous apparition in California was on a brief visit south to La Jolla, a seaside resort pronounced in the Spanish fashion La Hoya. Normally the sunniest of spots with the purest air, on this particular Saturday afternoon in January it was afflicted by fog which began to roll in as we drove through San Juan Capistrano, and although patches of sun broke it up in spots, by the time I unpacked my overnight bag at Sea Lodge the ocean fifty feet away had disappeared behind a thick, grey, misty barrier. Leaving my companion immersed in a television re-run of THE JOLSON STORY, I strolled on to the almost deserted beach and walked along it, just out of reach of the lapping waves, where strange little birds like miniature seagulls raced in and out of the thin layer of water. A jogger overtook me and vanished into the gloaming. An old man with a stick came the other way. There was also a solitary dog. The fog clammily embraced my hair and facial skin, and had brought in with it tiny wisps of some black oily substance which attached itself to the pupils of my eyes and made me feel half-blind and dizzy. As I took my glasses off to wipe them I heard a curious sound from the direction of the sea. Bobbing about on the waves, maybe twenty yards out, was what I took to be an enormous black jellyfish, or perhaps the corpse of one. As I watched, it seemed to grow larger, and began unmistakably to emerge. I had the impression, out of focus without my glasses, of a single giant eye, a coloured proboscis . . . it was a little like the alien in IT CAME FROM OUTER SPACE. I backed away as it seemed to sense my presence and advanced clumsily towards me, its base still in the water through which it dragged its squat, ugly being. I wanted to yell for help, but in accordance with tradition my voice had frozen in my throat, my eyes were hypnotized by what they saw and my feet seemed incapable of taking me anywhere. The fog closed in round my back like a wall as the unspeakable thing lumbered with difficulty out of the water towards me, looking more misshapen every second. Not until it stretched out a horrid black flipper in greeting did I recognize it at last . . . as a frogman in a wetsuit.

Readers may wonder why a cinema encyclopaedist includes no stories set in cinemas. I am inclined to say that I despair of producing frissons comparable with those achieved by Graham Greene in his story A LITTLE PLACE OFF THE EDGWARE ROAD. But the truth is that cinemas are rather boring places, empty of detail and personality: all the emotion is up there on the screen. I was once told an allegedly true story about a woman who was taken to the pictures and, because she had a stiff leg, chose the one single seat at the side of the circle where she could stretch out the deficient member by the wall without the likelihood of anybody falling over it. Her husband sat across the aisle, and halfway through the feature noticed his wife signalling to him in some distress. She was feeling very ill, sickly and breathless, and had to be escorted outside. He got her into the open air, where she promptly recovered, and indeed couldn't imagine what had been the matter; so after a little while they went sheepishly back to their seats. Twenty minutes later the same thing happened again, so this time they went straight home and called the doctor, who came but could find nothing wrong. Next day the husband called on the cinema manager with the intent of finding out whether there was possibly a broken gas pipe near the seat his wife had occupied, in which case it would be well to take steps to prevent other patrons from being similarly afflicted. The manager willingly went to look, but there was no such clue, and the husband sensed a hesitation in the man when he saw which seat it was. It didn't take long to get at the truth. That had been the favourite seat of a youngish woman who had been sitting in it when her purse was snatched by a passing thief, who stabbed her when she screamed. She died in hospital. A little perplexed, the husband went straight to the local newspaper office to check the story. When he saw the dead woman's name he took a photocopy home and after some hesitation showed it to his wife, who half-collapsed when she read it. The woman murdered in that seat was her own twin sister, from whom she had not heard for eight years.

I suppose I never wrote up that story because, even if true, it was too coincidental to seem plausible. Hopefully a few of the following pieces of fiction may strike the reader as more likely.

Leslie Halliwell
Kew, 1983

The Late Mr Llewellyn

This rather neat little story was told to me as an actual event
by an elderly lady whom I knew very well indeed and in
whom I trusted absolutely. She would be quite incapable of
making up such a thing, and in saying that, I bear in mind
her limited imagination as well as her extreme moral
rectitude. I should add that she was my Great Aunt Hester,
and the fact that she recently died, quite happily, at an
advanced age, enables me to share her remarkable anecdote
with a wider audience. She was amused enough by it to tell
it to me and to several close friends and family members
(some of whom didn't believe it at all) but she always
shunned the public spotlight.

I am speaking of a time fifteen or more years ago, when
Hester could no longer describe herself as middle-aged; but
luckily she had acquired no physical infirmities and was
possessed of a personality and drive as indomitable as in her
youth. Oddly enough, although we were two generations
removed, Hester was no more than twenty years older than
me, she being the youngest of my mother's aunts, and I
being an eldest son: so we were almost as close as
contemporaries. She had never married; she saw no need of
any official blessing on her fairly romantic and varied life. 'I
may be a miss,' she was known to assert, 'but I haven't
missed.' Quite the reverse: from what I heard, she struck
several bull's-eyes. One way and another she always had
enough money to live comfortably without working very
often to augment her resources. Throughout the war and for
some time after she was in the WVS and never earned a
penny, but she didn't go short. In her youth she travelled the

world, but from her mid-forties she restricted herself more or less to the British Isles, and indeed wrote a book about the lonely shores of Sutherland which was thought to be of considerable merit. Slim of figure and somewhat acerbic of tongue, she was always pottering in cathedral cities or driving off to some remote peninsula or another, buying antiques, lovingly restoring them, and re-selling them at a modest profit to people who would give them a good home. This passion extended to houses: in her later life she bought about six remotely rural sows' ears and turned them into silk purses, meriting a mention or two in *Country Life*.

From about fifty, she took with her on all her travels a paid companion–housekeeper. The first of these worthy ladies died after a few years, but the second, whom I knew only as Miss Rose, an efficient but rather mousey creature of indistinct personality, was faithful to the end. Aunt Hester's end, that is. At times the menage reminded me very much of that of David Copperfield's Betsy Trotwood, except that in this case there was a female Mr Dick (and no donkeys). Nor did Aunt Hester ever have a house on Folkestone cliff; but I remember with great affection a little misshapen Tudor barn on a slope of Leith Hill, a tiny Victorian villa squeezed into Salisbury's cathedral close (or rather just behind it), a draughty old farmhouse near Honiton, and in the main street of Chipping Campden a terraced property which seemed to belong in an *Alice in Wonderland* illustration, with a perpetual tea party on a lawn which might well have accommodated a white rabbit or two in the long grass. Inside all was silver teapots and copper kettles and horse brasses and antimacassars, and Hester briefly took to behaving the part by wearing a white bonnet, which didn't suit her at all and made her look old. She didn't care about that. She loved life while she had it, and couldn't bear to be bored. Indeed, I can't conceive that she ever was, not even for a minute. I miss Aunt Hester.

For whatever reason (probably the right customer) it was this Cotswold paradise she deserted, at the time of which I speak, to go to Tenby in Pembrokeshire. 'Why Tenby?' I asked her, for I well remembered her once announcing an intense dislike for all things Welsh, especially for Mr Lloyd George, whom she regarded as directly responsible for the death of her elder brother in the first world war. She retorted that she was inflexible on the point, but surely everyone knew that Tenby was not in Wales but in Little England Beyond Wales? Having come across the phrase in a guide book, I had to concede the point. On a short holiday visit to this country of cliffs and castles she had, I gathered, found herself the most delightfully situated thatched cottage on the slopes of the Prescellies – the hills, she reminded me irrelevantly, from which the Stonehenge monoliths were quarried. It had a wide and distant view of the sea, and from the garden there was a wonderful sense of open sky which made it the most rapturous place to be on a summer's day. I can confirm all this from a visit I made some months after Hester had completed her improvements, though I should add that in my view it was somewhat more than a cottage, having upstairs four bedrooms and two bathrooms, impeccably modernized and chintzified; downstairs it was all polished wood floors and casemented leaded windows. Although my suspicion was that it dated back no further than 1895, with a log fire burning it was the very quintessence of olde English comfort.

My story concerns the first weeks of Hester's occupancy, a period which was very nearly not extended. The house had previously belonged to Mr and Mrs Llewellyn, a fairly well to do old couple whose fortunes had been amassed in trade. Mr Lucas Llewellyn was in fact the deviser, producer and distributor of a form of toffee apple which in distant days had taken the Welsh resorts by storm. To this popular line he naturally added others, and by the time he retired in favour of his sons Mr Llewellyn could point to a range of products extending to some twenty-five items, including Welsh Allsorts, St David's Rock, and the famous Llewellyn's Lollipops, on the colourful wrappings of which his rubicund visage appeared in facsimile. Mr Llewellyn belied his benevolent image. He was in life a large, uncouth, rather bullying man, or so the estate agent told Hester in confidence; his wife walked in his shadow, and had withdrawn into a rather wizened shell. All Mr Llewellyn's talent and virtue, in fact, went into his toffee-making; when he had recently died, the vicar had had a job to recruit six men willing enough, and strong enough, to be pallbearers.

The widow's intention was to live with a sister in Tenby, all her relations being local; and Aunt Hester happened along on the very day that the property was first put on the market, before the details had even been typed out. An interview was promptly arranged with the grieving relict, and proceeded well despite Hester's initial dislike of the latter's Welsh chapel manner. Mrs Llewellyn proved indeed to be as devious as Hester was direct. The agent had said that valuable furniture and fittings were included in the asking price, but on enquiry these items turned out to be not only very few but of such dubious practical value that most of them must needs be put out with the dustbins. Hester did specifically remark on a carved oak sideboard which stood oddly in one of the bedrooms. The subject provoked a flood of tears, for it transpired that the item was Mr Llewellyn's own bachelor dresser, a piece he had brought into the family as a new bridegroom and used lovingly for nigh on fifty years. Alas, there was no room for it where the widow was going, and so she would be prepared to make the supreme sacrifice on the altar of commerce; but only if the right price were offered. The sum suggested was at the top end of the dresser's market value, but Hester was willing enough to pay it. She also took at the asking price, in order to show her willingness to fit into the widow's scheme of things, a wrought iron lamp standard and a butler's table. There remained the question of the house itself. The tour, led by the tearful widow, was especially embarrassing in the case of two small northward-facing ground floor rooms: these, it seemed, were piled high with the late toffee-maker's personal effects, sight of which was guaranteed to drive the widow into a further paroxysm of grief. She therefore begged Hester not to insist on an examination at that time. Hester shrugged, and promptly began negotiations with a once and for all price which fell ten per cent short of that being asked. It was received in a flood of tears by the widow but accepted by the agent on the way back to town, with occupancy available as soon as the deeds were drawn. Not until a month later was Hester able to make an unfettered tour of the property; she was displeased but not entirely surprised to find that the two prohibited rooms, now empty, displayed unmistakable patches of damp.

A little damp, however deviously it became her responsibility, was not something about which she wished to cavil, and when her surveyor commented adversely upon it she waved him away. A small army of workmen would shortly set to work at her behest, and could deal with the damp at the same time as the blocked chimney, the broken casements, and the locks which didn't always lock: the total cost would be reflected in her own asking price when she came to sell the property. Meanwhile the house had infinite possibilities and she proposed to explore them all, doing her own minor repairs and decoration once the property was sound, dry and well-protected. At least the attractively-styled thatch needed no renewal at the moment, according to the honest foreman of the team which went in to paint, to wax, to repair, to mow and to point. (In Wales at that time it was apparently possible to find men ready and willing to do such work at quite reasonable rates.) Within three months of her first sight of the house, Hester was able to drive Miss Rose down bag and baggage to share it with her, and to direct the arrangement of their favourite furniture to its most pleasing effect. Mr Llewellyn's dresser, as it happened, was given pride of place in the newly-designed parlour, full in the light of the windows which looked down to the sea.

The trouble began on the very first night. Hester was something of a television addict, and had left off her housewarming processes in order to watch Panorama, followed by the news and a Charles Laughton film. Miss Rose had just brought in the chocolate Horlicks when they heard the front door blow open. It was indeed a stormy night, but the lock was new, and Hester's lips set in displeasure.

'Goodness,' she said, 'a hurricane must have come up; and one of us must have failed to shut the door properly. You stay where you are.'

She went out of the room and was both impressed and bewildered to see through the open front doorway a cluster of bright stars hanging in the stillest of skies over the sea; the wind was clearly all at the back of the house, blowing from the north, and the actual storm had long since spent itself. She examined and tried the new lock on the door; it seemed to click easily and firmly into place. Yet it had opened of its own accord: how very odd. After several more trials she closed the door with her fingertip and rattled the handle hard: it stayed closed. With a shake of the head she returned to her fireside.

The next thing the two women heard was something being thrown about upstairs: slippers, it sounded like, or a book, and it was followed by the indistinct sound of footsteps, muffled as though heard by a slightly deaf person. Miss Rose promptly displayed symptoms very like hysterics, and Hester had to calm her with brandy, then bring her back with smelling salts; before she did so, however, she took the precaution of snicking the bolt on the parlour door and feeling very glad she had insisted on it as a double protection. She was then prepared to sit out the siege as long as necessary until the police arrived, but on the point of calling them it occurred to her that she had forgotten the back stair, being unused to having such a thing. Too late now: the footsteps were quite suddenly in the room next to the one in which they were sitting, that is to say in the kitchen. 'This is ridiculous,' said Hester, and arming herself with a poker she stormed into the still untidy centre of their future cuisine. There was of course nobody there: but as she stood in the doorway, more taken aback than she had ever been in her life, the footsteps appeared to brush past her, with a chill sensation, on their way into the parlour she had just left. More furious than scared, Hester ran to take Miss Rose in her arms as they watched a most curious spectacle: the drawers of the Welsh dresser were opening of their own volition, or as if pulled by an invisible agency. Each opening was followed by a slamming shut, as though a large and bad tempered man were impatiently looking for something and not finding it. The unseen presence then turned its attention, as Hester and Miss Rose crouched petrified, to almost every available cupboard on the ground floor, though halfway through this process its power seemed to ebb, and within ten minutes of its first calling attention to its activities, the disturbance died away much as a wave sends itself on the sand, leaving in its wake two extremely distressed gentlewomen.

What Hester said to Miss Rose, or heard in return, is immaterial; one can imagine which of them was first to recover. They spent that night in the same bed, and their sleep was fitful indeed; but Hester was not one to be intimidated, whether by beings temporal or beings spiritual. Next morning at nine she was at the estate agent's office in a fine state of indignation, dragging Miss Rose behind her in a

mixture of hysterics and perplexity. Perplexity was also the
agent's state after her recital, for in all his long years in
business, as he said, he had never before come across
anything *peculiar*. Mrs Llewellyn was duly called on the
telephone, and sharply repudiated any suggestion that the
house was haunted; if the new tenants had experienced
anything of that kind, she seemed to imply, then they must
have brought the malign influences with them. Nor was she
interested in reacquiring the dresser which had been so close
to her heart, not even at ten per cent off. One would have
thought that the whole story had been concocted expressly
to annoy her.

Hester was not even sure that the dresser was the centre of
the curious activity; but the ghost's interest in it did seem to
indicate a connection with the previous owner. She persuaded Miss Rose that it was probably a momentary
spiritual aberration, ascribable to the psychic disturbance
brought about by new ownership. Alas, that evening the
performance was repeated, more or less as before but about
half an hour earlier. The two ladies sat it out doggedly, Miss
Rose rather less so than Hester despite having been
previously fortified with brandy and peppermint. At the
height of the haunting Hester whispered to her, with a
conviction remarkable in the circumstances, that there was
no record of any ghost ever having hurt anybody, especially
when invisible. At that moment a brass ashtray came
whizzing across the room and fell into the coal scuttle.
Hester felt impelled to be cheerful, like the people who sang
'Nearer My God to Thee' as the *Titanic* went down. 'Just
ignore him,' she said. 'It's probably only that unpleasant Mr
Llewellyn who's got lost on some foggy astral plane and come
back to look for his wife. I don't suppose he was very
competent without her. We've just got to show him that
however much she knuckled under to him, he can't bully us
instead.'

The night passed as before, and on the following morning, observing that Miss Rose had not been entirely comforted by her impromptu repartee, Hester spoke on the telephone to the vicar. The Reverend Stanley was round within the hour, rather as though a good haunting was exactly what he needed to put some zest into the familiar round of baptisms and burials. That evening he came at seven and stayed until eleven, getting through more than his share of seed cake; but in his presence the intruder obstinately refused to intrude, and Hester was most embarrassed. The vicar pooh-poohed her apologies and left with her the audio tape recorder which he habitually used to try out his sermons. This came in handy on the following evening, when the full programme of thuds, slams and scrapes started at nine-fifteen and ended some fifteen minutes later with a massive reverberation when the front door was thrown to; yet sad to say, when Hester played back the tape later, quite convinced that she had pressed the right buttons, not a sound came through. In exasperation she packed Miss Rose off to a hotel for the following weekend, and determined herself, alone, to sit out the siege. The vicar had whispered something about exorcism, but she regarded that as the very last resort, fearing that some good spirits might be sent packing along with the bad, like a detergent which cleans too well and leaves a fabric in tatters. All she had to do, she told herself, was to make Mr Llewellyn (for she was reasonably convinced that it was he) understand clearly that the house now belonged to another and that if he was a gentleman he would take his leave once and for all. As for the dresser, he really couldn't have much use for that in the after-life. No doubt its presence had made it easier for him to return, but what he really wanted was surely the wife who had been his support for fifty years. She couldn't have much of an aura, Hester reflected, if the pull of the house was stronger than hers; but then it was difficult to imagine any man wanting that particular woman back once he'd rid himself of her. 'Birds of a feather, I suppose,' said Hester rather obscurely.

That night she paid the local handyman five pounds to sit in his car in the drive until midnight in case she called for his help by striking the large Burmese gong which she had moved to within reach of her armchair. The sound of it, she told herself, would surely deafen any ghost which had ears to hear. Neither handyman nor gong were in fact used. Hester had primed herself well with Dutch courage, and when the front door opened of its own accord at eight forty-five she took another gulp for good measure. Just as soon as the presence came into the parlour – without so much as a by your leave, she told me disapprovingly – she gave it a sizeable piece of her mind, starting off with a reproof for shaming two innocent ladies in front of their vicar by failing to appear as scheduled, especially as it must have been clear to any self-respecting ghost that all three only wished to be of assistance. 'If you *really are* old Mr Llewellyn,' she added, 'I can only say how glad I am that I didn't have to put up with your bullying ways when you were alive. I don't know what you're coming back for, but all I can offer you is one of your old collar studs which I found in a crack in the dresser. The dresser itself is paid for, and having been in trade you will respect that, I am sure. The same applies to the butler's table and the lamp standard. Everything else has been carted away, and your wife is in Tenby, at number 31 Bullivant Road, so please go and do some haunting there, and leave me entirely alone.' Hester felt that her provision of this last piece of information was only just in view of the damp patches, but the ghost showed no sign of noting it anyway. Hester's tirade seemed only sporadically to interrupt the normal programme of violent noises, though the manifestations did finish a little earlier than usual.

After that evening, Hester felt herself to be at least Mr Llewellyn's equal, and expressed herself as convinced that his power was limited to frightening those of weak mind and nerve. She did not include herself in that category; and so sent away her bodyguard and next evening she did her needlework unperturbed throughout the performance, looking up only once at a quiet moment to say: 'I've told you what I think of you, Mr Llewellyn. I have no further comment to make.' She did not look up again until the performance was over, when she sighed and rested her elbows on the chair arms. 'He must be on one of those very primitive astral planes,' she told herself, 'with an extremely limited sense of his powers in the other world. Ah, well, no doubt he will improve. After all, a puppy is blind for ten days when it starts its new life.'

On Sunday Miss Rose came back, shaky of appearance and manner but determined to desert her mistress no longer. Hester was grateful, but dubious of her friend's constitutional ability to stand up to much more supernatural battering. They therefore developed a plan of evasive action. The moment the front door first blew open, the two ladies deliberately put down their handiwork, donned their coats, and walked firmly through the open portal, out of the house, bent on a ten-minute moonlight stroll around the downland loop path, which never took them out of sight of the building. 'We're back, Mr Llewellyn,' called Hester cheerfully from the doorstep on their return, but there came no answering thud. The same subterfuge was accordingly adopted on the following evening, with a similarly satisfactory effect; but it was clearly absurd to be driven out of one's own house in the prime of every evening for the indefinite future, especially when there might be something engrossing on television. The dresser, being the apparent focal point of the manifestation, must go. On Tuesday morning she rang up an antique dealer, who said he would be along to view the haunted object on Friday. Hester instantly regretted her decision – she already had a warm affection for the old piece – but there seemed no other way. Much to her surprise, however, no performance took place that evening: not a rattled bolt, not a footstep, not an opening drawer. It was as though the unseen presence knew what she was up to, and was sulking. 'Don't worry, Mr Llewellyn,' she called sweetly to the flower-perfumed air, 'I'll see that it goes to a good home, full of strong men and dogs. They'll know how to deal with you if you bother *them*. And they'll pay me a very good price, probably thirty times more than you paid for it all those years ago. Isn't that annoying? But then, you no longer have any use for money, I suppose.'

On Thursday morning, after two nights of perfect peace, Hester took a chance and cancelled her Friday appointment with the antique dealer. That afternoon she was shopping in the village store and met her nearest neighbour Mrs Phillips, who lived in the house at the foot of the hill by the little stone bridge, and was clearly all agog to hear the latest news. 'I hear you've been having some goings-on up at Sea View,' she began ambiguously. Hester tightened her lips. Obviously either the handyman or the vicar, probably the latter, had been talking; and she must rename the house at once. However, there was now no possibility of concealment, and a distant friendship with her neighbour might prove useful, so she adopted a light and friendly tone. 'Oh, nothing to speak of,' she smiled, launching into a brief description of the extraordinary noises which had beset her; 'just a friendly ghost come to call on the new owners. I told Miss Rose it was old Mr Llewellyn come back to look for his wife.'

Mrs Phillips was looking at her somewhat strangely. 'Aye,' she said; 'he used to use her like a dish rag. Such a big man too, his tread made the house shake. And what day did the noises stop?'

'The last time we heard them was Monday.'

'Aye, well, that would be right, wouldn't it?'

'Right? Right for what?'

'Oh, did you not hear? Poor Mrs Llewellyn passed away very suddenly on Tuesday morning. Her husband, God rest him, doesn't need to come looking for her any more. Now he knows *exactly* where she is.'

The Beckoning Clergyman

I suppose it is during adolescence that we humans first come to grips with the important truths about ourselves. Our strengths and weaknesses, our inclinations, our obsessing desires. The demon of discontent does not make its presence felt until puberty, when the genes do their little dance, when girls suffer from puppy fat and boys from acne. Personally I never gave a serious thought to growing up until I was sixteen. Schoolroom studies and private hobbies had fully occupied me; I was an untroubled sort of boy, content with my family, my books and my own curiosity. Then something happened to make me take fresh stock of myself. But you shall hear.

I was born and brought up in the industrial north, where dark satanic mills used to cast sinister shadows over the lives of the working class (though without necessarily making them discontented with their lot). Lancashire was, before the second world war, and even during it, a very closed society of church, co-op and cotton spinners' union, with an occasional day trip to Blackpool to blow the soot out of one's lungs; and nobody in this polluted age can imagine the melodramatic horror of that all-pervading soot, which soiled lace curtains as soon as they were put up, and made it necessary for house-proud women to wipe their window sills twice a day. My father was a spinner, often out of work, but at the age of ten I won a scholarship to the local public school, and found my new horizons of the mind utterly absorbing if more than a little bewildering. Physically my experience was very limited, and this ignorance was extended by the war, which made any kind of school journey impossible and put a temporary end even to the co-op tours, which had been temptingly advertising a week in Lucerne for eleven pounds. In these days of Concorde it is undoubtedly difficult for the young reader to understand how little we knew of the world outside our little land of chimney stacks, which stretched ten or fifteen miles north, and about five miles south, of an imaginary line drawn between Liverpool and Manchester. It was a world into which the sun's rays seldom percolated, and I have seen skies a blazing yellow from the chemicals emitted into them; only during wakes week, when ninety per cent of the population escaped to the boarding houses of Blackpool or Morecambe, was it possible to climb up to the moors and gaze down into the long straight streets of our town whose two hundred or more mill chimneys had suddenly been excused from fouling the air with their smoke. The local paper once found a washerwoman of sixty-eight who claimed never to have been outside the town's boundaries at all; and my own mother had a life only slightly less narrow. In 1924 she was taken on a day trip by rail to the Wembley Exhibition, but otherwise, until in her old age she began to travel for visits with her grandchildren, she had never been further west than Morecambe, never crossed the Yorkshire border twenty miles away, never ventured south of Manchester, which was half an hour away by bus. She was genuinely aware of these limitations and encouraged me to have wider ambitions. As a growing lad I used to hover on the grimy footbridge outside the railway station, dodging the columns of steam and gazing down at the metal rails as they crisscrossed and led the eye away over bridges and around curves to destinations unknown. Of course my reading took me to mythical lands, to Brobdingnag and Utopia and Shangri-La, but also to places nearer home which seemed equally unreal. Hadley, the rural village of Richmal Crompton's *William* books, was a place I longed to visit, with its old-fashioned characters of squire, flirty girls, bashful boys, silly curate, and nouveau riche lord of the manor. Greyfriars, the boarding school of the *Magnet*, had drawbacks such as Billy Bunter and Mr Quelch, but a year in the Remove there was an experience I would have greatly valued: as George Orwell later said, it was always 1914 there, and everything would be the same for ever and ever.

You get the impression, I hope: an introverted lad, getting his exercise from lonely moorland walks with the dog, indulging gratefully in amateur theatre of all kinds, carrying the church cross three times every Sunday, waiting for his true talents, whatever they were, to be recognized. Perhaps the first person inclined to suspect their presence was the affable young vicar of St John's, a church which when my grandmother first attended it was set among rolling fields but which now, distressingly, found itself in the middle of an industrial slum whose newer residents even objected to the sound of its bells. (After my time it was desanctified and turned into a mackintosh factory, and in the seventies was demolished along with its entire neighbourhood, which was quickly turned into one of the new slums, an industrial estate.) The young man who in the first year of war came as shepherd to this depressing parish was an ex-rugger blue called Tom Aspinall, just married and with little idea of how to live on a ration book in the rambling Victorian vicarage with which he was presented. Many of the regular church spinsters were however eager to make helpful suggestions, and by his cheerful and varied activity Tom quickly made himself popular with young and old alike, though a few of the older ladies did raise an eyebrow when he introduced a joke or two into his sermons and impersonated Will Hay in our youth club concert. He prepared me for confirmation, and I seized every opportunity to accompany him on choir outings and Easter walks, as well as assisting him every Sunday at the eight o'clock communion. I don't say he treated me any differently from the rest of his charges of like age, but when during the spring of 1944, very soon before D Day, he announced that he would shortly be leaving us for St Agnes-in-Delahaye, a rural parish in Worcestershire, I think he must have sensed from my stricken look how suddenly and utterly the bottom had fallen out of my comfortable world. At any rate, he patted me on the shoulder and said we must certainly keep in touch. This was kind indeed, but I was surprised to have a letter from him about eight months later, saying that he and his wife had settled well in their new surroundings. Astonishingly, he invited me to spend a week or so with them during the approaching summer, and even suggested a date at the end of July. I hardly needed to be asked twice, especially as Tom's successor was a dour fellow who had promptly taken all the fun out of churchgoing; and mother's smile was a testimony to her pride.

For me the railway trip was a great adventure. Mother went to the savings bank to help me with pocket money: the return fare alone was more than three pounds, but I could manage to repay that over a period from my Saturday job. I had to change in Manchester (one mile's walk) and again in Birmingham. Disappointingly there wasn't much scenery to look at, and for once I was too excited to read much. Tom met me at Kidderminster just after five, and we drove to the rectory in his battered convertible, through five miles of country lanes. It all seemed like a dream: I had never smelled air so sweet. If only my mother had been with me to share the experiences – especially my first sight of the rectory! The church looked fine enough, standing proudly on its little eminence, but the rectory was sensational. I expected the whole Bennet family from *Pride and Prejudice* to gather in the front doorway, for the building was more or less in Jane Austen's period; or perhaps a little earlier, as some windows had been blocked up to avoid tax, which would mean that the building existed when William Pitt the younger was prime minister. The truth, I later discovered, was that it was built in 1738. To me, coming from a town with scarcely a building erected before 1870, such a sight was as breathtaking as the emerald city of Oz. Squarely and sturdily built, with a lowish roof and a central door with a small portico, the house had had perfect proportions, the white stone facings and sash windows perfectly complementing its plum-coloured brick. To the right, quite asymmetrically and regrettably, an extra wing of later sub-Gothic architecture had been added; luckily it seemed bland enough to be ignored, and in any case was luckily shadowed by an enormous chestnut tree. Such an excrescence could not have been contemplated on the left, for here the original house was built up against the churchyard wall, and indeed from the front path I could see the tower of the old church, parts of which, Tom said, were definitely Norman. I had a lump in my throat from just being there.

From the front gate – the garden was walled all round, by the way, which made it a perfect sun trap – it was about a quarter of a mile down an unmade path to the village of Eastlea Major where most of Tom's congregation lived. The village proved interesting if higgledly-piggledy, with one splendid junk shop which stimulated my lifelong interest in old brass. Tom's ordnance survey map showed me that the countryside around was spattered with other villages of greater or lesser historical interest, and I could see at once that my proposed six days would be all too few: why, it would take a whole day properly to explore the rectory itself, to take stock of its arches and carvings and corners, all mellowed by the generations. For a start, I had no previous experience of oak-panelled walls or even white-painted doors; and there was a custom-built library, with a collection of more than a thousand books which went with the property and had been handed down and augmented by one rector after another. At first dip I found myself holding a volume printed in 1698. Tom and Sue were amused at my excitement, but I couldn't subdue it. She, by the way, hailed from Grasmere, and Tom had met her while staying with her parents during a walking tour. A quiet but efficient woman with a sense of humour, she saw her duty as walking in Tom's shadow and smoothing his path. And quite a large shadow that was, for at thirty-five or so he towered massively above me and gave the impression of absorbing air enough for three normal people. Sometimes it made me quite breathless just to be in the same room with him: you know the sort of person I mean.

Well, they had given me what must have been the master bedroom, though they insisted not. I never saw theirs, but mine was at the top of the carved oak staircase, which creaked at every step. As I sat in the great bed, which was four-posted but not canopied, I had my back to one of the blocked-up front windows, and facing me was an antique wardrobe with linenfold panels. (These positions are quite relevant to what follows.) To the left of the wardrobe was the great double-width door to the staircase I've mentioned. The wall over to my left was almost all window, with – joy of joys! – oak window seats in which spare blankets for the whole house were kept. The view was north-north-westerly, so the room itself was always cool in summer, and probably freezing in winter: but if the morning sun was strong I got the benefit of seeing it full on the church tower with its multi-coloured surface patched with lichen and ivy. By stretching my neck I also commanded a spectacular view down into the surrounding graveyard, with a bend of the Severn in the distance. Back in my bedroom to my right was ample space for a rather nondescript chest of drawers, a dressing table, and in the far corner a small light grey door, which I was told was locked.

'It leads,' said Tom, 'to the part of the house we haven't

sorted out yet. Two front rooms facing south-west, which will be marvellous in the afternoon if we can bring ourselves to chop down that old chestnut. Then there's a corridor to the so-called new wing, that means it was built only a hundred years ago. I haven't the keys on me, but I'll show you around before you leave.'

There was a constant stream of parishioners to the front door, sometimes with presents of freshly-shot rabbits, which Sue had no idea how to handle, or with personal queries which Tom attended to in his study. On my first morning it rained, and he had a funeral: I watched from my bedroom window with solemn interest as the coffin was rested under the lych gate in the approved manner before being carried into the church. Tom's working dress was his long black cassock, shiny leather belt and dog collar; an occasional pipe completed the impression of a hard-working country parson. Twice he found time to take me on some brief excursion, though I was perfectly content to potter about by myself. Although the church wasn't exactly well filled even on Sunday, he took two services every day, holy communion and evensong, whether anyone else came or not. Naturally I volunteered to assist at these, as in the old days, even though the first was at seven in the morning (because many of Tom's flock were agricultural workers who needed to be on the fields by seven-thirty). 'Don't say I didn't warn you,' he grinned as we went to bed on the first night, and sure enough next morning at six-forty (as I later discovered) I heard the heavy creak of his weight on the old staircase and he burst into the room like a medieval messenger with news so urgent he could scarcely contain it. 'Come on, come on,' he called, drawing the curtains. 'Time later for lingering in the bathroom: you have fifteen minutes to get yourself into the vestry.' Clearly I stirred insufficiently to be convincing, for in an excess of enthusiasm he fell upon the oversize bed and tore the covers from me. In so doing he accidentally put his full weight on my projecting foot and half sprained my ankle. I hobbled around rather pointedly all day. On the next morning something similar happened, except that this time he bruised my calf with his knee. I began to wish I had brought an alarm clock so that I could be up and about before his visitation; I hardly felt I could complain to him outright.

And now we come, at last, to the nub of the anecdote. As it chanced, on the third morning I was awakened very early by the singing of birds, and observed with pleasure that the fragments of sky, visible through the gaps in the curtains, were of the brightest blue. It was as though a play were about to begin: I expected the drapes to open and allow me to see some celestial pageant. They didn't, so I got up and drew them myself, drinking in with my eyes the superbly composed scene of church, and mossy gravestones, and low green hills, and distant river. My watch showed that it was just after six, and I felt almost magically awake. Opening the heavy door as quietly as possible, I tiptoed down the corridor to the bathroom; when I got back, I opened a window and did some breathing exercises. Then I climbed back into the venerable bed and decided to read for a while, my plan being to listen for any telltale creaks so that when Tom lunged through the door I could spring out of bed and yell in approved George Formby fashion: 'Haha, never touched me!'

I had brought with me an orange-covered Penguin paperback of *Wuthering Heights*: my English master had told me for exam purposes that I should acquire a few authors of whom I had read every word, so I had chosen the Brontës and Jane Austen because they didn't write very much. Besides, *Wuthering Heights* was marvellous melodrama. I plumped up the pillows and began to read, coming after about twenty minutes to Cathy Earnshaw's dream of her own death:

I was only going to say that heaven did not seem to be my home; and I broke my heart with weeping to come back to earth; and the angels were so angry that they flung me out into the middle of the heath on the top of Wuthering Heights; where I woke sobbing for joy.

I paused for a moment to consider this powerful passage, and marked it in the margin with my pencil; it was probably worth learning by heart, for there were ways in which a cunning student could make it relevant to almost any question on the English novel. As I began saying the words over to myself, I heard a creak.

I should have said that my spectacles were on the bedside table and not on my nose. Then as now, nearly forty years later, I needed glasses for distance work, but for reading I usually found the print blacker and bigger without them; opticians tell me that this is quite usual. So, on this occasion, I was reading without glasses, which meant that if I looked up I could quite adequately see everything across the room, even the church tower outside, but I saw it in slightly vague or fuzzy outline, like a dirty old oil painting or a bleached-out print of a film. And what happened was this. I heard a creak, as I've said. I put down my book and looked towards the oak door leading to the stair. I grabbed the bedcovers at the same time, ready to toss them aside and leap to my feet as soon as Tom entered. But it wasn't the oak door that opened. It was the small grey door on the right, the door which led to the disused part of the house. And Tom . . . looked in.

I say Tom looked in because that is what I thought at the time. I could clearly see what I recognized as his fresh complexion, round features and light-coloured straggly hair, which seemed enough for my brain to go on without further question. The door handle was in the corner of the room, so as he leaned round the door I didn't see much of his body, just the dog collar, the cassock and an inch or two of the shiny leather belt. For a moment he gazed silently at me, with an expression I still remember but can't quite analyse. Then, just as I shifted weight in order to propel myself out of bed, he seemed to beckon, though I don't remember with which hand. Anyway, before I could get to my feet he moved back out of sight and closed the door again.

I felt somewhat bewildered. Was he possibly a little annoyed because he could see that I was awake and had spoiled his little game? Funny fellow, I said to myself, reaching for my glasses and getting up at once. It was now by my watch a quarter to seven. I dressed in leisurely fashion, creaked my way down the stairway to the side door, and joined Tom in the vestry just after five to. He was already robed, and silently motioned me to hurry up. We had a congregation of three that morning, and as we came out into the warm sunshine half an hour later, I stretched languorously in it to give myself an appetite for breakfast before strolling back the few steps to the rectory.

'You were very quiet about waking me up this morning,' I ventured.

He shrugged. 'Woke up late myself. I thought I'd let you have a lie-in for once. I was surprised when you turned up on cue.'

'But you did look in to see if I was awake?'

'Not me.'

I stopped in my tracks and frowned. 'But somebody did. Somebody I thought was you.'

'Well, it wasn't me, and if it had been Sue I'm sure you'd have noticed, and there's nobody else in the house, unless Martha Dilworth has taken to doing some extra unpaid early morning cleaning.'

'No, no, it was a man. In fact, it was a clergyman. I saw the collar.' I gave him a full account of what happened, and of course he accused me of dreaming it, which I stoutly denied, or of imagining it because I was expecting him.

'In any case,' he added, 'you say it was the small door that opened, and that's locked.'

'Do you mind if we check?'

He didn't, so we went straight up to the room, and not only was it now locked but the key was on the other side, which he couldn't quite understand as it shouldn't have been. 'Still, nothing supernatural about that,' he said. 'I must have forgotten to turn it last week when I was rummaging about up here. And I expect after all I shut it from that side and went down the back stairs to the kitchen. But perhaps the lock's faulty. Do you think the door could have blown itself open?'

'And blown itself closed again?'

He pursed his lips. 'Unlikely, I grant. Well, it's locked now, so let's see whether your clerical friend comes back tomorrow.'

The funny thing was that he did. Only this time I didn't wake up early enough to catch his entrance. I just came to my senses gradually, looked at the window (sunny again), half sat up in bed, and found him staring at me from the doorway. Same attitude as before. Same impression of beckoning. Same quiet exit. And when I got up and checked, the door was definitely locked.

I was pretty quiet at breakfast that morning, and didn't have much appetite for lunch either. I tried to cheer up simply because I sensed that Tom and Sue felt responsible for my welfare, but it wasn't easy: some half-repressed fear was heavy on my consciousness, and I didn't know how to cope. Tom cancelled his afternoon appointments and took me to Bewdley, where we enjoyed ourselves in the remoter regions of an antiquarian bookshop: I remember picking up a 1903 copy of *The Diary of a Nobody*, which I still own. After dinner, Sue disappeared while we men had our port. Tom was formal that way. Presently he took a deep breath, assumed his most rectorial attitude, and said: 'Look here, would you prefer to sleep in another room tonight?'

I shook my head with a fair show of vehemence. 'Not for the world,' I replied, feeling more than a little foolhardy as I said it. 'If it *is* a spook of some kind, it doesn't seem to want to harm me, and anyway I doubt whether it really *could*, except by scaring me half to death. Now that I'm ready for it, it can't even do that.'

Tom sighed as he puffed on his pipe. 'Have you any idea why this may be happening to you and not to Sue and me? You know, we slept in the room for a week or two when we first moved in, and we saw nothing.'

I raised my eyebrows rather vaguely. 'Because I've never lived in a house as old as this before, I may be more receptive to the atmosphere. I mean, you studied history and architecture and religion, and you're much more sophisticated than me. Perhaps you know too much, and it sets up a barrier.'

Full of his own thoughts, Tom tapped his pipe clean on the side of the chimney grate. 'Mind you, I'm not admitting yet that you saw anything, though I grant you thought you did. I still think somehow that it's all in your own mind. Maybe you imagine subconsciously that a house so old should have a ghost, and so you subconsciously invent one.'

'I can't swallow that. To me it was as real as you are – well, almost. And I think it's developing. This morning I got a stronger impression that it was beckoning me, like Hamlet's father.'

'Well, if you don't mind I think I'll share the development with you. Then at least we'll be sure it isn't me, or my astral body. I'll be in your room at six-thirty tomorrow.'

He was, and I was up and fully dressed, having slept rather badly. We sat in the window and talked of this and that. Twenty to seven passed, and no sign. I flopped restlessly on to the bed, and Tom strolled round the far end of it, chatting. Just as he began to retrace his steps, and paused with his back to the grey door, I could see over his shoulder that it was beginning to open, and I meaningfully motioned him aside. This time I had my glasses on, and could see the figure with total clarity. Despite the colouring, it certainly *wasn't* Tom's astral body, or anything to do with Tom at all. The hair was brushed forward instead of sideways, the nose was longer and slightly crooked, and I could see now that this was a thinner and older man altogether. Beakier, too, like a bachelor schoolmaster. The face was still almost expressionless, but I somehow saw in it a tinge of purposeful malice, mixed with that melancholy which I have always thought quite proper for ghosts. The eyes looked straight at me, and I realized with a start that the flesh surrounding them was not quite opaque: I could almost see the picture rail through it. The right hand however was definitely raised in my direction, the index finger crooked. With the boldness of youth I stood up, intending to move towards the vision and greet it in some way. I had taken only two small steps when I realized that it had gone. I saw no movement; it simply wasn't there any more; it had dissolved. And the door was closed again.

I exhaled very slowly and turned to Tom. 'So you see,' I said.

He looked apologetic. 'I saw nothing,' he said quietly.

I felt very lonely then, and I believe I broke down and wept. After breakfast he tried to insist that I should either see a doctor or move to another room, but I wanted one more go; and meanwhile, now that I'd had a clearer view of the face, I thought we might try a little detective work. 'If he's a priest,' I said, 'and if I'm not dreaming and he really is a ghost, then it's very likely he's connected with the history of this house. So mightn't he be a past rector? And if so, couldn't we track him down through the church records?'

Tom was plainly worried by the way things were going –

perhaps he should have consulted his bishop before this – but he agreed to take me to the vestry and go through the framed pictures of past incumbents, of which half a dozen were on the walls and another score or so tucked away in various drawers. 'Assuming you're on the right track,' he asked, 'was there anything to suggest a particular historical period?'

I thought hard. 'I imagine the cassock and belt haven't changed much over the centuries, and there was nothing else to latch on to.'

I took half an hour or so to go through the photographs. They were of church picnics, football teams, mothers' unions and the like, and almost all were graced by the central presence of the rector of the day. The only one I thought possible was rather blurred, apparently a blown-up snapshot of the rector shaking hands with a player just off the football field. There was no inscription, but the scene looked fairly modern. 'It could be him,' I said, 'though he seems shorter and rather fatter than I thought. And he's wearing a hat, so I can't sense the colour of the hair.'

'Mm. Now, who would be able to help us? Perhaps Mrs Senior who should be cleaning the church by now.' We went out into the nave and showed the photograph to a generously proportioned elderly lady who was polishing the brass altar rail.

'Oh, yes, sir,' she said at once. 'That's my nephew there, playing with the church team against – now who were they playing that day? I forget, but he'd know: he lives over near Hereford now, but he's a good lad, he calls on me every month on his way to London.'

'Well, Mrs Senior,' said Tom, 'I'd certainly like to meet your nephew, but it's the rector we're interested in now. I take it he *is* a rector of this parish?'

'Lord, yes, sir, why that's Mr Widdowes. I remember him well. The Reverend William Widdowes. Though he wasn't a chap I could ever get on with, if you'll pardon my saying so.'

'I'm sure we will. And when was he here? Is he on the scroll?'

'Oh, he will be, sir. Very particular about that, the church council is. The signwriter always comes in as soon as the gentleman's left. Not that Mr Widdowes ever did exactly leave, not in the normal way.'

'Why, what happened?'

'Oh, I couldn't tell you, sir. Except that the bishop came down and told my Henry – who was on the PCC then, God rest his soul – at least, I suppose the bishop told the church council, but my Henry told *me* – that Mr Widdowes, who'd gone on holiday, wouldn't be coming back and that for the time being Mr Hadfield from St Mark's over at Netherwood would be looking after us, but because of the short notice we'd all have to go *there* for Sunday mattins, and there'd be a bus laid on from the church gate. My Henry didn't think it was right, but there was nothing else to be done. It was nigh on a year before we got Mr Winter, and then off *he* went to the war, and never came back. So old Mr Beddington looked after us, more or less, till you came along. Of course, he didn't live in the rectory, for it was too big for one old gentleman, especially in wartime. Mrs Gentry down the road made him comfortable.'

'So Mr Widdowes must have arrived during the thirties. Here we are.' We had arrived at the west window, to the left of which was an inscribed wooden plaque showing all the rectors of St Agnes-in-Delahaye since Geraldus di Parmentis, 1133–46. 'Here he is: William Widdowes, 1936–38. He certainly didn't stay long. Well, that places him for you, Nicholas, so now that you have the bit between your teeth, let's be off and try to confirm the identification.'

Tom took me to the newspaper office in Worcester, and it needed no more than five minutes' research among the photo files to prove to my satisfaction that William Widdowes and my visitor were one and the same. And while poring over the rather boring scenes of fête openings and the like, we were struck by the fact that, almost always, the same thin, almost weedy young man was standing next to or near the rector. Only once was he identified, as 'R. Gudgin'.

We were fairly silent on the drive back, but Tom did once say: 'Assuming I'm coming round to your view of the matter, I can well understand why my predecessor Winter wouldn't see anything. The best way I can sum him up, according to report and my own very limited enquiries, is to say that he had no soul. His attitude to the church was entirely political: he would do anything he could to get preferment. He would be far too insensitive to receive such visitations as the ones you've described, unless they brought with them an invitation to Lambeth Palace.'

'Did he succeed in his mission?'

'The last I heard, he was bishop to one of the emergent African states, and very welcome. Going on to Beddington, who died only a few months ago, he was an old codger long since retired, a wartime substitute for anything better. No, to all intents and purposes the rectory had been starved of raw intellectual activity for more than ten years when Sue and I arrived; and even we don't seem to have been on the right wavelength.'

The rectory was not starved of activity that morning when we arrived back for lunch: Sue and two willing lady helpers were dashing madly about, dusting corners, sweeping paths and arranging flowers. The cause of the urgency was that the bishop's secretary had called to say that his eminence would be passing by at around four, and might he pop in for a cup of tea? 'Couldn't be better timed,' said Tom. 'I was thinking of giving him a ring. He may be able to shake the dust off this whole curious story.'

The bishop, who insisted on being called Bertram, was an

elegant man in his fifties, with a touch of the matinee idol about him. Prematurely white-haired but with a most agreeably gentle voice and manner: one really couldn't be in awe of him for long. Tom spirited him away into the study as soon as he arrived, then I was sent for and asked to tell my story again while we sipped our tea out of Sue's delicate Coalport cups. The bishop nodded from time to time but didn't interrupt. Finally he said: 'Well, at least your chap was friendly. I've known some that weren't, and once I actually attended an exorcism where some pretty inexplicable and unpleasant things happened.'

I was relieved. 'So you don't think I imagined it?'

'Oh, by no means. Let me qualify: since Tom here didn't see it at all, I imagine the vision came into your brain through some sense other than that of sight, but that's a quibble for the psychologists. I'm sure it did come, and that you didn't provoke it except by being there and by being, for whatever reason, receptive. I never knew this man Widdowes, but my predecessor told me about him. Not at all suitable, apparently: I can't imagine how some of these chaps get ordained in the first place.'

Tom stirred. 'Might one ask in what *way* he was thought unsuitable?'

The bishop pursed his lips. 'Oh well, he was rather a snob for a start, and that's one thing you can't afford to be in a country parish which doesn't even have a lord of the manor. Then he was a terrible nuisance about accommodation. You're only too well aware of the rather ugly extension to this house, added a hundred years ago to fit the requirements of a minor canon with a large Victorian family. It was of no earthly use to Widdowes, who was a bachelor, and indeed it had been closed off for thirty years or more, but he wanted it all structurally checked and redecorated. He said it was in danger of falling down, which of course it wasn't, for the church dilapidations board had inspected it regularly.

However, to placate him, and because the parish had just lost its church hall to a speculator, the bishop ordered some work done, and they'd just started on it when this strange thing happened.'

'What did happen?'

'My dear chap, aren't there any gossips left in this parish? Widdowes simply disappeared. Went on holiday and didn't turn up back on the due Saturday, so people came to church next day and there was nobody to take services. The bishop rang the hotel at Torquay, but they said he never even arrived. And the police couldn't find a trace of him. It was all in the national papers, but I imagine the Loch Ness Monster took precedence: it *was* the silly season, after all, and there didn't seem to be any scandal attached to Widdowes' disappearance, just a totally unsolved mystery. Not nearly so juicy a case as the famous rector of Stiffkey, who finished up on Blackpool beach being eaten by a lion.'

'And he was never heard of again?'

'The rector of Stiffkey? Yes, he died.'

'I mean Mr Widdowes.'

'Not a single solitary word, either of him or of his friend.'

'What friend was that?'

'Ah, *there* was another reason for his unpopularity. He lived here with a male cook-housekeeper he'd brought down from his previous parish. I rather got the impression he was a distant cousin. Did everything for Widdowes: secretary too, apparently. One of those shadowy people you can almost see through: the then bishop told me he couldn't describe him at all when the police asked, except to say he had a shifty look, which perhaps wasn't very charitable. Luckily there were some photos about, not that they did any good.'

'Gudgin!' I exclaimed with conviction.

The bishop was startled. 'That was indeed his name. How did you know?'

We explained. 'Two bachelors,' said Tom: 'sounds more like a Catholic menage.'

'Except that Gudgin wasn't ordained, though Widdowes did apparently put the idea forward. I don't suppose that would have worked at all, because the parishioners here took an instant dislike to him. That may have been because he was a close-mouthed man who never went to the pub; they were undoubtedly used to having a local in the rectory who could pass on the latest gossip. Not that there was any, at least nothing ever filtered through to the bishop except the odd anonymous complaint. These days there would certainly have been talk about two men living together – certain assumptions would have been made – but in a country village in the thirties I don't suppose there was anybody sophisticated enough to harbour that kind of suspicion, any more than they would have cast doubt on the relationship of . . . Sherlock Holmes and Doctor Watson, shall we say.' The bishop chuckled.

'As to that,' said Tom with mock solemnity, 'I am told there is a New York school of thought inclining to the belief that Doctor Watson was a woman.'

'Only in America.' The bishop smiled and turned to me. 'Well, young man, you're the kingpin of all this curious activity, so what do you have to suggest?'

I cleared my throat and said I thought it might be helpful if we had a look at the locked up part of the house, so that's what we did. All the disused rooms were on the first floor – the big room on the ground floor was nearly in a fit enough state to be used for parish meetings – so the three of us progressed rather cautiously through my bedroom and unlocked the grey door. We passed into a musty corridor, rather narrow, but I don't think claustrophobia was the reason I felt suddenly faint, as though I were being overpowered by some unseen assailant, or as though a whole tribe of geese were walking over my grave. I got my breath back almost immediately, and didn't think the others had noticed. To the right were two dark medium sized rooms overlooking the wilderness end of the front garden: both were absolutely empty. Then at the end of the corridor, opposite a small bathroom, a door on the left gave access to a very large room indeed, the size of the other two put together. Whatever the exact date of the so-called new wing, there was little evidence that this room had been used then or since. The ceiling had open beams, the walls were roughly plastered; and there was a rather nasty smell of raw paint and unseasoned wood and sawdust and damp and age, together with some other odour we couldn't fathom, almost like the sweet sickly fragrance of a saw-mill.

'Let's open a window,' said the bishop. 'And leave it open for half a year. One thing's for certain, we'll find no buried treasure, for nobody could ever have lived in this atmosphere long enough to hide it.'

I bent down and looked into the fireplace: there was no trace of soot in the chimney. 'I don't suppose your ghost lives up there,' said Tom, 'you're thinking of Father Christmas.'

I stood up seriously. 'But there isn't anywhere else for him to hide. And I'm quite convinced he meant me to find something. Something behind the grey door.'

'You don't feel his presence now?' asked the bishop reflectively.

'I did in the corridor, but not here. Perhaps he's only fully operative in the early morning. Perhaps that's the time of day he died.'

'Right,' said the bishop. 'Then let's give him one more chance to make himself understood. Tom, I suppose you couldn't find me a bed for the night?'

There was no doubt that Tom could. The bishop's dinner speech went off as planned, ten miles down the road, and he was back with us by eleven. We all went to bed on mugs of cocoa, and at Tom's insistence I borrowed a sleeping pill.

Consequently he had some difficulty waking me at six-fifteen, but by the appointed time the three of us were dressed and waiting. It was an overcast morning and no birds sang: I found myself shivering a little. 'If it doesn't sound too silly,' said the bishop from the window seat, 'try to *will* him to tell us what he wants.' Nobody answered.

'He's here,' I blurted out suddenly, having just turned my head towards the grey door. 'But not so clear as before. Can nobody else see him?' They shook their heads; I conquered an inclination to shiver. 'The door isn't open this time. I simply get a misty impression of him, this side of it, as though he were very lightly painted on to the door itself. Like a transfer. He's perfectly still, but I sense that he's going to move, and he wants us to follow him. I don't think he can come again. It's as though he's exhausted his potential for a while: tomorrow he may not be visible at all.'

I was already standing. As the others rose to join me, the figure faded away. I felt cold perspiration on my forehead. 'Perhaps the three of us have diffused the impact,' said the bishop. 'Let's move towards him in the hope that he'll lead us to whatever he wants us to see.'

'He's already gone,' I cried, reaching for the handle of the grey door and pulling it towards me. At the far end of the little corridor I saw, or rather sensed, my visitor, his head almost lost against a little stained and leaded window through which the sun was streaming. As we creaked and thudded along the old floorboards we sounded like the charge of the light brigade, and not surprisingly my ghostly visitor was completely gone by the time we reached the spot. I stood there quite helpless and dismayed, remembering the time I tried water divining with no better luck.

'Well,' said Tom, 'it's either the bathroom or the big room on the left, and I suspect the latter.' We went in, but I knew instantly that the trail was cold; here there wasn't even the echo of a spiritual sigh. Instinctively I tried taking a deep breath and holding it, but I couldn't reactivate the vision. The bishop laid a comforting hand on my shoulder, and shrugged. 'Perhaps it's me he doesn't like,' he said.

He and Tom turned and moved towards me – I was still by the door – but I held up my hand. 'Wait a minute. There's something still making itself felt. Something behind me. Not in the room or by the door itself, but out in the corridor. By the stained window. Under it, in fact. I feel very strange, as though a magnetic force were pulling through me. He can't be seen any more, but he's still here. I'm sure he's still here.'

'Which way?' said Tom abruptly, clearly feeling his reponsibilities towards me, and unwilling to send me back to Lancashire in a strait jacket.

'Towards the wall. I've got to move away. Sorry.' As I took a few steps down the corridor, the force which had been holding me seemed to snap like elastic. I took some deep breaths and nodded to Tom not to worry.

There was a long pause during which it seemed to me that none of us could think what to do next. But it was broken at last. 'That strikes me,' said the bishop reflectively, 'as a very small stained glass window above a very thick wall. Nor are either of them right for a Victorian extension: the whole effect is too clumsy, too medieval, like a half-crown souvenir of the Vatican. I wonder whether this is the part of the building the men had started work on when Widdowes disappeared.' He ran his fingers gingerly along some very lumpy plasterwork. 'It all seems much newer than the rest, and don't you think the workmanship is worse than one would expect even from an amateur?' He stooped to pick up an old length of wood from a corner, then began to rap the wall with it until, about two feet from the floor, he found a spot which sounded hollower than the rest. Changing his grip, he glanced at us and aimed again. At the first strong rap with the wooden billet the wall caved in, and the three of us staggered back in nausea and horror from the truly revolting smell which emerged.

You will scarcely need telling what the police found when they so speedily responded to the bishop's summons. Eventually it was possible to identify the decomposed, plaster-choked body by its teeth. What really happened to bring the Reverend William Widdowes to this ghastly end, and what became of the mysterious R. Gudgin, nobody could hope to discover after so long a passage of time.

The rest of my visit was both trying and somewhat unreal. Sue asked me to stay on for a few days until she could make up her mind whether it would be possible for her to go on living in the house; meanwhile she wanted somebody by her side whenever Tom went out on his parish duties. In the end the Aspinalls did stay for a while, though not so long as they had intended. Meanwhile the bishop performed a quiet exorcism ceremony in that musty corridor, and I had no further visitations.(We didn't even mention them to the police, by the way; the bishop thought it was best to let them assume we had simply been exploring and had caved in the wall accidentally.)

A year later I visited St Agnes-in-Delahaye again, and the brief supernatural reappearance of Mr Widdowes was so distant that we were able to talk about it almost as though he had materialized to some third party. In fact there was very little to say: the thing had happened, and that was it. Just one thing puzzled me, and I broached it to Tom as we sat sprawling in front of the fire on my last night:

'I grant you not many people had stayed in the house since the murder, but of those who did, why do you suppose Widdowes waited for me?'

Tom went through a big performance with his pipe before replying: knocking it out against the fire, refilling it, tamping it down, etc. Then he lit it and looked up at me through the curling smoke. 'Perhaps because you were the first visitor to whom he felt . . . sympathetic.'

I pursed my lips and raised my eyebrows, but couldn't quite decide what he meant, and he didn't elaborate. Nor I think did we ever return to the subject, though I thought about it quite a lot. A few years later I began to think I did understand Tom's half-expressed drift. Certainly when I rang him a couple of years ago to announce that I'd been appointed editor of *Gay News*, he seemed quite genuinely pleased for me but not in the least surprised.

House of the Future

'They say the police found the most frightful mess. And what made it worse was that everyone thought they were an absolutely devoted couple.'

George could scarcely be sure at first that he had actually heard the words. He was rather self-consciously enjoying the tactile sensations provided by the fabric of his new house. Or rather, the new extensions to his old house. Basically his heavily mortgaged home was the kind of superior early thirties semi one would readily expect to come across in Kew, and twenty years ago, in 1963, George had paid no more than six thousand pounds for it. Now, having unexpectedly come into a considerable sum of money, he had spent nearly five times that amount on extending the kitchen, rebuilding the conservatory as a dining room, and adding various little touches of his own which resulted in vistas somewhat reminiscent, he thought, of the eighteenth-century mansion of Sir John Soane in Lincolns Inn Fields. The enterprise seemed likely to be a good investment, in an economy which had property values increasing by a steady ten per cent each year; but the important thing was that it would give enormous pleasure to him and to Nelsa during every remaining day of their lives. He fingered with affection the carefully designed, immaculately leaded, folding window which divided the dining room from the den. Then he took the little circular tour of his own devising. From den into quarry-tiled kitchen; from kitchen left into the narrow corridor, past the new toilet into the dining room; from dining room left again into Chinese-carpeted lounge; from lounge to hallway; and back into the den. His Cairn bitches padded obediently behind him, though they probably saw little point in going anywhere only to arrive so soon back in the same place. At least they must be grateful to have behind them the appalling physical upset which had bewildered them throughout last winter, with different groups of strange men treading mud into the hall, leaving the side gate open, knocking down walls only to replace them with corrugated iron, and leaving behind them each evening a chill half-house covered with choking dust. Yes, thought George, if we had really known what to expect we might never have said yes to that ingratiating young architect; but we learned a lot, and now we can begin to enjoy the results. For months there will be missing lampshades and bookshelves and rugs, until we find just what we want, and there will be awkward wall spaces until decorations find their natural home, and some of the house plants have died, but at least the whole structure is now usable, and liveable in, and recognizable as the satisfying fruit of our original design. George tended to be a little pompous in his unspoken soliloquies.

The new dining room was faced in old yellow brick, part of which was the outside wall of the original house. It had a long integral door and window unit giving a panoramic view of Nelsa's neat medium-sized garden. Its pewter wall brackets had been the fruit of a search through lighting emporia in the entire south of England. The table was of heavy old oak, and had been the subject of a long battle with Harrods when it was twice mislaid, then arrived French polished and had to be replaced. The skirting board which concealed the central heating was carefully shaped and stained to match the reproduction oak furniture which George and Nelsa had lovingly collected over the years as opportunity offered. The chairs, for instance, had been picked up for seventy pounds when their real value was nearer four hundred. It was a room which suggested no particular period or style, except that it harked back to the distant past, to a time when craftsmen were proud of their work and houses were built to last. The skylights were a modern touch, set in a fabulous timber roof; they prevented the oak from seeming heavy and gave an airy, relaxed feeling to the room, at whichever place one sat round the table.

It was in the dining room that he had first heard the voices clearly, though there had been some curious incoherent mutterings one afternoon in the den, mutterings which he had put down to the central heating system misbehaving itself. When he mentioned the experience, he remembered, Nelsa had changed the subject rather oddly; he fancied instinctively that she might have heard something herself and didn't want to be reminded of it. These disturbances had begun only after the men had left, possibly because while they were in residence no voice could have been heard above the hubbub. Almost immediately afterwards George had gone abroad on business, and this was virtually his first chance, jetlagged as he was, to survey the details one by one. Nelsa was at the local shops, getting fish for tea, and he took the opportunity to sit in each chair in turn, to try all the doors and windows, to stroll down the new yellow brick path, not to Oz, but to the circular patio beneath the pear tree at the far end of the lawn. He returned to the dining room and closed the outer door softly, locking it behind him. He put the key in an ornamental jar and looked around once more. This was a space in which he was going to spend a great deal of time, not only eating but writing, sorting out papers, paying bills, sipping post-prandial coffee or merely slumping baronially in his carver while discussing art and life with his more intimate friends. It was a room of his own design, his finance, his execution (almost); a refuge for him from the pressures of the world; a unique summation of all he held to be best in the life of twentieth-century man.

And he certainly didn't want any supernumerary voices in it.

At least there weren't any now. Or were there? He thought he heard something, fragments of female speech, but much lower than before. 'They say you can see where the blood was' . . . did the voice really say that? How absurd! Or was it – the air was still and a window was open – could it be two women in the side street just three garden walls away? The first voice had been too loud for that, though, too close. Perhaps there was an inbuilt echo, an accidental trick connection of pipe or joist which brought in sounds from the house next door (and must therefore do the same in reverse)? But his semi-detached neighbours had been away for a month. Had a radio been left on upstairs? He wandered through every room in the house, but if a radio was to blame he couldn't find it. He went back to the dining room and gazed at the carver with its back to the wall between the Welsh dresser and the lounge door; that was the vantage point from which he had first heard the voice. He lowered himself into the seat and placed his hands gingerly on the arms. There was only a faint buzzing in his ears, but as he slowly stood up the voice came through so much louder than before as almost to pierce his eardrums.

'Of course, they did a big conversion job here in the early eighties, not long before it happened. He probably couldn't pay the bills and went demented.'

George dizzily raised his hands to his temples and almost slumped to the floor, his faced flushed with shock and frustration. It *was* a woman's voice, it wasn't Nelsa, it wasn't the radio, it *was* in the room with him. Where the hell was it coming from? And what was that about the early eighties, as though the early eighties were the distant past instead of now, this year, 1983? George strained his ears, but the room was now almost deliberately silent. He took little slow steps around the edge of the carpet, testing apprehensively for further experience, but none came. Still the room was filled with a curious sensation of anticipation, rather like a radio between programmes, when nobody speaks but the capability for broadcasting is almost audible.

Nelsa came back soon after, and he told her what he had heard. She raised an eyebrow in that actressy way of hers, but made no remark as she stacked her purchases in the freezer and set about the preparations for tea. George laid particular stress on the remark about the early eighties. 'As though the conversation was taking place in the future,' he said. 'A kind of reverse haunting.'

'Unless the woman was talking about the eighteen-eighties,' said Nelsa casually.

George emitted a loud scornful laugh. 'I don't think they talked much about houses being converted in the eighteen-eighties,' he said. For the rest of the evening he made a conscious effort to force this unexplained but unimportant series of events out towards the fringes of his mind. It was absurd to think that a ghost could haunt backwards, unless one believed in Professor Dunne's time continuums. Which, after all, J. B. Priestley did. Or of course, the voices could be thought of as actual, in which case he and Nelsa must be ghosts, pretty solid ones. Could it be, he thought as he gazed out of the window, that by changing the physical identity of the house to the shape it would occupy in the future he had somehow opened it to influences from that future by putting it on the same wavelength? A pretty theory indeed, logically satisfying but totally implausible.

Next afternoon George hung about the dining room as much as he could without actually settling. He felt no influences at all. There was in fact no sequel until six days later, when he had virtually forgotten the whole affair and came home early from the office to sit wearily at his big oak table and sign cheques. The final one, to the architect, had just been put into its envelope and sealed when the voice came again, as a murmur in his left ear, just as though the speaker, this time a man, were lolling by the kitchen door.

'It seems a shame to demolish this rather splendid work, but it's so old fashioned and of course we can re-use the bricks.'

George rose, ran into the lounge, and dragged Nelsa from her television set to bear witness, but the room was still again. His wife now seemed decidedly unconvinced by George's description, and almost pointedly refrained from suggesting that he'd been working too hard. 'Do you suppose,' she said dubiously, 'that the old kitchen radio we threw out got accidentally dropped into the cavity and boarded over?'

He shook his head. 'Even if the battery hadn't died after a month it would hardly spout the odd sentence and then lie doggo again.'

'Then what do you suggest?'

'I have no idea. But I did see a few science fiction movies about time warps.'

'And didn't, I trust, treat them as anything but fantasy.' Nelsa moved rather thoughtfully into her kitchen, and later rang a psychologist friend of hers and invited him and his wife to dinner the following Friday. George was persuaded on this occasion to give an account of the voices, but the psychologist drank several glasses of excellent brandy without shedding any light on the matter. After that, George took to sitting alone in the dining room whenever he could – casual callers thought he must be waiting for his dinner – but another fortnight passed before a further fragment of conversation came through. It seemed to be the same female voice as the first time, speaking on the same topic.

'I never bothered to read up the gory details. Sex came into it, of course, it always does. He imagined she had a lover. Maybe she did. I'd rather not know.'

Nelsa heard nothing of this instalment from George, but she did begin to notice a small change in him. He no longer made jokes. He gave her no affectionate squeezes. His expression was continually abstracted, as though he were listening for something. When he did look directly at her it would be with a glance of sudden suspicion, almost at times of hatred. She noticed when she left the house on little errands that he was more than usually interested in her destination, and when she went to her sister's on Thursday he insisted on driving her all the way instead of merely taking her to the bus. What she did not know was that he was keeping a diary note of the disembodied remarks, which came to him more frequently now, always in the late afternoon or early evening, and always when she was out.

'I personally can't imagine why anyone would let a perfectly good house stand empty all these years just because a murder happened in it.'

'I think those old-fashioned attitudes to sex were ridiculous. I mean, Gregory has two mistresses to my *certain* knowledge, and if he doesn't tell me about the others it's only because he likes to appear moderate in all things.'

'No, they'd been married for years when it happened, but they'd never had children. She'd been away, I think, for a day or two, and it happened immediately she got back.'

Nelsa was suddenly called to nurse her ailing mother in Basingstoke. She was glad to get away from George, who was increasingly moody and had no conversation whatever. The truth was that he felt more dead than alive, as dead as the dead grandparents in Maeterlinck's *The Blue Bird*, who only stir and flex their muscles when some live person thinks and talks about them. Callers noticed his torpor but said nothing in case he took their concern amiss. The only thing that could stimulate him now was the voice from the future. Something in its timbre sent a thrill through his veins, turning him from a virtual zombie into a being well capable of action. It spoke to him, or through him, just before Nelsa got back. He heard her coming up the path, and by the time she had unlocked the door he was waiting for her in the shadows of the hall, with a knife in his hand. The voice had not told him in so many words that this was the way the murder happened, but he sensed that it was, and although in a distant way he still loved Nelsa, there was no point in trying to tamper with historical fact. If the voice said there had been a murder in the house in 1983, then a murder there would have to be. Besides, the voice had taken to laughing about the ancient violence – a high-pitched, tittering kind of laugh – and if there was one thing George couldn't stand, it was to be laughed at. As Tolstoy's Karenin said, the deceived husband is a comical role, impossible to play with dignity. He would change that. His blow would be struck on behalf of deceived husbands the world over. He drew himself in behind the grandfather clock, but obviously not quite far enough, for while holding the front door open Nelsa paused, peered into the semi-darkness, and called his name. 'Is that you, George?' she repeated.

This was it. He leaped out into the passage in a murderous rage, his right arm raised high with the knife in it. Nelsa screamed, but she was a resourceful woman and, something he'd momentarily forgotten, two inches taller than George. She grasped his upraised arm and managed to stand her ground, wrestling him, screaming. George was astonished to find himself helpless, for she had pushed him back against the panelling and he had lost his balance. While he struggled desperately to regain the upper hand, he heard a foot kick the bootscraper and saw another figure rush in through the open doorway, a tall man whom he didn't recognize in silhouette but who was clearly a figure of strength and authority. The stranger grasped the arm with the knife in it. George kicked out at his private parts, but the man was nimble as well as tall, and twisted George's arm so that George not only dropped the knife but was sent reeling. George came back at the stranger with redoubled force, but without caution, noting with mild surprise that Nelsa was shouting: 'Kill him! Kill him!' He took the naked blade full in the stomach. Nelsa's contorted face was the last image implanted on his retina as he crumpled to the ground, consciousness ebbing away quite slowly, slowly enough for him to hear the voice for the last time.

'Oh no, she got off. Claimed self-defence, and lived in this house till the day she died.'

George smiled. He had nothing against Nelsa apart from this little problem, and he certainly wouldn't want her to suffer for his own misinterpretation of events.

'Of course, it's my belief her lover did it, but he was never identified. You see, there was evidence that the husband had been batty for a long time, and probably dangerous. Kept on hearing voices.'

The Centurion's Road

Since I have never approved of people trying to eat their cake and still have it, I shouldn't really approve of this story, which can be based, according to your interpretation, upon temporary delirium or upon a genuinely supernatural event. Or on both, since it has a 'clincher' of a rather ambiguous kind. Since it is true, however, and since it happened to me, I have no alternative but to place it before you and invite your rational explanation – if you can find one which fits the facts.

I was in Monte Carlo, attending an annual six-day market concerned exclusively with the so-called industry in which I work. The nature of the industry is quite irrelevant. It happens to be television. We were all staying, hundreds of us from fifty nations, at the newish and more than slightly appalling Loew's Hotel, a featureless convenience which bestrides the sea on concrete pillars. Inside, it suggests Las Vegas without the style; its gambling hell isn't even air-conditioned. I was allotted, and was occasionally able to find, a pleasant room overlooking the Mediterranean; the trouble was that all the corridors looked the same, none of them ran straight or even at right angles, and there was next to no signposting, so I soon got into the sort of trouble that besets me in the streets of Paris. My favourite Cap Estel down the road would have been much more civilized, but the market was at Loew's and that was that. In fact, a whole floor had had its bedrooms turned into office suites for the duration of the enterprise.

It can be imagined that after three or four days of dodging high pressure salesmen in these confined spaces I would have seized any excuse to absent myself for a while. As it happened, I was able to do so while salving my conscience, for an old salesman friend named Will Taylor grabbed my arm in the lobby and murmured something about a rather complex offer he could make if I had an hour or two to listen. He must have read my thoughts, for he promptly added: 'Why don't we take a day off to do it, the three of us?' He meant to include his wife Shirley, who has always been perfectly pleasant company. The upshot was that we all cleared our decks for the very next day, the weather forecast being good. Will said he would hire a car if I didn't mind sharing the driving, which I didn't; and we agreed to make the most of the day by starting at eight-thirty and getting back in good time for dinner at the Hôtel de Paris, where the mostèle is usually quite delicious.

Italy is only about twenty miles east of Monaco along that winding coast road, and none of us had ever been into that part of it, so it was an obvious choice. Having bought a road map, I was appointed navigator, and suggested that we went as far as San Remo for an early lunch, then north into the hills, and back along the Grande Corniche if pressed for time. After a false start when we had to turn back for Shirley's passport, everything went well. We finished our business before we even reached the Italian border: I rather thought we would. We did notice, with a smile or two, that the moment we got into Italy the whole character of the countryside changed as though by magic. We were at the foot of the same hills, but the streets were dustier, the people dirtier, and the whole mood less formal, with lines of washing marring most of the urban landscape. Nor were we much impressed by San Remo (the local preference, by the way, seems to be to spell it as one word): the streets were so narrow that we hardly expected to get through without a scratch, and when we found the beach it was cluttered and unattractive. We were successful however in finding a little harbour restaurant which agreed to feed us at eleven-forty five, and after some fish soup and a plate of green lasagne we felt much more relaxed. We'd asked the waiter to bring a local white wine, not too dry, and although I myself wasn't too taken by the result it did have a most attractive label, which I examined closely. It depicted what looked like a Grimm's fairy tale castle rising up behind a river bridge, and under the picture was the name Dolceaqua. (That's pronounced Doll-chay-ack-wa and it means gentle water.) Between us we got out of the non-English-speaking waiter that it wasn't far away, four miles north of the road we'd driven along; a very ancient village, apparently, now noted only for wine-making. When we further asked, in our apologetic Esperanto, whether the hills to the north held any especially picturesque places, he looked long and hard at our map and finally indicated that we should climb out of San Remo as far north as Perinaldo, and take the very narrow track (much gesturing here) as far west as Apricale; if we then turned south at the bridge the road would bring us back through Dolceaqua to the coast. This seemed both practical and desirable, a round trip of twenty-five miles at most; we would even have time to shop in Menton on the way back. We tipped generously, and left.

I drove on this lap, and very soon wished I hadn't. Although our road was clearly signposted from the town square, within the next five minutes I twice found myself in dead end alleys full of taunting urchins and large ladies carrying bundles of washing, all shouting instructions at once, like something out of an old Anna Magnani film. Even when we found the main road at last and rose swiftly above the town, Will had a quiet chuckle or two at my difficulties on hairpin bends, of which there were at least a dozen before we found ourselves steering more or less directly north, crossing and recrossing the route of a cable railway which surprisingly served one of the less accessible villages ahead.

Once I was used to the difficulties of driving in this part of the Riviera it was a delightful experience in near-perfect weather, and I was adversely affected only by the overpowering odour of Will's pipe and by a slight nausea which it seemed must have been caused by the rapidly increasing altitude, though according to the signs we never exceeded two thousand feet all afternoon. The car had an open roof, and afterwards I wondered if I'd had a touch of sunstroke, but if so there was no physical sensation to suggest it. In fact, the higher we climbed, the more mentally exhilarated I felt. When we got through the vineries, and forests, and uncultivated heathland to a steep escarpment from which we could view across a massive dip what looked like the whole range of the Alps, we were all struck dumb with wonder. The high snow slopes were disconnected by haze from the black hills below, so their design seemed as fanciful, their location as impossible, as that of a Himalayan lamasery: we would not have been surprised to turn the next corner and find ourselves in Shangri-La instead of Perinaldo. Up here, the impurities of the overcrowded coastal strip behind us were not merely forgotten, but inconceivable. Here one could fancy oneself uncontaminated by the twentieth century with its dubious history. These isolated hilltop communities had developed at a more sensible pace, and either by good luck or good management had avoided the attentions of the developer. In Perinaldo, with its utterly medieval ambience, nobody seemed to be awake; from its charming terrace Apricale was visible across the valley, clinging unbelievably to a steep slope, its fairy tale buildings pink in the afternoon sky. We teetered along the narrow track towards it, and eventually passed below it, edging westward on a road which was little more than a low ledge on the mountainside. These were lost civilizations, about which whole books could doubtless be written. A north Italian *Akenfield*, perhaps, reincarnating all the sons who had gone off to successive wars, and all the local aristocrats whose monuments lent dignity and awe to the little churches.

'Of course,' said Will, as though deliberately breaking in on my thoughts, 'it's my belief that this area, historically, is even more interesting than it seems on the surface.'

'The surface seems pretty interesting to me. What do you mean?'

'Only that the old Romans must have passed through here on their way to fight the Gauls and the Hun, and on their way back from Britain come to that. If you look at a map of Europe, these valleys are the only sensible route, the only possible one in winter when the alpine passes must be snowed up and frozen. They certainly run in the right direction. Stop a minute.' I braked the car and we both got out. 'Walk back a few feet on to the height of that little bridge. Now, see this rocky stream below, rushing its way to the sea? Don't ask me what it's called, but it's a safe bet the Romans camped by it, and followed it down to Ventimiglia. They probably even built the original bridge at this spot. And look down there on the left bank: it isn't just a towpath as we understand the term, it's a real Roman causeway with a rubble base. You can see the old broken stones in places, deliberately laid, probably by an army. They'd have brought the rock from up the hill behind us where it's loose, rather than quarry it. It would be worth the effort, you see, to get all those troops quickly down to the sea; they probably went home by boat from there.'

I nodded: Will's enthusiasm was infectious. 'Two thousand years ago. I hope we find a better road.'

'Oh, we will. According to the map there's a T-junction about a mile ahead. Turn left when we get there.'

It was always a pleasure to listen to Will's outpourings, because he justified his theories by research. After the jolting we'd had on those mountain tracks, it was even more of a pleasure to find that he was right: the T-junction appeared on cue. We turned left towards the sea, and saw that very soon the stream which we had recently crossed approached our road and followed it closely, down on the left. Will was consulting the map again. 'Now we're about three miles from Dolceacqua. Gosh, what a view!'

It was indeed. I pulled up again where space had been made for the traveller to enjoy the combined sight of road, river and mountain. Ahead in the distance, as we looked into the sun, we could see crowded old towers which must be Dolceacqua. Below us on the left the shallow river, twenty feet wide at this point, burbled its way over rocks and round boulders, while almost sheer from its opposite bank the mountain rose steeply to the heights on which we could still see perched the roofs of Perinaldo.It was a panorama too big, too bulging, for a canvas; but I would have been happy to sit where I was for an hour and absorb it from the life. Meanwhile Will had noticed something else. 'What did I tell you? Look across there, on the far bank. You can actually see a length of the old road. See, the bank's fallen away and exposed the rubble foundation. And further down there's even a stretch of low wall. God, if it weren't for my wonky ankle I'd love to walk that bit, just to say I'd trod where the Romans trod.'

I smiled as I slipped into gear. 'You could do that on Watling Street.' Sympathizing with his excitement, I drove slowly into Dolceaqua, noticing at one point stepping stones on either side of a long flat rock which rose grandly from the river. The little town itself presented us with a mixture of emotions. It was a discovery, no doubt of that, though the ribbon development on the main road was miserable: the river stayed close on the left, but on the right we were affronted by half a mile of poor-looking dun-coloured houses and small shops, all covered with dust from the road. It was rather like coming into Matlock, except for

the absence of ice cream parlours and souvenir shops. The
revelation was across the river, over a hump-backed stone
footbridge, where the dream-like towers which attracted us
on the wine label turned out to rise from a deliriously
ancient walled village which had had the luck to let
civilization pass by on the other side. From where we sat it
seemed the most delicious jumble of old crooked alleys,
patios and turrets, the more overpowering because it was
cramped on a little eminence which forced the passer-by to
view it impressionistically from below. Momentarily I
envied the people who lived there, people going about their
daily lives in the same traditional ways as their ancestors
had done centuries ago. It was a world not yet taken over by
the Riviera nobility, a world I longed to be part of for a
while. I knew the longing would pass quickly on close
acquaintance – the alleys no doubt were dank and
insanitary – but just a night here would, I felt, be an
experience worth cherishing, something to remember when
I was back in the drab world of commerce.

'That looks like a halfway decent hotel up ahead,' I said.
'I'd be delighted to treat us to bed and breakfast in it, unless
you have to be back at Loew's in a hurry.'

Shirley was a little taken aback at the suggestion – she was
probably looking forward to violin music while she ate the
sophisticated meal we had planned at the Hôtel de Paris –
but they both fell in with it easily enough. We didn't have
any night things with us, but even Dolceacqua must stock
toothbrushes, and we could be back in our luxury bathrooms
early next morning. It transpired however that our sudden
plan was doomed to disappointment. The little hotel, the
only one, didn't have rooms. They would be happy to
accommodate us for dinner, but otherwise their five
chambers were full. The manager, who spoke disappointingly
good English, obligingly offered to put one room at our
disposal until eight or so, but someone was coming from a

late plane to occupy it for the night. We shrugged and accepted: a few hours in this unexpected haven would be better than nothing. We all managed a wash and brush up, and then Shirley decided she needed a nap. Will and I had a couple of hours to kill, but with his weak ankle he didn't want to go much further than across the bridge. Over a campari we consulted the barman about local sights. In particular I asked whether I could cross the river at the rock a mile back and then walk to the old village along the far bank.

The man looked surprised. 'You mean along the Centurion's Road?'

Will looked at me with an expression of triumph. 'It *is* an old Roman road, then? We'd worked that out for ourselves but we weren't positive we were right.'

'Oh, yes: it has been here longer than any of the buildings you see. Once upon a time it was the only road from the mountains. Further up stream, it has fallen away, so none of the local people use it any more, but above the town it should be passable, if you have strong shoes. I crossed the rock myself last month, to fish.'

'That's for me, then,' I said. 'A little adventure before supper.'

Will looked doubtful. 'Are you sure you'll manage on your own?'

'What harm can I come to? It's a mile to the rock and a mile back down the other side. Give me an hour – fifty minutes even – and I'll look for you where the Centurion's Road comes out into the old village; then we'll have a drink over there. If I'm any longer, then I'll have had to retrace my steps. But I expect I'll make it.'

The bartender smiled, as though to make some comment about mad dogs and Englishmen. 'Give my regards to the centurion if you see him,' he said.

I pricked up my ears. 'There's a story, then?'

'Oh yes, a good one. It was always said that the last centurion who guarded that road in Roman times still does so. You will see a tablet to him in the village church, and there are postcards in the shops. The likeness is imaginary, you understand. His name was Antoninus, and the legend goes that instead of returning to the south when his service ended he retired here, and set himself up to care for the few travellers in this region, even giving them money if they needed it to continue on their way. We keep up the story for the tourists, but there are few of them these days: the hotel is busy only because the wine business thrives. That is more than can be said for the rest of Dolceaqua.'

'I take it then that you haven't met Antoninus yourself?'

The bartender chuckled. 'I do not travel that way. But I wish you luck. And I will lend you a stick in case the going is rough.'

A quarter of an hour later, at four o'clock, I set off, at the same time as Will, pipe in mouth, strolled blissfully over the footbridge: he couldn't wait to examine the church. The main road was of course a fairly dull trudge over tarmac, but it took me less than twenty minutes to reach the rock, and all the stepping stones were firm. For five minutes I stretched myself out on the flat boulder, dangling my fingers in the surprisingly cold water and gazing downstream into the afternoon sun, which was still very strong and caused a blinding reflection on the water. Then, remembering that Will was waiting for me, I carefully made my way across the torrent to the far side, using the borrowed stick to steady myself. In a few moments I found myself stumbling over fragments of what was, quite plainly, an old cobbled road about six feet across, with some evidence of a gutter on the river side. I was so excited to be in the presence of two thousand years of living history that I had to make frequent pauses for breath. It wasn't easy going, for between the worn and uneven pebbles the earth was sometimes very soft, but the stick was a blessing. The direct rays of the sun in my eyes made me feel dizzy and hot, so I slowed down, bearing in mind that I would have to wear the same clothes for dinner. To make matters worse I was trailed by great clouds of unfamiliar black flies, which refused to be beaten off and settled stickily around my neck. I have noticed before that insects tend to be attracted to yellow shirts, but this crowd was exceptionally persistent, and they seemed to lurk along the whole line of the road rather than in odd spots. I remember wondering whether their remote ancestors had troubled the centurions.

I had been on this return part of the journey for ten minutes or so when the cliff to my left grew steeper, and I realized that I was going to be troubled by an old landslide, possibly a result of last winter's storms, which had not been cleared away. I picked my way over it easily enough, for at its worst it was only seven or eight feet high, but I sank in the soft earth almost up to my knees at one point. Another problem was that the soil had brought down with it bushes of some gorse-like plant, which had reset and flourished to form a spiky barrier which was sometimes difficult to penetrate. I was glad I wasn't wearing shorts. The sun still seemed incredibly hot for the time of year, and I felt a little sick from it, also very strangely out of breath even considering my exertions. Suddenly a shooting pain in my stomach made me realize that this was only a culmination of the odd discomfort I had been feeling for the last ten minutes, and possibly also a development of the nausea I had felt after leaving San Remo. The heat, then, was not from the sun at all, but from within myself; it could have had something to do with the fish soup. Perspiration was standing out from my forehead, and I felt weak around the knees. I was suffering from some kind of flash fever. Panic seized me. I must press on while I still could, so that Will could get me to a doctor, or at least back to the hotel. In terms of distance I had made little progress since the rock: at least half a mile remained before the village, and I wasn't sure that I could make it. Now I was rounding a corner of the mountain: perhaps I would see the village before me, and all would be well. But what I saw was another slide, immensely bigger than the last: many tons of rock and earth had fallen not merely on to the pavement but across it into the river. This was a real climb even for a fit man, a case of three steps forward and two steps sliding back. The stomach pains were sharper now, and my efforts to mount the slope made them worse. I was dizzy, and my energy had drained away totally. If I fell here, I would be hidden from the main road: I might not be found for days. (In my panic I had forgotten that Will was waiting.) I must get on; and somehow I did, up over boulders, slipping in the scree, afraid at one point that I might disturb a great cornice of soil which hovered dangerously above me. Frequent halts were necessary, but I dared not sink to the earth, or I might not get up again. At last I reached the top of the slope, or very near it. Another step would surely allow me to see over the top to the village beyond. I took that step with my right foot, feeling like the conquerors of Everest, on to a square rock which seemed firmly lodged; but it gave way, my ankle twisted, and I slid cursing back down the slope I had so arduously climbed, resting eventually on my side in a hollow near the bottom.

Now I was really unable to move. I had no strength left at all, and those damned flies came at me in squadrons, even getting into my mouth as I gasped in pain, pain from my stomach and pain from my ankle. If I cried out for help, my voice would be drowned by the rushing water between me and the infrequent travellers on the main road. A wave of despair and weakness passed over me, and I lay shivering and helpless. I was about to close my eyes and give in to sleep when my twitching left hand closed over something hard, and I saw an object glint in my outstretched palm. At the same time the flies seemed to vanish and a strange smell surrounded me, not a smell from nature exactly but a male human smell of sweat and old leather and metal polish. With an effort I looked up. The sun was shining on what seemed like a helmet, blinding me to what lay underneath. Had a local policeman found me? Did Italian policemen wear helmets? I neither knew nor cared. *Someone* had found me, that was for sure, and even if he was a bandit I was more than willing to leave myself in his care . . .

I didn't eat any dinner, but by the time Will and Shirley came up to see me (I had been moved by now to the manager's own spare room) I was feeling very much better after being extremely sick. An Alka Seltzer took the nasty taste away, and I was certainly fit to be driven back to Monte Carlo. I struggled to sit up in bed, anxious to convince my friends that their worried looks were unnecessary, that the crisis was over. Will had brought up a small brandy, and my sipping of that finally reassured them.

Memories of what happened finally came back quite vividly, though in fits and starts. 'How did you find me?' I asked Will.

'Oh, it wasn't difficult. When you got to be twenty minutes late I began to stroll upstream along the Centurion's Road, and there you were, laddie, dead to the world but looking quite comfortable, lying on a rock just where the river bends. Actually you gave me a bit of turn at first, but I soon saw you'd be all right.'

'A rock? I don't remember that. But you had to clamber over that enormous rockfall to get to me?'

'I'm too old for clambering, I can tell you. No, you were on the flat, not four hundred yards from the old village. I saw the big slide, and wondered how you'd managed to get over it in your condition.'

'But I didn't. I couldn't: I fell back.'

'Well, don't worry about it. You must have made a second effort and managed it. You wouldn't remember, the state you were in.'

'No . . . I hadn't the strength. Unless I levitated.'

'What?'

'I have a distinct memory of floating, or rather being carried.'

'Carried? By whom? Certainly not by me, and I didn't see anybody else around.'

'Perhaps you wouldn't,' I said slowly. 'This was someone who smelt of old leather and wore a helmet.'

Will gave Shirley an odd glance, but all he said was: 'I don't know who you think would be capable of carrying your fourteen stone. Anyway, your efforts were well worth while. Tell us, where did you dig it up, and are there some left for me?'

'Dig what up?'

'The relic we found clutched in your hand. I think it's a Gordian coin, and quite a big one, in the most marvellous condition as though it was minted yesterday. I doubt if Christie's have seen one like it. You wouldn't like to come back tomorrow and look for some more?'

Blood Relation

'The question is,' said Ambrose Chauntsinger, 'ought I to tell anyone about it? The police, I mean?'

His voice trailed away and stopped. I exhaled a cloud of cigar smoke and looked studiously at the intricately moulded ceiling. 'The question is, would they believe you?'

'That's it exactly. I mean, you don't seem very convinced yourself.'

I hastened to reassure him. At the very least, his was an interesting story, the sort you don't come across every day, and while it wasn't exactly easy to believe, neither was he the kind of man capable of inventing a gigantic lie for no obvious reason. Under cover of catching the waiter's attention, I tried to get behind those rather pale eyes. A bachelor type of the old school, by no means queer but in view of his paunch|a bit past it anyway. Something of an adventurer in his youth, I imagined: in middle age he had probably come to terms with the real world and was by all accounts doing a useful job as a social worker in one of the outer London boroughs, while devoting as much time as he could to personal writings which by his own admission had so far failed to find a publisher. A solid, quiet, polite person who had tried, he told me, like Somerset Maugham, to arrange his life into a formal pattern with a pleasing climax, and who like Maugham had utterly failed, for despite Chauntsinger's enthusiasm for fresh experience, events were now passing him by. A lonely fellow, else why would he be entertaining a casual acquaintance to dinner on a Friday evening? Come to that, the same could be said of me; why else would I be making an unenthusiastic selection off the

Garrick Club's menu after the obligatory tour of thóse famous Zoffanys? We now lounged uncomfortably in a creaking old hide settee, and I had been wondering how soon I could get away when he came out with this curious story, after which I couldn't wait to wring him dry of every detail.

I didn't know him well at all. In fact we had met on a plane only a few months before, coming back from New York. I would have been willing to doze off as usual before the Stilton even arrived, but he had kept me talking, with the result that we both sat through a most inferior film about a Jewish wedding and kept ourselves stimulated with glass after glass of 86 proof Bourbon. I got the impression that, unlike most of us in first class, he was paying for his own ticket; and indeed he soon let slip that that was so, that a year ago he had come into a sizeable fortune from a mysterious older cousin he had hardly met. This had enabled him to rent a flat at the Albany, which he had always wanted to do, to vary these surroundings with a shared weekend place on the Thames at Teddington, and to take tea at the Dorchester every day if he wished. With his every statement he seemed more and more like a character out of *The Prisoner of Zenda* or *The Thirty-Nine Steps*, idling in London on a plentiful allowance, salving his conscience with voluntary work, and waiting for romance to turn the corner and bump into him. Though now that it had, he seemed pretty ill-equipped to deal with it.

Look here, the details of his life and personality don't have much effect on this particular story, beyond what I said at the beginning, that he wasn't the type to make such a thing up. Let's just add that he was well past fifty and had spent most of his life in America after being there at the age of twelve when war broke out. His parents had been killed in the blitz two years later, and for convenience he adopted the single-syllabled surname of the American friends who brought him up. He made a solid career in the tourist business, and only of late years had he grown restless. With the death of the last of his foster parents he determined to spend his declining years back in England, readopting his splendid family name which would have seemed so inappropriate in the land of simplification.

Some little while after his return to the old country, he was surprised to find himself called for jury service. I too had thought that the status of householder was required before this honour, or duty, or nuisance, could be legally imposed on one, but it seems that the rules were changed at some stage and that anyone on the electoral roll is now eligible. Ambrose was not displeased to receive the summons, for he hoped shortly to bring out a book of new fanciful solutions to unsolved real-life murder cases, and a little court experience could only be useful to this end. And so it was with an inappropriately light heart that he presented himself one rainy Monday soon after nine at the Crown Court in Surbiton, a little square building in a pseudo-Palladian style, with a yard of grass around it and a simple but elegant marble staircase in the lobby. Ambrose was disappointed to be hustled through to the back yard and thence to a concrete hut whose elementary amenities included a long and dismal jurors' waiting room with bare pockmarked tables laden with overflowing ashtrays and elderly magazines. Metal windows, tightly closed, ran down one side of the chamber, and sitting on metal and canvas chairs, wreathed in cigarette smoke, were a score or so of assorted citizens, no one of them engaged in conversation with another. It was, said Chauntsinger, like a low life version of the old play *Outward Bound*, in which the dead, not knowing they are dead, mingle vaguely in the lounge of an ocean liner floating on the seas of eternity.

Presently, a matronly lady in a black academic gown

came in and announced herself as one of the court bailiffs. She proceeded to read out names from a handful of cards, which Chauntsinger perceived to be coming up in reverse alphabetical order. Williams, Stone, Quincy, Norris, Morrow, McIlhenny, Haslam, Finch . . . he braced himself for the inevitable stumble over his own name, but when his turn came there was none, just a change of inflection, an extra loudness, a question. He looked up to find the good lady gazing at him in unmistakable surprise, holding the look for a second or two even after he had indicated his presence. Then Bennett and Allan completed the list, and they were all being shuffled off upstairs to hear what was termed 'a speech'. This turned out to be words of wisdom and nuggets of advice from the snaggletoothed clerk of the court, including not to worry if the defendant didn't like the look of you and exercised his right to have you replaced, not to forget to claim your expenses on the last day, and not to discuss the case with anybody at all until after the verdict.

At length the preliminaries were over, the jurors-to-be were sent back to the spectators' benches, and counsel and defendant took their place to hear sentence passed on a case which had ended the previous day. Be upstanding for his honour Judge Elsted, called the clerk, and there swept into his place of honour an elderly man in impressive regalia. Sixty-five, perhaps – it was a little difficult to tell under the wig – and with pendulous cheeks which gave him the appearance of a toothless old bull mastiff, an impression he sought to dispel from time to time by a rapid grin which was not so much of a spontaneous rearrangement of the flesh as the apparent result of an electric current having been shot through the body; or, Chauntsinger thought, like the glint on the brass nameplate of a coffin. At any rate he spoke clearly, if quietly, with due regard to the poor acoustics of the courtroom, and from the way he laid into the poor

convicted sneak thief in the box, Chauntsinger guessed that
his summings up ought to offer some small entertainment
value.

Now the clerk was calling his twelve new jurors, by some
form of random selection, and the judge's hooded eyes
examined each one carefully as he stepped as quietly and
meekly as possible into the box. (The clerk had advised that
this particular judge was intolerant of squeaky shoes.)
Suddenly a man just seated was asked to step down: the
defendant had objected to him. Since the defendant was a
teenager accused of intending grievous bodily harm to the
police during a street fight, and the disappointed juror a
white-haired man with a stick, Chauntsinger guessed the
reasoning to be that youth might be more lenient to youth.
Suddenly he heard his own name called, and again there
was that upward questioning infection but no stumble. He
looked up to see the clerk gazing open-mouthed at his card,
and behind him the judge raising his eyebrows so high as to
make his face an entirely different shape. Then the moment
passed, and he stepped into the box unchallenged; one more
followed him and then, after twelve oaths had been
haltingly read, the charade was ready to begin.

Chauntsinger said he called it a charade because,
although he had enormous respect for the law, at this local
level of shoplifting and gang fights and brandishing an
offensive weapon it seemed to involve excessive wastage of
the court's time and the taxpayer's money. During the first
four days they heard three cases, in each of which the
defendant was under twenty, of foreign origin, from a poor
district, and very plainly guilty from the word go. Pressure,
he felt, should be brought on such people not to force the
court to spend a day or more in proving them criminals, but
to go before a single judge and accept his verdict direct from
the evidence. As it was, though the judge was careful to
make interpretation of evidence the jury's own business

('Next, ladies and gentlemen, you saw the defendant's father give evidence. What did you make of him? Was he a man you could believe?'), it was quite clear from his swingeing comments in sentencing that he had been in no doubt from the beginning how matters stood. The only justification Chauntsinger could see for stretching these particular defendants over the rack of law was that the counsel got well paid work (often poorly executed) and the jury got a new experience which might be summed up as an extended and only tediously absorbing parlour game on the level of *What's My Line?*

The necessary concentration was sometimes hard to come by, for reasons that were purely physical. The jury box seats were small, close-set, and uncomfortable. The ceiling lights were too strong and too low, causing one to quail from them after minimal exposure and to run the risk of the judge's thinking one asleep. A headache usually resulted by lunchtime, and after the first day Chauntsinger brought dark glasses, which provoked a scornful glance from Judge Elsted. Perhaps the worst physical discomfort was that the court was cold in the morning but by afternoon insufferably hot. The week's initial rain quickly gave way to unblinking sunshine which defied the venetian blinds behind the jury box and made the back of one's neck burn from continued exposure in the same position. Aesthetically too the court was disappointing, not at all the multi-level Victorian puzzle box of carved oak which Chauntsinger had expected. It seemed to have been furnished during the austerity period which followed the second world war. All the chairs and desks at ground level looked like schoolroom rejects, and there wasn't a shaped handrail to be seen anywhere, just straight polished tops, with sides of poorer wood covered by peeling vinyl. Even the judge's solemn throne was an up-and-across affair upholstered in plain red. No, this dismal room with its poor acoustics entirely failed to suggest the majesty of the law. Its best feature undoubtedly was the panelling on the three non-window walls: plain enough, but clearly of solid oak and most pleasing to the eye. It rose from the floor of the court about twelve feet, so that even the judge on his dais was dwarfed by it, and the defendant facing him seemed insignificant indeed in his unnecessarily capacious dock. Above each of these two protagonists the top edge of the panelling rose in a semi-circular upward sweep, the intention above the judge being to accommodate a handsome painted shield featuring the lion and the unicorn and bearing the time-honoured phrases *Dieu Et Mon Droit* and *Honi Soit Qui Mal Y Pense*. The defendant's end had no adornment whatever. Running around the three walls, from window to window, the panelling was surmounted by a heavy wooden architrave or cornice, projecting six inches or so into the room and giving an ornate but top-heavy impression. Chauntsinger's eyes inspected it for damage, but there was none, and its splendid lengths of oak had been immaculately dovetailed.

Lunch was taken each day between one and two, and it was announced to the jurors that within walking distance were three pubs offering respectable fare. On the second day, having made his choice of these, Chauntsinger found himself walking back alongside the lady bailiff who had first welcomed the jurors. In order to avoid discussing the current case he complimented her on the smart way in which she had dealt with his very cumbersome and unusual name, which gave so much trouble to telephone operators. He enquired whether she had come across it before; she seemed a little uneasy and managed to change the subject. Chauntsinger persisted: she had pronounced it so perfectly, omitting the 'U' and 'T' sounds, as was right and proper but not at all obvious. She half shook her head and expected she must have heard it somewhere; were there many Chauntsingers about?

Here my friend had to confess partial ignorance, having

been out of the country for so long. He had always understood his family to hail from Alton in Hampshire, where he knew there was still a street with the same spelling. He had himself however been born in the north country, and of his branch of the family only his Aunt Alice soldiered on at an advanced age; she had lost the name by marriage fifty years back. He had occasionally sought it in telephone directories, usually without success, and he really thought that the old cousin, who had left him a fortune after not seeing him since childhood, might be the last of the line, apart from himself.

So matters rested until Friday, which frankly seemed a long time coming, for one case was very like another, and the court stenographer required all evidence to be given at dictation speed. It was during Friday afternoon, when the sunlight was exceptionally strong through the venetian slats, that Chauntsinger began to worry about his eyes. From his place in the middle of the rear tier of the jury box he could without turning his head look only straight across the court, past the counsel towards the circular railway-style clock on the opposite wall. To see the judge he had to strain to the right, while a glimpse of the defendant involved an equal strain to the left. What with sunlight aided by ceiling lights, the illumination in the room should have been bright and even, yet Chauntsinger increasingly found it difficult to get a clear view of the defendant, who was perpetually in some kind of shadow. He knew the accused to be a vacant-faced youth with a multitude of spots and a mop of unruly hair, thought by the police to have stabbed a friend during a pub brawl in Putney High Street. Chauntsinger did not particularly wish to examine his unattractive face in detail, yet it worried him that for some reason he couldn't. When he looked in that direction, all he saw was a foggy greyish haze, or rather a cloud; a cloud of finite size, though he could not have said for sure where it started or finished. Certainly it seemed to be as high as the panelling, more or less following the bulge of the architrave above the defendant, who was just dimly visible through the encirling gloom, apparently impervious through pure dim-wittedness both to his own vulnerable situation and to the barbs of the prosecuting counsel who was now summing up his case. At this moment Chauntsinger realized that the ticking of the court clock had become louder, and was indeed dinning remorselessly into his brain. Also, the defendant's unattractive face loomed larger through the curious fog into his consciousness, except that it was now not the defendant's face at all, there being much less hair, sharper ears, and an older, craftier look. There was also something unnaturally shiny about the upper teeth . . .

'Thank you, Mr Lewis,' said the judge crisply. 'I need to consult with the shorthand writer, so we will take a five-minute break before my summing up.'

Saved by the bell, thought Chauntsinger. He shook his head and filed out with the other jurors for a stretch in the corridor. Outside, he mentioned the weather and asked the man next to him whether the courtroom hadn't seemed to get very dark at the defendant's end; the man hadn't noticed, and indeed when Chauntsinger looked back into the room, the dock was flooded with sunlight. Only a slightly sticky feeling round Chauntsinger's collar was left to remind him of the panic which had been about to seize him when the judge had so luckily interrupted.

The summing-up was brief, the verdict guilty, the sentence three years. The weekend passed without any relevant event, and Monday brought a fresh case. Had Mr Alf Franklin stolen, as the police alleged, the expensive refrigerator which had been delivered to him by mistake? Or had he, as he claimed, merely signed on behalf of the man upstairs, and later handed back the item to the two men who had returned to correct the error and then vanished with the appliance? The available evidence was scanty and the witnesses too few to make the result interesting. Lunch came and went in its undistinguished way, and at three-twenty the defence counsel, an anaemic young woman with a cold, was still drearily picking at the police allegations, despite several testy interruptions from the judge. Chauntsinger gazed solemnly at the clock, and it was borne upon him that this was the time on Friday when he had his odd turn. Immediately he groaned inwardly: whether in some intuitive way the mere thought of it had brought it back he knew not, but his back was beginning to perspire and the area of the court to his left was growing dark. The cloud was denser than before, and it brought with it, as though overflowing the dock, a sense of malevolence which he could scarcely associate with the cunning little cockney being tried, who was almost totally obscured by the slowly whirling black mist, though where his face had been the other face hovered vaguely, the face with the crafty eyes and something odd about the teeth . . .

Once more there was a useful interruption. The lady counsel sat down to general relief, her opponent contented himself with a few swift reminders of what he had said earlier, and the judge summed up at a pace which suggested he had a date on the golf course. The jury's decision took no more than ten minutes; back in court, the defendant was discovered to have a list of previous convictions as long as your arm, and got off lightly with eighteen months. By twenty past four it was all over, and there was a general dash for the exit. Chauntsinger's Rover was down a street opposite, but his emergence coincided with an unpredicted shower, so he sheltered for a minute in the vestibule and was presently joined by the clerk of the court, who cursed at the weather and readily accepted Chauntsinger's offer of a lift to Norbiton Station. Chauntsinger took his time on the way. 'From the way you started when you first saw me last week,' he said pleasantly, 'I had the impression that you recognized me, or thought you did.'

'Oh. Well, no, Mr Chauntsinger. I expect it was just your unusual name.'

'Which, like the bailiff, you pronounced absolutely correctly, with no prompting at all.'

The clerk grinned rather nervously. 'I suppose I thought it might be the other one come back. Gave me quite a turn.'

'What other one? I'd like to meet another Chauntsinger. He may be a relation.'

'I doubt whether that could be arranged, sir. You see, he's dead. And I trust he wasn't no relation of yours, for a more evil person I never clapped eyes on.'

'I see. How did you meet him?'

'Why, as a defendant. Him, not me. In that very court, before that very judge, something over two years ago it would be. He came from a little village called Send, near Guildford. A big man, and bald as a coot, with sharp ears and baleful blue eyes, and a kind of broken gold tooth that caught the light. Looked like one of those mad doctors you used to see at the pictures when I was a lad. Stood up erect in that dock he did, over six feet of him, and if looks could have killed, he'd have taken the lot of us at one fell swipe.'

'And what was he charged with?'

'Why, assault was the only thing they thought would stick, assaulting the police when they came to enquire into the goings-on at that great house of his. I drove round to have a quiet look at it one Saturday afternoon: huge grounds, with a electrified fence, but the building very dilapidated. It was in all the papers at the time. You see, there'd been complaints about hysteria and nervous breakdowns and the like among local children this Mr Chauntsinger made so-called friends with, and when there was an outbreak of damage to graveyards and church altars and so on, everybody naturally assumed he was at the back of it, him and his funny friends. They used to visit him weekends; otherwise he lived alone, with two servants who were as spooky as he was. Anyway, one Saturday around midnight some neighbour rang the cops to complain about flashing lights and weird noises, and chaps with red hoods cavorting on the front lawn, and spilling on to the main road, scaring passers-by.'

'Which put it within the province of the law.'

'Quite so. Well, when the cops arrived all was quiet. They knocked on the front door and this Chauntsinger came out himself, very arrogant. They told him what they'd come for and he said nonsense and slammed the door in their faces. Of course, they made him open up again, but this time a gang of his friends came out and beat them up quite badly. Well, that was it, of course. The pity was he was the only one we could manage to charge, the others still having their red hoods on, and he wouldn't name them. Said it was all imagination, in fact. Reinforcements came and he was carted off to the station. And what do you think was found down in the cellar? A regular museum of witchcraft, with what looked like the remains of an animal sacrifice. The judge ordered it all confiscated, and quite right too.'

'So my namesake died in prison?'

'No, sir, that he didn't. What happened was, the judge made it clear in his summing up that he didn't much care for him, and when it came to sentencing there was a fine old argy-bargy. Judge Elsted told him in no uncertain terms that he and his kind were a menace to all decent folk and needed putting away for as long a time as possible. Chauntsinger said nothing, but I for one got the feeling that bars weren't going to hold him for long. The judge hadn't even finished when he started making a speech, something about being a new messiah. Quite quiet he was at first, but talking through his teeth if you know what I mean. The judge wasn't standing for that, so he told him to stand down,

and when that didn't work he ordered him to be restrained.
Well, it took three coppers to get the fellow under control,
and even then, when they got him to the door, he was still
yelling at the top of his lungs, and what he was yelling was a
curse on the judge. Calling on Beelzebub and folk like that
he was, to come down and smite the judge with the great
blackness–'

'The what?'

'The great blackness, sir. I remember the phrase very
distinctly, though I've no idea what he meant. Standing
with his arms curved up, he was, as though to pull
something down from the ceiling, with cops all round him as
much use as little yapping dogs. Everybody in court was
scared stiff: I was myself. There was something very nasty
about the fellow, you see. And then suddenly, sir, he
crumpled up to nothing. One moment he was this all-
powerful monster, and the next he was dead in a heap on the
floor of the dock. A fit of some kind: the police doctor
couldn't put a name to it. I'll never forget the look on his
face as he lay there, his lips all drawn back in what looked
like a snarl, and that big gold tooth of his glinting like a
diamond in the sunlight . . .'

Before they parted, Ambrose ascertained the first name of
this other, diabolic, Chauntsinger. It was, as he knew it must
be, Rowan. Now he understood why the lawyer had been so
reticent about the manner of his benefactor's death; but
there was still much that was oppressive and obscure. It
became quite appallingly clearer on the following afternoon.

A new case had begun, burglary this time. The defendant's
claim was that he had been rather drunk after the pubs
closed, and had unfortunately fallen through the glass door
of the shop where the police caught him red-handed with a
bag full of expensive stock. The judge permitted himself a
weary smile to the jurors at this point, but justice continued
to be seen to be done through lunch and well into the

afternoon. Chauntsinger had forgotten to notice the time when he became aware of a raging headache over his left ear. Such afflictions were sometimes caused by pressure from his spectacles, so he took them off and placed them on the shelf in front of him. The pain however did not abate, and he found it increasingly difficult to follow the evidence. Instinctively he recognized his discomfort as having a connection with that – what was the phrase – that great blackness which had assailed him during the previous two afternoons in court. He put on his spectacles and looked hard at the sullen defendant through the inevitably encircling gloom. The first thing of which he became aware was the tooth, the great gold tooth, gleaming menacingly at him; the second was the bald dome over the impossibly older face with its sinister, penetrating eyes. None of these items belonged to the sallow youth of Greek origin who had been accused of burglary and was so plainly guilty of it. This was a face of more mesmeric and mature evil, not perhaps malevolent to Ambrose personally, but wanting him, willing him to perform some awful mysterious act which would clearly be against his conscience. The sun on his neck made him feel faint; the mystery of what the face wanted made him feel dizzy. Strength, perhaps; it wanted his strength. Certainly he felt drained, as though power were passing out of him, or rather being drawn out towards that strange dead creature who had borne his name. He sat hypnotized, transfixed, knowing that no one in the court room save himself was aware of what was going on. It was happening perhaps on a different plane, a plane on which, for the moment, only he and the awful spectre in the dock existed.

As the energy drain continued, to the point where Chauntsinger began to fear for his life if it became much more intense, the blackish mist round the monster began to solidify and harden, not to a texture absolutely tangible but to a heavy smoke which seemed to condense and hang like soot at a point a little above the creature's head. At the same time, whatever physical unpleasantness had been happening to Chauntsinger seemed to cease; he was safe now, weak and still and impotent but quite comfortable, waiting for his normal heavy and healthy breathing to return him eventually to the land of the fully alive. Meanwhile there was no way in which he could move a muscle.

What was happening now? Why, the monster had stretched its arms above its head. Chauntsinger could see its tapering hands, hands studded with heavy rings, closing relentlessly together, and between them was the smoke, kneaded now almost to the semblance of black dough, flowing upward with some awful new will of its own until it settled lumpenly on the wide architrave of the arched panelling. It lay there quivering softly; at the same time the human or semi-human apparition in the dock disappeared, or rather melted away, leaving young Constanides quite clearly visible. The black thing, Chauntsinger saw, was shaping itself into a monstrous caricature of an animal, like a giant caterpillar. There was no head, no eyes, no tail, yet it had intelligence: it was working out its next step. Within seconds the plan of action was determined. It moved. Not towards the window with its flood of light, but away from Chauntsinger into the far corner, into the shadows which were its natural field. In doing so it arched, and seemed to propel itself as a caterpillar does, sliding its front silently along the wooden rail, then by some muscular action bringing up its rear. Round the corner and over the doorway it progressed, like a ghastly mockery of primitive life; then after a pause for consolidation of strength it began its journey along the rest of the far wall of the court, over the clock, over the heads of the defence witness and the attendant policeman, and eventually round the other corner towards Judge Elsted, who was sunk in contemplation, one elbow on the bench before him and the index finger of that arm sunk deep into his cheek. The judge! He must of course be the final destination of the black thing's progress! Chauntsinger wanted to cry out in warning, but he could not. He was paralysed: he could only watch. The thing soon reared itself up the final slope of the semi-circular moulding above his honour. Extra effort was now evident in its progress, a sense of suppressed excitement which pulsated its whole being. It had now reached its highest possible vantage point above the shield, and from this it insinuated its top part forward until at one moment Chauntsinger felt it must fall; but somehow the essential part of it remained gripping the architrave while the rest spread itself more thinly, yet still menacingly, forwards and downwards until it again seemed grey rather than black, like a dense canopy obscuring the colours of the shield. Chauntsinger felt his hands tremble as they lay in his lap; he was thinking that if the thing came near to him he would surely die of horror and revulsion. At last, part of it seemed to belch and billow so that it was almost able to touch the grey wig, and at this point a great sickness in Chauntsinger rose to his throat. The spell which had bound him was half broken, and with a deep guttural sigh he found himself rising to his feet, his arm outstretched towards the judicial dais, a strangled cry forcing itself from his arid throat . . .

He woke to find himself in a strange cheerless room, lying uncomfortably on the floor with a rough blanket over him. His whole body throbbed with a vibrant nervous sensation, but his head was lighter and he felt a sense of great relief, as though an intolerable oppression had passed. Suddenly he was suffused with embarrassment at the scene he felt he must have caused. The lady bailiff was sitting on a nearby chair, talking to a man in white: they must have sent for an ambulance. With difficulty he raised himself on one arm, wondering what he could tell them, but the man seemed to have little interest in him, and with a glance and a smile left the room. The lady bailiff came forward with a comforting look, though her eyes were red as though with crying. She began to talk to him, almost to babble, about the heat in the court, and how air conditioning was to be fitted next month, and how it was all too late and she could never work there again after what had happened. And what had happened was that Judge Elsted was dead, it seemed from a heart attack, no doubt brought on by the intolerable atmosphere, which even she had noticed was lying like a shroud on the assembly. Clearly, it was thought, Chauntsinger had been the first to notice the judge's fatal malady, and on rising to his feet to give the alarm had himself fainted from the sudden exertion.

I stubbed out my cigar, which was beginning to taste foul. 'Well,' I said, 'I hate to say so, but if I were you I'd keep all that to myself. Unless you want to find yourself listed as a psychiatric case. It sounds like a job more for an exorcist than for a policeman.'

Chauntsinger nodded sadly. 'You admit, though, that it has a certain logic?'

'I suppose your theory is that the supernatural thing, whatever it was, used your strength to propel itself into action, and indeed must have waited for you because you were of the same bloodline as this black magician relative.'

Chauntsinger managed a smile. 'They do say blood is thicker than water. And I suppose he expected a favour in return for what he left me.'

'But there's absolutely no way you can prove any of it.'

'None at all. And it's not as though anybody else is in danger: it was only the judge who was cursed. I did go up to see Aunt Alice, and asked her whether she remembered anything about Cousin Rowan. She didn't even seem to know he was dead, but then she's eighty-seven and entitled to her fancies. She said she didn't recommend me to look

him up. It seems the family more or less paid him to leave
the country thirty years back, after some scandal that was
hushed up. Personally, she said, she'd never been able to
stand him since he stayed with her as a smallish boy and put
rats in her bed.'

The Temple of Music and the Temple of Art

My friend Membury is a bachelor bookseller who runs what is possibly the best antiquarian establishment in the south of England. Though the word 'antiquarian' these days usually connotes no more than 'second hand', his is a richly rewarding and well selected stock, and Membury himself, with his bald head, pointed beard and pince nez, certainly looks the part. His clientele by now must be world wide: he won't post any parcel worth less than ten pounds, and if he takes a dislike to a customer he is quite likely to be so rude as to turn him deliberately away. On the other hand, if he finds himself psychologically in tune with an impecunious browser, he has been known practically to give away expensive volumes. I have gladly put up with his eccentricities for twenty years, and most of my own library has been built up from his shelves. Whenever we meet, which apart from my visits to the shop is usually on the first Monday of every month for a theatre, followed by supper at a little place for parliamentarians I found in Westminster, we converse in lively fashion on everything to do with the arts. Our only serious dispute has been on the unduly large occult section which he has allowed to accumulate at the back of his somewhat cramped premises. I disapprove of such interests, not because I don't believe in the supernatural but because I think that concentration on it leads to fanaticism. My wife agrees, and is always trying to get Membury married off so that his thoughts can wander along healthier routes. Membury however is serious in his belief in reincarnation, and once told me over two or three glasses of Courvoisier that to his positive knowledge he had led previous lives in ancient Rome and at the court of Louis XIII. To my mind this conviction resulted merely from his finding those periods of absorbing interest. I do so myself, but make no claim to be descended from Tiberius Caesar or Cardinal Richelieu. I closed the subject on that occasion by asking Membury to ensure that next time I come back, I do so as an extremely pampered dog. I could do with a rest.

Membury had long passed fifty and was becoming, shall we say, a trifle corpulent. Since in the manner of most bachelors he was obsessed with the state of his health, he resolved to shut his shop for a week in May and take a cure. After perusing several brochures he settled on the homeo-pathic clinic at Arlingham Hall in Norfolk, a few miles northwest of Thetford. A bumptious mutual friend claimed to have lost a stone a week there; most of it, I imagine, from his head. At Membury's request I took my Pevsner to dinner, and looked up Arlingham over the Stilton. It certainly had features of interest. A house had stood there since the time of the Domesday Book, when it was known as Pasford (and in the vicinity there still exists a ford which has to be passed). Later it became Rallingham, after the family which owned it; later, by a curious but not uncommon process of etymological dyslexia, the name amended itself to Arlingham. As the family were Royalists, the old castellated house was thoroughly slighted (lovely word) by Cromwell's mob, and more than a century passed before the family fortunes were sufficiently rosy to permit demolition followed by a grand rebuilding, to the design of no less eminent an architect than Sir John Soane, whose superbly appointed mansion in Lincolns Inn Fields (now a museum) is one of my most frequent ports of call in London. The famous diarist Parson Woodforde was thought to be among the first guests at Arlingham when it was formally reopened in 1791, though he fails to record the fact in his journal and indeed died soon after, hopefully not as a consequence. Unfor-

tunately the Arlingham family itself died out in the
nineteenth century and the house and grounds passed into
other hands, those of a wealthy Nottingham lacemaker, who
conceived some most unfortunate additions, including an
asymmetrical south wing and a half-hidden third storey for
servants, which sits most oddly behind the original Soane
balustrade. In the present century an American millionaire
acquired the property, and insanely added to the central
roof a massive copper dome which conceals an astronomical
observatory, used twice before the owner's sudden death
and thereafter only a blot on the landscape to discourage
further potential buyers. In two world wars the house was
used as a military hospital, and in the early seventies it
became the property of an oil-rich Arab who, in gratitude
for his son's rapid recovery from a form of skin cancer,
deeded it for twenty-five years to the current residents, a
group of homeopathic practitioners. Living rent free, they
were obliged to shun the profiteering motive, and Arlingham
was known among connoisseurs of health retreats not only to
offer its guests the widest range of treatments but to do so at
the lowest possible price.

'Well, it all sounds very interesting,' I said. 'Osteopathy,
acupuncture, massage, saunas, the lot. And you're off on
Saturday? If you'd given me warning I might have come
with you.'

'No chance of that, old chap,' said Membury. 'They're
booked up half a year in advance: I was just lucky to get a
cancellation. But we'll go again in the winter if you like.'

I pulled a face. 'When it comes to the crunch I like to
know what I'm letting myself in for. Especially in winter: I
catch cold easily. Tell you what: I have to drive up to
Norwich on Wednesday week and stay over; may I pop in
on my way to share your luncheon lettuce leaf and a cup of
slippery elm?'

So I did. The peanut salad wasn't bad, actually, though

the manager put me off it, while I was waiting for Membury to emerge from his ultra-sonic massage, by showing me round the kitchen garden and demonstrating what they dumped on the vegetables to make them grow: everything organic they could find, including blood and urine samples. At lunch we nibbled sedately in a rather dour room done out in Wedgwood blue. I was always told that blue is the one colour you shouldn't associate with food, as it occurs in almost no natural substance; but no matter. Membury was most amiable but seemed to be in a state of suppressed excitement. I put it down to the fact he'd allegedly been on a fast for three days, or to the effect of the vibro massage. But it turned out to result from his addiction to historical detective work. After lunch – they didn't believe in serving drinks with it, not even water, which irritated me – we walked round the rather pretty gardens and Membury told me what his excitement was all about: the Arlingham temples. Two very remarkable small buildings they were too: as soon as I saw them I shared Membury's curiosity. An identical pair of gazebo-like structures in stone, the temples were symmetrically arranged at the far corners of the formal sunken garden, which lay to the rear of the house and central to it. The French windows of the dining room actually commanded a view between the two temples to a distant treeline framed by two broken columns; you know the sort of thing, all very much of Soane's period, Romantic with a capital R. Membury said the oblong garden, still framed by thick box hedges, had originally contained a maze, but more recent owners had swept this away to accommodate a vast blue-tiled open swimming pool, which was now being restored to use after decades of neglect. The whole arrangement was dominated by these two curious structures, which were perhaps a hundred feet apart and each about twenty feet square, in a distinctly Palladian style. So far as Membury had been able to discover, they were contemporary with the main building, though the plans had been lost. Both were domed, which is probably where the American had got the idea for his ghastly great rooftop observatory, but the designs were otherwise strictly formal and classical. The buildings were locally known as the Temple of Music and the Temple of Art, and these names were thought to date from the eighteenth century, though the precise reason for them had been lost during the house's frequent changes of owner. Why Pevsner had failed to mention them is a mystery, for they undoubtedly had a fascination for the eyes, and must have been particularly striking at sunset. Regrettably, although the stonework showed little sign of age, the interiors were half-derelict and judged somewhat dangerous, though Membury had been allowed on request to take the only key and explore. The Temple of Music, the northerly one, had an upstairs room, with *two* stone spiral staircases, which seemed excessive unless there were fire regulations in the eighteenth century too. The upper storey must have been used for packing things away, the lower presumably for small chamber concerts, or to house an orchestra playing at garden parties: wide French doors on three sides would give the effect of an open pavilion. The Temple of Art was quite a different matter, and certainly had a less cheerful aspect, for clearly it would lie in the shadow of a high wood for most of the day. To begin with, an inscription had been carved over the portal: DOMUS DEMONIS. That didn't seem to have much to do with art, but Membury, with his particular proclivities, found it very interesting indeed, especially as what appeared to be the face of a bearded demon was carved in stone in the lintel below it. The interior was however disappointing. At the east side a metal spiral staircase led up to a solid stone balcony; otherwise this was a one-storey building which could have been used as a chapel or, indeed, a small art gallery, with illumination from what amounted to a clerestory below the dome. The building had long been stripped of all decoration apart from the floor, whose oddly coloured stone slabs, some of them shaped from highly polished marble, were arranged in a curious concentric pattern, unique in my experience. Sadly, the most obvious recent intruder was water, for the roof leaked badly in one place and virtually every window casement needed its wood renewing; also, I counted eleven cracked window panes, though whether from frost or from vandalism it was impossible to say.

Membury had found himself entirely preoccupied, both between and during treatments, with the historical puzzle presented by the two buildings. The very limited Arlingham library, which mostly consisted of sporting volumes happily disposed of by a nearby US Air Force base, had absolutely nothing to divulge on the matter, and any family prints which might have been expected to hang on the walls of the old house had been either stored or sold by the Arab owner. It was Membury's instinctive theory that the Arlinghams of the late eighteenth century could well have been close friends of the notorious Dashwoods of West Wycombe. Sir Francis Dashwood would certainly be known to them, and as minor nobility they must have been well aware of his Hellfire Club which operated surreptitiously in the West Wycombe caves for high-ranking deviants who relished its monkeys dressed as nuns and other erotic extravaganzas. The onlie begetter of such diversions for the young sparks of the period, Sir Francis seemed to draw the line at actual devil worship, but who was to say how baleful his influence might have been when propagated by a disciple among the bored country squires of Norfolk?

Being no driver, Membury had come to Arlingham by train and taxi. His suggestion now was that if I could spare a couple of hours more he would cut a two-o'clock yoga class so that we might pop into Thetford for a joint reconnaissance of the public library. I had no appointment in Norwich before my evening lecture, so that's what we did. The Thetford librarian seemed so pleased and surprised by our interest that he actually made us a pot of tea while we perused all relevant documents, but they were few indeed and he had no personal knowledge of the Arlingham family. It seemed that all documents for the period immediately following the reconstruction of the house had been lost, so mysteriously that local historians favoured the deliberate suppression theory. There was no hard evidence either way, even in the surviving letters of contemporaries. The library held copies of a contemporary local newspaper of sorts, which might have been expected to carry any sensational story, but did not. There was plenty of testimony to the opening ceremony in 1791, and to some amendments a year later, but nothing at all about the temples. Then came this curious ten-year blackout, which could hardly be accidental. One engraving of the period did survive, but showed only the front of the Hall, looking much better without its dome.

I took Membury back to his Scottish douche and went on my way. We did not meet again for another fortnight, when I allowed him to invite me to a vegetarian restaurant on Putney Hill, recommended by the powers that be at Arlingham. It was ghastly, but at least I was able to smoke my cigars, to accompany which they provided some tolerable so-called fruit brandy. Membury clearly had a most exciting story to tell me, but as was his wont he let it pour out in such a jumble that I think I had better give it in my own way.

After my departure he had returned to his treatments pondering over the name Arlingham, and wondering why, from the time he first heard it, it had seemed to represent some lock to which his mind might provide a key. At six o'clock he went to his room to prepare for the evening snack – in a health clinic one can scarcely dignify the meal with the word dinner – and while dressing stood for a while at his rear window looking down on the pool and the two temples. His room, being in the asymmetrical south wing, gave a view similar to that of the dining room but one storey elevated and further to the right, thus presenting an oblique impression of the formal garden, with the Temple of Art partly obliterated by a tall cypress. It was a pleasant evening, with the sun making long shadows. He thought of the day nearly two hundred years ago when Arlingham Hall in its present form was first opened to family and friends. He pictured the distinguished personages helping themselves from an open-air buffet and parading around the simple maze in their satins and brocades, with powdered wigs and trailing gowns, the bright colours gleaming in the sun, no doubt to the accompaniment of cheerful music from the open doors of the appropriate temple. He was still gazing into this delectable vision when in the distance a bell rang to command assembly, and at once the figures of his imagination faded. All save one.

The obstinate exception was a girl in pale green, standing near the doorway of the music temple and looking across to its twin. Whether a complementary figure was standing in the other doorway Membury could not from his vantage point be sure, but in any event the girl disconcertingly began to turn away from her first objective, until she was looking straight up at Membury. The distance between them must have been almost a hundred yards, and if she had existed in the flesh he would have had little possibility of scrutinizing the details of her face; as it was, her features were fully revealed to him, as though a telescopic lens had suddenly been placed between them. The unexpected effect quite took his breath away, and by the time he recovered himself the girl had gone. The face however stayed with him very clearly. Neither beautiful nor aristocratic, but composed and most would say pretty; probably quite attractive when animated, but at present on the sad side. The most troublesome thing was, it was a face he seemed to have known all his life.

The next morning he woke up early, and remembered at once that the day marked his first entitlement to a hot savoury lunch, which was indeed a comforting thought after existence on barmene and bean shoots. Not that he was particularly hungry, but it had occurred to him to wonder whether his experience of the previous evening could have resulted from light-headedness through the body's unaccustomed physical deprivation. He certainly remembered feeling a little dizzy when he looked at the girl in green. Membury bathed, donned his underwear and dressing gown, and was ready for the day's action. He glanced out of the window. No garden party there today; despite the season there was actually a touch of frost on the grass. He was moving away from the window when his eye dropped to the gravel path immediately below. The girl in green was standing there, looking up at him, plaintive and open-mouthed.

In his excitement to get the window open Membury banged his forehead quite hard on the glass, which luckily failed to break. By the time he recovered himself from this accident, the girl was nowhere to be seen. Eventually Membury emerged from his room and walked very slowly and thoughtfully down the narrow corridor to the thermal pool. After an active morning during which he determinedly sampled the sauna, jacuzzi, solarium and underwater jetstream, he was ready for his lunch. This proved to consist of a disappointing and saltless combination of macaroni and mushrooms, indifferently cooked, but at least it made him feel physically stronger, and seemed to ensure that no more impressions from the past came his way that day. Contradictorily enough, he awoke the next morning with some kind of chill round the waist, and at his consultant's suggestion cut short his treatments and retired early to bed with the homeopathic version of a hot toddy and a couple of paracetamol tablets. Saturday morning found him fully restored and eager to be home; however, there was a full schedule of treatments to get through, followed by a final consultation and the all-important weighing out. Nine pounds lost; not bad at all. He hurried to pack before the last supper: soup as well as salad were promised. It was six P.M., and someone from the new intake was already waiting for his room. A quick shower, and then to dress. It would be interesting to see what some members of his group would look like fully dressed; in many cases the choice of dressing gowns had been eccentric to say the least. A cloud had passed over the sun, and he was wrestling in the gloaming with a recalcitrant tie when he happened to glance into the Victorian cheval mirror which stood in a dark corner. Reflected in it was the girl in green.

For a period of about five seconds he did not dare turn round, but stood there frozen, one hand at his neck knot. Then he took a deep slow breath and looked straight at her reflection in the glass, establishing that she had to be standing right behind him, to the window side of the bed, not blocking his path to the door and yet somehow steeling him to remain. Determined to challenge her, he turned slowly to fix her with a stare at least the equal of hers. This time she had one arm upraised as though to touch him, but the expression on her face said that she was afraid for some reason to do so. With a mixture of satisfaction and dismay he noted that she was transparent; through her body he could see his pile of books heaped on the dressing table. He took a short step towards her. She uttered a word. Her lips did not seem to move, yet he heard the whisper. The word was: Daniel. And then she was there no longer.

'And so,' I said with a questioning inflection, 'you left and came home, with the puzzle unsolved?'

'I couldn't stay: my bed was spoken for. Besides, at the

rate she was approaching she might have taken me over before I told you the tale. Now that you've heard it, do you think I'm potty?'

'Do you?'

'No, but I do think that part of me belonged in that period, and very likely in that house. I forgot to tell you, something else peculiar happened on the day we arrived. We were given a tour of the house, and the fellow in charge said there were no known ghosts, but one secret panel, which he didn't suppose we'd find unaided. Something made me ask if it was in the library, and when he said yes I went straight to it, absolutely on my own. It was between two bookcases, and led to the tower stairs. And I knew! I *knew* that! The chap was a bit upset, thought I'd been put up to it or somebody had told me. I mumbled something about knowing a few architects' tricks. But the fact was I knew the house, the older part of it, even though I'd never even been within ten miles of it before.'

'And what about the name Daniel?'

'That didn't seem to surprise me either. It somehow fitted. I've got to find out whether there was a Daniel Arlingham. Do you think Somerset House . . .?'

I took some papers from my pocket. 'Don't bother. While I was in Norwich I did some research of my own. The reference library had a collection of holograph manuscripts covering the missing period, including a diary by a local gossip named Jonathan Porter. He seems to have been an educated man with a big library and a narrow mind, rather like John Aubrey or Augustus Hare. The journal was left to his heirs with an injunction that it shouldn't be published till fifty years after his death; by then of course nobody thought it worth publishing at all, and it's a miracle it survived. But listen to what Jonathan has to say about Arlingham Hall in July 1793.' I began to read quietly.

I fear that the noble family of Arlingham has again fallen on evil times. The last two children born to Lady Anne died in infancy, and 'tis a certainty she can produce no more, being in my imagining nearer fifty than forty, and all her life stronger in spirit than in body. Now tragedy has struck her first born, young Daniel, who would have reached his majority this summer. It appears that last year while in the city he did fall in with evil influences, of a kind shunned by all Christian men. Who will say what practices were carried out in his Temple of Dionysus, which Sir Alfred had been persuaded to give into Daniel's absolute charge? Such things are better unspoken. But to add to the account, Daniel did conceive a most unwise affection for a village girl who by all accounts doted upon him. She was ill educated, but of sober, hard-working parentage, and he proposed to make her his wife. His father naturally withheld consent, but Daniel did fly into a passion and arranged for some species of heathen wedding ceremony to take place one night in the temple. Just in time did his father find out about this intent, and so went down with his dogs to clear the congregation away. In the ensuing scuffle Daniel did fight with his father and the dogs did intervene, with the unhappy result that the boy did fall badly over a low wall and was found to have broken his neck. The girl did wail piteously over the corpse and the father, repenting him of his wrath, did adopt her into his family. The temple was stripped of its infamous decoration and young Daniel interred beneath its floor, the structure thus becoming a mausoleum for one who died so tragically and so young. Alas, the girl did not recover of her grief, and one month later did pass away also. Unhappy Sir Alfred then had her buried beneath the opposite temple, so that the lovers, in death, lay opposite each other in the handsome garden which might have entertained them for a score of summers. All this was done in secret, and I know it only because old Dr Cook, who attended both, asked me on his death bed to be his confessor, having regretted the concealment which was connived at by family and servants alike. And none shall hear it from me until no harm can come to any man from its revelation. For which of us can know himself to be incapable of such misdirection of his life? There, but for the grace of God, etc., etc.

I passed the papers to Membury. 'They allowed me to take photostats,' I said. 'That girl clearly wants her Daniel back, so you'd better be off to Somerset House and see whether you can trace any Arlinghams among the Memburys. And meanwhile, if you want untroubled dreams, I should think twice before returning to Arlingham for another cure. What have you heard about Pendlebury Manor?'

Remembrance of Things Past

I am a strong believer in the effect of place on the human spirit. Personally I can think of half a dozen atmospheres in which I function extremely well. There are also many environments in which I can scarcely function at all. These include my office (usually) and any dinner party for more than six people.

In a similar way, it seems to me, people likely to be susceptible to psychic influences will be far more so in certain places than in others. I included in an earlier setting the true story of a friend of mine who shall be called Haslam, who on his first visit to an annual television market in Monte Carlo encountered, or thought he encountered, the ghost of a Roman légionnaire, in an ancient village some twenty miles to the east. Well, there can be all kinds of explanations for an isolated occurrence, but I'm in the same line of business as Haslam, and in the following February when we were both in Monte Carlo a series of events took place which persuaded him and me that he did have some psychic second sight of the kind not given to all of us.

I thought he wasn't looking at his best. Nothing serious, rather as though he'd been taking too little sleep and fresh air, and very possibly too much to drink. Certainly too much French cuisine, with all that cream and red wine. You know the syndrome: the French call it 'crise de foie'. I spotted him first in the hotel lobby, about two evenings into the event. I was standing on the steps looking down into the maelstrom – most of the hotel is built below road level – and there he was, walking nervously along the main corridor, glancing occasionally over his shoulder as though he suspected somebody of following him but didn't care to see who it was. I remember thinking that Haslam, whom I knew just a little better than casually, had the lightest of characters and would probably be incapable of saying boo to the proverbial goose. It so happened that we were both guests that night of the same American salesperson, and if I say that it took three cars to get us all to the restaurant you will know that I did not enjoy myself, especially as the hostelry selected was an elaborate but gaudy reconstruction of a Roman villa. It was in fact called the Villa dei Cesari, and the major domo was decked out like a Roman legionnaire, which made me ask Haslam whether he looked anything like the ghostly figure in the tale he'd told me the year before. He said yes, pretty much, and was silent; so I went on to mention, in the way of small talk, that after lunch that day I had been driving back from Eze – the mountaintop Eze, not the *sur mer* variety – and on passing through the high junction town of La Turbie had noticed high over the rooftops some massive broken Roman pillars with a partial coping, which I presumed were sombody's expensive eighteenth-century folly.

Not necessarily, said Haslam, stroking his upper lip thoughtfully. He remembered, he said, hearing something about a genuine ruin up there, and indeed during the previous market thought he had caught a glimpse of it from the hotel roof way down below in the bay. He had been told however that getting up to it involved twenty minutes of tricky driving, and as he wasn't exactly a demon at the wheel he had lost interest. I said that the hairpins weren't too bad, and that I was more than willing to drive him up there on the following morning, which was Sunday. It turned out to be a gorgeous day for that time of year, and I enjoyed the exhilaration of zooming ever higher up those great beetling cliffs, with glimpses of the Monaco skyscrapers looking like Lego constructions far below. The road we took is in fact the only way up for miles on either side, which is presumably why the little town of La Turbie was built at the top of it; at one time it must have marked the only direct descent to Monaco from the Alpes Maritimes. Alas, time and corniches and aeroplanes have reduced La Turbie's status. The tourist will now find it at first glance an undistinguished and straggly community with a lot of through traffic and some remarkably extensive modern housing developments which may for all I know appeal greatly to those who enjoy living on the very top of a three-thousand-foot rock with a total southward command of the Mediterranean.

Finding the monument wasn't difficult: it towers above the shopping area from most angles. We drove up a cobbled side street and parked right by its surrounding wall. It was looked after by the French equivalent of the Ministry of Works, and there was a hut where we paid five francs each to pass through the turnstile. We also bought an illustrated brochure which referred to the monument as the Trophy of the Alps, although the noticeboard on the wall had called it the Trophy of Augustus. What seemed not to be in doubt was the purpose of its original erection in the declining years of B.C.; it was to mark the triumphal return of Caesar Augustus from his peaceful settlement of Gaul. Indeed, the guide book rather lyrically described the object as the oldest surviving fragment of French history. (Haslam and I admitted to each other our shame at never having heard of it before.) I suppose the description depends on how one interprets the word 'survive', for what remains today in La Turbie (the name of the town is simply a corruption of trophy or *trophée*) is almost entirely a loving nineteenth-century reconstruction of the north wall. It must once have been a massive cylindrical building with no windows but every imaginable kind of stone decoration. A browse round the little museum made it clear that nobody knows for sure what

it originally looked like, what practical purpose it might
have been made to serve, or whether or not it was
surmounted by a statue. One vast bronze door which had
been reconstructed *in situ* makes it likely that people did go in
and out of it for ceremonial purposes; but the only real
certainties now are that the original building held one of the
most romantic and commanding positions imaginable to
man, and that the remaining ninety-foot ruin is worth an
hour of anybody's time. Worth it if only to stand on the cliff
edge, casting one eye on the trophy and the other down the
dizzying slopes to the tiny principality where rich parasites
feed off one another and microscopic chunks of real estate
change hands at astronomic prices. Such is the state of the
Mediterranean world twenty centuries after the trophy was
built.

Haslam showed a consuming interest in the ruin, and
lingered in the museum long after I had retired to smoke a
pipe on the one seat provided at the highest point. I thought
his complexion was still a bit ashen, and said so; he laughed
this off by saying that he certainly shouldn't have breakfasted
off what the French call a kipper, the result being a sick
stomach which he was sure would pass with the help of a
fernet branca before lunch at some local restaurant. We
decided first, when he had had his fill of the trophy, on a
quick tour of the shops, and were delighted, on passing
through the exit turnstile, to find that the most direct access
lay down a cobbled street of great apparent antiquity,
though much of it may have been as artificial as the scenery
in a provincial pantomine. It was so narrow that the
projecting first floor eaves seemed from certain angles almost
to touch. A sign designated it as the Via Julia, which seemed
a pretentious label for a passageway not much more than a
hundred yards long; but perhaps it had had that name since
the days of Julius himself. Clearly closed now to all but
pedestrian traffic, it led down a gentle slope to a couple of

steps where it joined the main street: even from the turnstile we could see the modern traffic flashing past. Architecturally the little street was a jumbled mixture of styles, but they all blended admirably. The predominant feeling was medieval, and the sense of history was accentuated by rather absurd plaques which had been let into some of the walls to denote particular associations: the cousin of Napoleon III, for instance, was thought to have dined in one of the houses towards the end of a journey south. All in all it was a magnificently showy street, and I didn't see how it could be entirely fake: in Roman times there would have to be an approach to the trophy from the natural crossroads, and this might as well have been it. It was all very tastefully preserved: no postcards, no sticks of rock, no Kiss Me Quick hats. A couple of the houses advertised lodgings, one was a lawyer's office, and there were a few small shops including a baker and a greengrocer. I tried to think of something to buy, simply for the experience of entering one of the buildings. Fruit would do, and I turned to ask Haslam whether he'd like a pear or an apple. What I saw gave me a nasty shock. In the middle of the street, just where it began to narrow, he was standing in a slightly crouched position, his knees bent, as though someone had begun to let all the air out of him but had then relented and replaced the stopper, leaving a shrunken facsimile of the original. His eyes were tightly closed and his hands clapped over his ears; he seemed to be in terrible sudden pain. From his lips came a low moaning sound of a timbre I didn't care for at all: it suggested a human being entirely out of control. As it happened, there were no other people in the street at that moment, so any help had to come from me. I grabbed him and shook him, and when that did no good I could only guess that it would help to drag him back towards the trophy, where he had obviously felt pretty good, perhaps because there was more air. He stumbled and fell to his knees on the cobbles, but didn't seem to notice the pain of that. His knees were certainly too weak to support him for the moment, and I had to steer him to a broken pillar which served as a seat. What on earth was the matter, I asked?

He made a noise and a gesture as though he were going to be sick, but the feeling passed. In a minute he looked up, took a deep breath, and half smiled. 'I really have no idea,' he sighed, 'but it was more frightening than anything I've experienced in my whole life. Stark terror would not be an exaggerated description of the way I felt.' He related the experience slowly, with as much detail as he could remember. He was following behind me, picking his way across the cobbles, and when the street narrowed he stretched out his arms in a playful attempt to touch both sides. Then several things seemed to happen very suddenly and at once, as though at a prearranged signal. First, he felt that the sky overhead had become much greyer, and the air colder. Then his eyesight and hearing became less acute, so that although he knew I was just a few steps ahead he could no longer hear me whistling (a bad habit of mine; I didn't even know I was doing it) and I was visible only as a blurred outline which almost instantly changed; it was no longer me at all, but some alien form passing from right to left and carrying a loaded basket. He stopped in an effort to confirm and clarify this strange evidence of his senses, and as his vision cleared he saw to his amazement, in an angle of the right hand wall, a shop which had not been there. It was open-fronted, and as far as he could make out a butcher's. There were women chatting in front of it, women in unfamiliar costume, chiefly consisting of pale grey and blue ankle-length smocks. In their hair they all wore metal bands which glinted in the light. The fear began when he observed that the street was half-filled with these strange people, but that I had entirely disappeared. Also, the three- and four-storey houses had somehow become bungalows; he could see over them, across the valley to the snow-covered Alpine peaks. Three of the first group of women approached him without seeming to notice him. They chatted in an unfamiliar language, and he noticed that on their feet they wore open-toed wooden sandals which clacked on the cobbles. As they were almost upon him, still oblivious to his presence, he stood back to let them pass; and as he did so he sensed, or heard, or felt behind him the welling up of a harsher male noise. He turned towards the Trophy, to see advancing upon him an untidy phalanx of uniformed Roman soldiers, each holding in his right hand something like a pike, and in his left a shield. He thought there might have been about twenty of them, but he could clearly see only the three in the front rank as they came at him at the double, muttering under their breath some kind of rhythmic marching chant. If this is the changing of the guard, he thought to himself, they have a poor eye for suspicious strangers: even the forward line saw him not at all. He was in fact in imminent danger of being trampled by these massive fighting men, and yet he was somehow transfixed; his feet would not move. Now he could almost smell the foul breath of the men, see into their mouths and their nostrils. When they took that last step at him he shuddered, but what made him cry aloud was their charging through him as though he were no more than a wisp of smoke. In doing so they were draining his breath away, dragging some part of him with them, straining his sanity. It was at this moment that he felt, on some other plane of consciousness, my hand on his arm, and luckily my live personality willing him back to the twentieth century proved stronger than the weird vision.

There was nothing one could usefully say to such a story, it seemed to me, except to suggest that we should, while I gripped his hand, retrace our original steps to the waiting car and thus avoid the lower stretch of the Via Julia. We got as far up the cobbles as the Trophy exit, where he collapsed on to a convenient seat. There was nothing I could do but wait. I waited the best part of ten minutes. Then Haslam felt strong enough to stand, but he wanted first to test the water, so to speak, by taking a few cautious steps back into the old street and finding out whether his previous experience could be repeated. He had ventured no more than ten feet when I saw from his expression that it could. I hastily persuaded him back to the car, and this time we made it: his strength visibly returned as we got further from the Via Julia.

We decided against a restaurant; it seemed best to see how he felt on the way back to the hotel. He was quiet but thoughtful on the way down, and I broke the silence by asking whether he'd frequently had paranormal experiences of this kind.

'Only in this neck of the woods, it seems,' he said wryly. 'I have no idea why.'

'You told me about Dolceaqua. Do the others have a Roman connection?'

'There was only one other, and it didn't. I was staying in Cannes at the time, and one day when we seemed to be sitting just inside the western edge of a rain belt, I took a long lonely drive to the west in search of some sun, not to mention inspiration for a book I was trying to write. I headed north from La Bocca, turned left at Pegomas, and found myself on an incredibly twisting mountain road which after some real corkscrew bends for twelve miles or so, and some dazzling views, landed me on a road which skirted a very pretty reservoir before allowing me to turn west again into a quiet, fertile country landscape. North of the road were several hilltop villages, and as the rain had stopped by now you can imagine how they glistened in the fresh sunlight. The mountain road had been a bit nerve-racking – at one point I actually saw a new-looking car at the bottom of a ravine – and I felt like a restful lunch; so I

turned into a higgledy-piggledy sort of small town called
Fayence, which lay at the top of a series of hairpin bends not
quite so alarming as today's. It was all very rustic, and
marvellous for pottering about. The antique shops yielded
nothing, but I did find a charming little bistro called La
Taverne, where the only waitress was the smart young
proprietress and the only cook her husband. Their specialities
were pâté and goat cheese, the latter melted on toast; a kind
of French rarebit, you might say. I don't think that
accounted for what happened later, even though I did wash
it down with a *marc de provence*. I wanted to get back to the
coast road at Fréjus, but on my map that looked likely to
provide more hard work. The patronne however was
reassuring. The gradients were easy, she said, and the views
magnifique; on either side I would see striking landscapes with
small hills and a few rocks; then a section famous for a
special kind of mushroom, and beyond Bagnois-en-Fôret
splendid country for the hunt. In view of this I set off with
great expectations, opened up my windows and sunshine
roof, and really drank in the country air. Everything was as
the lady said, and after forty minutes or so I was coasting
through Bagnois at a canter and feeling like a true
Provençal. A couple of minutes later I passed the town sign
of another little community which I didn't recall seeing on
the map. I was going to stop and check it – it was one of
those French tongue-twisters and I couldn't keep it in my
mind – but just then I had to brake in order to pass a man
and woman on horseback. They were dressed in hunting
colours, which bore out the lady's remark; but although I
didn't see their faces there was about them something
strange which I couldn't quite put my finger on. Almost
immediately I came over a rise, and saw the village spread
out before me in a hollow; the streets were very narrow
indeed, and it didn't look as though there would be
anywhere to park. I felt like a stretch, so I left the car at the

top of the hill where the road was wider, took my stick and strolled on down. There wasn't a soul about, which isn't really surprising in a French village at three in the afternoon: everybody takes the siesta very seriously. However, I was hoping for a shop where I could buy a glass of milk or a coke, for the sun was really baking by now. The buildings were of soft light-coloured stone rather reminiscent of the Cotswolds, and they seemed to take the heat in and throw it back at me. At the foot of the hill I looked forward and up again into the narrow main street with a T-junction at the top. Facing me on the other side of the junction was what looked like a town hall, and in front of it an ancient statue which made me wonder how a car could possibly be manoeuvred round it. Suddenly I was aware of the clip-clop of hooves breaking the afternoon stillness, and from the right-hand arm of the T there came into view two dark, gleaming horses, their fine heads surmounted by purple plumes. You will perhaps not be surprised to hear that they were drawing behind them an ornate hearse, with a coffin in it.

'There was a driver, of course, in a top hat and what might have been a black frock coat. He steered the horses anti-clockwise round the statue and down the street towards me. By now I could see that quite a number of mourners followed on foot, and now I suddenly realized what was odd about them and about the couple on horseback I had seen previously. They were all dressed in costumes of a century ago, the men with luxuriant moustaches, the women generally plain and sombre. Crinolines and wide bonnets abounded, with a blue velvet suit for the small boy who stumbled along behind the hearse carrying a wreath. I looked around me wildly for evidence of the twentieth century, but there was none. No painted lines on the roadway, no television aerials, no cars. My own car would be out of sight over the hill crest, and I was in a panic to get back to it, especially with that dismal procession bearing down so relentlessly upon me. I turned and ran, feeling every second that a thick cold cloud was about to envelop me from behind. In the circumstances I was amazed to find the car where I left it, and even more so, as I turned the ignition key, to see a shiny red Lagonda whizz past me towards the strange village I had just left. But as I ran back to the crest of the hill there was no village to be seen, just the Lagonda in the distance leaving a trail of dust and scattered chickens outside a broken-down farmhouse at the other side of the little valley, which was given over entirely to some kind of vegetable crop. There wasn't even a T-junction any more: as soon as it got over the hill, the road bore down and away to the right, following the line of the valley for about a quarter of a mile before climbing again and heading toward Fréjus. Very hesitantly I returned to the car and drove on through the site of my recent scare. I felt nothing except the sun on my face. When I got to Fréjus I made some enquiries and found that there had been a village on the spot until the eighteen-fifties, when the lord of the manor had died in an outbreak of plague and the village became a particularly virulent centre for the disease, so virulent that the authorities ordered it cleared and razed to the ground.'

Telling the story had clearly tired Haslam, and there were a dozen hairpin bends to go. I pulled into a viewpoint and gazed at the ocean. 'You never experienced this kind of thing in London?'

'Never.'

'Do you have any special feeling for this part of France?'

'Only that most of it's over-rated, and especially the Côte d'Azur itself between Cannes and Nice. The only possible connection that comes to me is that I was born in Lancashire, that my father and grandfather were cotton spinners, and that the local accent has a lot of corrupted French words, which are said to be due to an influx of refugee huguenot weavers in the seventeenth century. Even the name Haslam seems to be more French than anything else. So it's just possible that my ancestors came from this part of the world.'

'Mm. I suppose it's also possible that these things have a physical cause, something affecting the nervous system. There are things in the air that our bodies aren't used to. You felt sick this morning, and I think you said that happened also before you saw the centurion. Twice when I have been in these parts I've taken to bed with a mysterious ailment which one doctor called sinus fever caused by mimosa pollen. All I'm sure of is that it left me dizzy, dreamlike and utterly drained of energy, and when I closed my eyes the most fanciful images billowed in and out. I was so weak, I remember, I didn't even have the strength to keep my head erect.'

'Oh, I haven't felt like that, though I have been physically out of sorts all week. That's because I haven't had much sleep. I keep hearing unaccountable noises.'

'Unaccountable? In Loew's Hotel?'

'Very much so. Noises of trains, mostly. Two men arguing sometimes, steam escaping, chug chug and all that, just as I'm nodding off. Doors slamming and whistles; hurried footsteps. Voices in greeting and welcome. But mostly the pure train sounds. And as you know, the only line is deep in a cutting on the other side of the hill.'

I nodded silently and pulled the car into gear. We descended without speaking until twenty minutes later we were driving by the formal gardens on whose edges are found the Casino, the Opéra and the Hôtel de Paris. I found a parking space and stopped. 'Do you mind taking a short stroll?' I said.

I led Haslam past the front of the Casino and turned left where the pavement leads on to a stone balustraded garden terrace facing out to sea and to the headland of old Monaco town. 'When I first came to Monte Carlo fifteen years ago,' I said, perching on the balustrade by a pillar, 'it was on a day trip by train from Nice, with a friend in the film business. We strolled all over the place and eventually found ourselves, rather footsore, at this very point, which I instantly recognized as the setting for the climax of a film called *The Red Shoes*.'

'I remember it. Ballet melodrama, with Moira Shearer, and that wonderful German hissing out all the best lines.'

'Anton Walbrook, that's right. She's torn between love and duty, and finally her Hans Andersen shoes drive her mad. She's due on the stage of that astonishing theatre round the corner, but instead she runs from her dressing room and follows the fairy tale she should be performing, by throwing herself over this very balustrade into the path of an approaching steam train. Rather a lot of tomato ketchup was used: I had to look away. Now on that first visit I naturally looked for the train tracks and they weren't there, so I assumed there'd been a spot of photographic trickery, matching this real terrace with a train from somewhere else entirely: in movies the quickness of the editing often deceives the eye, and *The Red Shoes* certainly had its share of painted backdrops. I never gave the matter any further consideration until this very week in the lobby of Loew's I heard two Frenchmen chatting and one used the phrase *la vieille gare*. I was intrigued enough to ask him later, when I caught him in the bar, whether there had once been a railway station nearby. He turned out to be one of the assistant managers of the hotel, so of course he was really genned up. "But of course, monsieur. Almost on this very spot. The first floor of the hotel is on the level of the old platform, they say, from room 1040 to room 1090. The track was relaid in the sixties, to make way for the new plans which included the hotel."'

Haslam looked thoughtful. 'And below us now is the roof

of the hotel. And I'm in 1082.'

I put my hand on his shoulder. 'Then if you want any sleep this week I think you'd better try to move. It seems to me you must have some rare and inexplicable sensitivity to things that have happened in certain places. I wouldn't worry about it. It might be rather comforting.'

Haslam looked glum. 'It might be, if I understood it. For instance, who can the two men be, the two I hear arguing?'

'What do they argue about?'

He shrugged. 'It all goes vague afterwards. But there was a petulance about the way they spoke – in French, by the way – which made me think they might be homosexuals. I don't remember any words because I couldn't catch many. There was a guttural quality too which suggested that French was not their native tongue. And I think one of them addressed the other as Vasily, or something of that sort.'

I was lighting a cigarette, and almost choked on it. 'Nijinsky's first name was Vaslav,' I said. 'And he and Diaghilev must have been inside that opera house more times than they cared to count. And quarrelled just as often. And left Monte Carlo from that station which once occupied the space now filled by your bedroom.'

I didn't see much of Haslam after that, but I know he did change his room. That was just over a year ago. He didn't turn up at this year's market, because he'd left the business. In fact, he disappeared entirely for a few months, and then somebody showed me an ad in the *Spiritualist News*. It was Haslam all right, calling himself a consultative medium and giving an address in Villefranche. Next time I'm down that way I must ring for an appointment.

Brain Scan

Hancock didn't mind the idea at all, providing the Harley Street man meant what he said. And what the neurologist said, after shrugging his shoulders and sniffing, was that he'd tried every test he could think of and come up with nothing beyond a slight irregularity in the electro-encephalograph results, which in fifteen per cent of all cases were irregular anyway. As for finding out the root cause of Hancock's chronic eye irritation, which was sometimes so severe that he had to lie down in a dark room until it passed, Dr Barnard-Robbins had to admit failure, which meant that in his opinion it couldn't be very serious. Hancock remembered that the dermatologist whom he had once consulted with a problem itch had finally summed up his researches by saying: 'Funny thing, skin.' He hoped Dr Barnard-Robbins was not going to make a similarly profound statement about nerves. Instead the good doctor took him somewhat aback by adding: 'The only further thing I can suggest, just to double check, is a brain scan. You're medically insured, I suppose?'

'Oh, yes.'

'Then why not have it done? Only takes a few minutes, and it may well throw up something. If it doesn't, then at least we'll have tried the lot. You see, I'm absolutely sure there's nothing seriously wrong with you. Just one of those minor mysteries: where would we chaps be without them? Probably your first Moorfields diagnosis was right, and it's episcleritis, in which case one of these days it'll go away of its own accord. The only thing is, episcleritis is usually associated with rheumatism, and there's no trace of that in you. None at all.' Barnard-Robbins sat back and fell briefly into what used to be called a brown study.

The receptionist made an appointment for Hancock without difficulty, and three days later he found himself driving through rush hour traffic towards the Buckingham Hospital in North London. This was, he felt sure, a total waste of his time and of the insurance company's money, but it would be interesting to sample one of the latest developments of medical science. He was more worried about the other thing, the German thing, but he was damned if he was going to waste time on that by spending months on a psychiatrist's couch. Especially as in that case he couldn't get back the fees.

He thought back to that terrifying night when, during the last month of his active CID duty, he'd had to kill a man for the first time. And fate had made his victim a German, and he hadn't even died right away. That was neat, and Hancock didn't like things too neat. He personally had nothing at all against Germans. He'd never even been to Germany. He'd meant to, and to learn their God-damned guttural-sounding language as well. But there had never been time. His mother now, she'd hated Germans until the day she died, and with good and sufficient reason. After all, there was no denying that a German had killed her husband, and left him to die slowly, in agony, in the Ardennes. The boy who did it probably had a guilty conscience for the rest of his life; the reverberations of the incident might even have sent him to an early grave. Hancock would never know, and didn't want to. War was war, after all. But Hancock had missed his father, and he never had managed to understand the Germans, not even after seeing *All Quiet on the Western Front* twice at the National Film Theatre.

After Mother's funeral, all the hatred had been forgotten. And then, out of the blue, near the end of an honourable

career, had come this curious parallel incident, after
terrorists had been caught in Woolwich looting a military
arsenal. The siege had been long and arduous, and shooting
and tear gas had been the end of it. The man Hancock had
shot certainly had a gun in his hand, but he may have been
intending to toss it to the ground and give himself up. He
may have been blinded by the tear gas. It was too dark to be
sure, and everybody was on the brink of hysteria. Hancock
had bravely gone to see the man in hospital, and found
himself saying defensively that he had nothing at all against
Germans and indeed had no knowledge of them. Then the
dying man had taken him entirely by surprise when he half
sat up in bed and enunciated wryly, in that too-perfect
English which was always being caricatured: 'Fear not, my
friend: I promise to show you what it is like to be
German . . .' He never spoke coherently again.

But did he really die? The hospital records had said he
did, but there were five terrorists in there, and it was just
possible they could have confused the documents. For
Hancock was sure that he had seen his German, not once
but several times, recently, in London. There was his
distinctive dark brown overcoat that no Englishman would
wear: Hancock remembered it from the night of the
shooting. If it wasn't the man Hancock had seen in the
hospital, it was his twin brother. The trouble was, it was
never possible to check. The man was always on top of a
passing bus, or separated by heavy traffic on the other side of
Charing Cross Road, or glimpsed from a taxi as he crossed
Trafalgar Square and was lost in the crowds of tourists.
Once he looked really sinister, on the opposite side of the
Serpentine as Hancock strolled in Hyde Park. It was too
much and too often for coincidence: the man was following
for a purpose, letting himself be seen from a safe distance, as
some sort of reminder. A devious psychological trick,
Hancock called it. Gestapo tactics. And yet there were

moments when he thought it wasn't a trick at all, that the figure which followed him was Hans Dorf but that Dorf really was dead, that he'd come back to haunt Hancock and carry out whatever curse he'd put on his killer that awful night at the hospital when he'd finally collapsed in a fit of coughing after yelling out a lot of words that nobody in the ward could understand except that they meant hatred.

And there he was again, walking down Hamilton Terrace just as Hancock drove across it at the lights. The brakes were jammed on at once, but by the time Hancock leaped out of the car, the brown overcoat was nowhere to be seen. If the man *wasn't* a ghost, thought Hancock, he must be a nut, to wear a coat like that on such a warm summer's day. Five minutes later he was lucky enough to find a meter round the corner from the Buckingham Hospital, which proved to be a spiky modern building with all signs inscribed in both English and Arabic, an indication that the proprietors knew where their best interests lay. No national health here, thought Hancock half-admiringly: they'll want your cheque before you leave the building. Before you have the treatment, if they can get it. At least the place was efficient. A few personal details to the receptionist and he was taken straight to the treatment room, even though he was twenty minutes early.

The huge sterile-looking apparatus seemed very formidable indeed. A high vinyl-covered bed, and where the head should go, a machine mercifully obscured by a vast steel plate. In the middle of the plate was what looked like an inverted rubber chamber pot. Glasses off, shoes off, up on the bed please, head into the dome, that's right, as far up as you can, press your head right in, nothing to hurt you at all, just an unfamiliar noise. The nurse threw a light blanket over him, pushed up under his buttocks some plastic shape to keep him in place, and turned some kind of tap which slowly adjusted the rubber dome into a tight-fitting skull cap. Explanations went on the while. Four pictures of six minutes each, from different angles, nothing at all to worry about, but keep very still, no movement above the waist, try to relax entirely and think of something else. He asked for a pillow under his neck, it was given, and the machine whirred lazily into action with a repeated horizontal plopping movement like a very slow typewriter. The first pass, only, seemed to push his head a little from left to right, which was clearly the direction the first 'picture' would take. The sound of each pass reminded him of somebody saying 'a kumquat'. Repeat, repeat, repeat: a kumquat, a kumquat, a kumquat. Twenty-four minutes of this? A kumquat, a kumquat . . . that would be, at something in the region of one second per pass, more than twelve hundred kumquats, which was enough for anybody. He was bound to get an itch somewhere before it was all over. He was alone in the room, but aware that nurses in blue uniforms were watching him from behind a glass panel. The first six-minute period came to an end, and the nurse hurried in to take a reading. Perfectly still, Mr Hancock. Then the kumquats came at him again, from right to left this time. In a way it was all rather relaxing, providing he could avoid boredom, which might lead to restlessness. He thought back to a film he saw the previous week, and passed the time by recounting the plot to himself. That worked: the break came before he expected it. Two to go. During the third picture-taking he amused himself by mentally ticking off the titles of all the Sherlock Holmes stories; during the fourth he took himself on an imaginary tour of Scotland. Now it was surely time to go. A few minutes, indeed! But no: now a doctor came in, introduced himself, and explained that three more pictures were necessary 'for comparison', and a good result would necessitate the injection of some dye into the bloodstream. So lie back, Mr Hancock, nothing to worry about, let us know if you get any painful reaction, you may possibly feel a

sensation of heat. Hancock hated injections, but there was
absolutely nothing he could do. Nobody even gave him time
to speak: his arm was bared and he felt the needle, which
was to remain in his arm, uncomfortably, throughout the
next 'picture'. Luckily it was out of his sight, though he
constantly felt it was about to fall out and spoil the
experiment. The arm ached somewhat already, but he
dared not move; he was in the grip of the apparatus, more
immobile than ever. His head, his body, now his arm, were
all under tight control: almost the only movement he could
make was to wiggle his toes. The dye presumably had no
anaesthetic properties, but he felt that it had. He was
entirely at the mercy of those in charge. Brain scan? They
should call it a brain *wash*, for they had taken all the juice
out of him, as a hypnotist does from his subject. They had
washed out his brain, they and their kumquats: only the
shell of Hancock remained. He could only hope that they
would have the consideration to replace the filling before
they sent him home. Perhaps they would squeeze in a
different filling: chocolate cream or toffee and mallow would
be nice. What *was* he rambling about? Good thing he wasn't
nervous: some people would be having kittens at this kind of
science-fiction treatment. At least he had relaxed, almost too
much, almost out of his mind. Was this the last picture? He
thought there had been another break, but he wasn't sure.
Where was the doctor? And who was this man in a dark
brown coat who stood so close? The edge of the dome
prevented his seeing the face, but the coat struck a chord of
recollection. The German? How could he have got in here?
What could he *want* in here? To show Hancock what it was
like to be German, to be beaten in two world wars, and to
recover so rapidly from them? Hancock really wanted to
understand. But not now. Not while his whole body seemed
to vibrate with the machine around his head. The wonderful

machine that was making him well, taking away pain
forcing him to relax as he could not remember relaxing for a
very long time . . .

When the machine finally clicked into repose, Hancock
was virtually asleep; the nurses recognized the fact and
smiled at each other. All right, Mr Hancock, it's all over.
We folded your arm up when we took out the needle, so that
you wouldn't get a bruise. There, now your head's free,
doesn't that feel good? I'll just pull the bed away so that you
can sit up. Up you get. Watch the little steps.

Hancock allowed his knees to be swung over to the left,
and sat up. 'Das ist alles?' he asked. 'Kann ich zu Hause
fahren? Danke schön, gnädige Frau. Auf wiedersehen.'

The Blackamoor's Drum

This happened not too long after the second world war, when helpless British youths of eighteen were still being prevented by the government from getting on with their careers; instead they were called up to a two-year period of 'national service' in the armed forces. This was to most of them a spell of purgatory for which nothing in their previous sheltered lives had prepared them. As one of this unfortunate number, who for some forgotten reason had chosen to serve and suffer with the army, I well remember my astonishment at the vast number of total illiterates inducted along with me, and my first day of shock and bewilderment at their spoken language, each sentence of which was likely to include three or more helpings of the same four-letter word. I was even more aghast when six months later, having opted for the allegedly 'cushy' Education Corps (and been sentenced at once to several arduous weeks of Guards training in a remote Scottish castle with the most primitive and ineffective form of winter heating), I found myself actually teaching the rudiments of English to these 'G. D. wallahs'. The initials meant that, having no education, they were fit only for general duties: gardening, latrine cleaning, that sort of thing. As a so-called 'professor' or 'schoolie', with three stripes on my arm, I did my best to maintain class discipline while instilling in them what I could of the three Rs, but it was an entirely thankless and unattractive task. Since our location was a cheerless wooden barracks on Salisbury Plain, a mile or more from a small scattered village called Winterbourne Dauntsey, there crept into my life a certain depressing monotony which even regular visits to cinema and theatre, via the twice daily bus into Salisbury, could not absolutely assuage.

Naturally I took every opportunity I could to escape from this drudgery, even if escape meant no more than climbing to the top of a nearby prehistoric mound called Figsbury Ring and losing myself (with a good book) in the long grass. I always had books with me, even on guardroom duty or in the mess hall: Jane Austen and Raymond Chandler sometimes helped me to swallow the frightful food without really tasting it.

Luckily, army life lent itself to quite elaborate wheezes or 'skives', and in view of my impending transfer to a higher university sphere I was able every three months or so to get myself allocated to some kind of cultural refresher course, all expenses paid, and often at some delightful country house of absorbing architectural interest. Here one met real people who talked of poetry and art rather than betting and the grubbier forms of sex.

It was during my last September in uniform, a very warm month as I remember, that I went to Tidworth for a course of a slightly different order. Over three days the Army Bureau for Current Affairs (ABCA for short) hoped by psychological methods and visual aids to enable me (and others like me) to become more effective teachers. The main concern of the Corps was to remove as far as possible the shock to its officers of their inevitable return after demob to the chilling austerities of civilian life, and to raise its illiterates to a level from which they might hope to understand the more elementary forms of government bumf and propaganda. The course required no effort from me except that of staying awake during the lectures; the venue was the extremely unattractive one of Tidworth Camp, a sprawling brick barracks housing a multitude of central units plus sufficient spare accommodation for the purposes of this conference. Aesthetically the hostel block seemed far from prepossessing, but its standard of comfort was in fact somewhat higher than Cambridge later provided. Each man luxuriated in a self-contained bed sitter with bath off a highly polished corridor, and mine was a corner unit with a splendid view over the camp perimeter to the countryside beyond, which at this point was dominated by a low conical hill about five hundred feet high, the top of it possibly half a mile from my window. I judged it to be, like Figsbury Ring, an old funeral barrow, but nobody in the mess or the Naafi had any information on the subject, so on my first afternoon I went for a solitary walk to the top. It was only a fifth of the size of Figsbury, with a flattish if rather bumpy top. In the middle was an indentation of a kind I had never seen before, almost cup or cauldron shaped and about twenty-five feet across. I would have thought it a bomb crater had it not been so perfectly central. The whole mound was almost certainly man made, but I am no archaeologist and had only the vaguest notion of the uses to which our dark age progenitors might have put it.

Returning to base for tea (with what the army called cakes) I saw from the notice board that we were to have an inaugural meeting at seven, with more meetings on Saturday morning and evening, but that my Saturday afternoon would be free unless I wished to join a coach party to see Southern Command play Northern Command at rugby, which I certainly did not. I would head instead for the local library and look up the origins of the strange hill, together with any other local oddities of antiquarian interest. At seven, in case I found nobody to talk to over dinner, I followed custom by taking a book with me, Dennis Wheatley's *The Devil Rides Out*, which had been enthusiastically recommended to me by a specialist in such things. It may not be the best written book I know, but once you find yourself in the grip of its narrative it is certainly among the most frightening. I took it out with my coffee into the comfortable if rather garish lounge to which we were assigned. Almost immediately someone sat down heavily next to me on the settee, and I looked up to see a sallow, Jewish-looking chap with bulging eyes and a lot of dark curly hair.

He was regarding me askance. 'Hot stuff, isn't it?' he said crudely, nodding at the volume in my hand.

I nodded and smiled, as equivocally as I could, wondering how a chap like that could have become a sergeant in the Education Corps.

'Do you believe in that sort of thing?' he went on, rather eagerly.

I said I hadn't given the matter a lot of thought, but enjoyed some kinds of ghost stories as entertainment and was certainly prepared to keep an open mind. (I suppose I should have known even at that age that I would find my way into politics.)

'So you've never seen a ghost?' he demanded, a note of disappointment creeping into his voice.

I hesitated, which was my downfall, for I then felt obliged to tell him of a childhood experience which might, or might not, have been supernatural. The details have no place in this narrative, but they were obviously sufficiently intriguing for this curious man to become entirely absorbed with me. I had made a sad mistake. He was not my type at all, and I really had no desire to cultivate his acquaintance; but after my story there was no means of escape, for his grip on me was as firm and fierce as a hawk's on its prey. He explained that he was fascinated by the occult and had an aunt who was a medium but would not so far let him participate in her seances. He had dabbled with friends in hypnotism and table tapping and ouija boards, but the results to date had plainly been disappointing. I said I couldn't help him there.

'Aren't there any haunted houses around here?' he asked plaintively. 'I'd never been this far out of London until the army tipped me off the train at Swindon.'

'Well, I'm a stranger too, but I know a few of the stately homes. I don't think it's a terribly productive area for ghosts, more for public schools and hunts. Oh, I don't know, though. Tidworth. Wasn't there a programme on the Home Service a year or two back? I'm sure there was, part of a series on authenticated ghosts: the demon drummer of Tidworth, that was it.'

He was practically bouncing on the settee in excitement. 'Tell me about it.'

'I don't know that I can. I mean, I've forgotten the details. It was supposed to be true, though. The local squire was the central figure, and he had a funny name. Montresor? No, that's Poe. Mompesson, that's it.'

'Mompesson?'

'Sir John or Sir James Mompesson. Family must have been French originally. Or possibly Italian. It's all coming back now. He was the local magistrate, back in the days of Charles II, and one day a little blackamoor came up before him, charged with some minor offence. He belonged to a travelling circus of some kind, and used to beat his drum either to announce their arrival in town or, I suppose, to start the acts during the performance. Anyway, a drummer he was, and Sir John – let's settle on John – was a hard man and gave him a stiffer sentence than he thought he deserved. So he cursed Sir John with great venom. A week later he died in prison. And after that Sir John up at the hall was haunted by the demon drums. Never in the room he was in, always in the next one. Went mad in the end and tried to hang himself, but they cut him down in time.'

Elkan – that was the fellow's odd name – regarded me fixedly. 'Did you just make that up?'

'I assure you I did not. Mind you, I can't vouch for the BBC.'

'Oh, they wouldn't say it if it wasn't true,' he said naïvely. 'You're sure it was Tidworth?'

'Well, I think so. Of course, it might have been Tadworth. Or Tidmarsh. Or Tolworth. Anyway, it was three hundred years ago. Not many ghosts seem to hang around that long.'

My acquaintance walked back to my room with me after the evening lecture. He talked all the way, and I groaned when we returned to the hostel and I found he was my next door neighbour. Despite the solid wall between us I could hear a lot of puffing and grunting after I turned in, and I guessed he'd added yoga to his more occult pursuits. The meeting of the sun and the moon, I believe it's supposed to mean. Lot of hogwash. At breakfast he plopped down next to me again and asked what I was doing that afternoon. And would you believe it, I fell into the trap again.

'Oh, just strolling. I want another look at the top of that hill, for a start.'

'Why?'

Idiotically, I could think of no reason but the real one. 'I discovered something odd last night. I was reading *The Devil Rides Out* until two o'clock.'

'I thought you looked a bit pale. Thought you'd been up to something.'

I ignored his inference. 'You remember the open air black mass near the end?'

'Do I not! Sent quite a few shivers down my spine. I've always wanted to go to a black mass. What about it?'

'Only that if you follow the geographical directions given in the book, guess where they bring you? To the lane right outside our windows. In fact, it's my guess that Wheatley knows this part of the country extremely well and set his diabolical party on top of that hill.' I pointed through the breakfast room window in the direction of the mystery mound.

'When can we go?' He was already standing up, and I had

to laugh as I hauled him back into his seat. There was no way now that I could avoid his company that afternoon: I would have had to spit in his eye to dissuade him. And so, after a ghastly lunch of rissole and baked beans, we set out together. He was restless in the library, as one might have expected; I did all the research, not that there was much to find out. The hill, like Silbury, was a complete local mystery; borings made in Victorian times had yielded no information whatever about its origins, and there was no mention of black masses at all. Despite this totally negative hour, Elkan still wanted to go to the top, and although I knew we would find nothing, I accompanied him simply for the sake of lying on my back in what little breeze there was that day and imagining myself in a warm corner of heaven. He buzzed around looking for burnt bones, until I reminded him pretty sharply that *The Devil Rides Out* is a work of fiction, and that Wheatley himself states categorically in the preface that he doesn't personally believe in black magic and has never been to any of its ceremonial occasions. My interest was simply in his knowing the location and adapting it for his own purposes.

Elkan finally dropped his considerable young bulk down on to the grass. 'This is pretty disappointing after all. Let's go to the other place.'

'What other place?'

'The other place you were talking about. Tidworth Manor.'

'In this heat? I don't even know for sure that it was here. Anyway, it wasn't Manor. House? Squire Mompesson of Tidworth – Hall, that was it. Yes, it was here, I'm sure of it.'

I sat up and surveyed through the heat haze the large straggly village which lay before us. The camp down to the right was the largest development, but in the left-hand portion of our view, west of the High Street, were several large old houses, any one of which might have been the

Hall. The only suggestion I could make was that we might scramble down the hill to the main road and ask somebody. We rolled down most of it, being young and finding that method easier than walking; but the main westbound road was empty of pedestrians. What do people do on Saturday afternoons in Tidworth? We crossed the road and were a quarter of a mile up a narrow lane before we met anybody, and that was a yokel cutting a hedge. He said that he actually came from Andover, but thought we were on the right track and we should bear right at the next fork. We did that, but I was sorry to be walking away from the camp all the time, for the heat was really baking and I was intent on getting back in time for a bath before supper. Ten minutes later we stopped a man on a bicycle and he said we weren't far from 'Old Tidworth Hall' but were headed towards the back entrance: apparently we'd had the grounds to our right for some time, and should have stuck to the main road, which passed the front drive on its way into the High Street.

'Look here,' he added, 'if you climb over this stile in the hedge, follow the field round to the right till you come to another stile, then head diagonally across that field in the direction of the church steeple. You should come out on Kings Pin Road just a stone's throw from the drive.'

'Thanks very much. By the way, is Mompesson a common name around here?'

'I've never heard it.'

Well, we trudged over two lumpy fields as directed, and I was feeling pretty hot and in need of a bath by now. The house eventually came into view on our left, behind a thick elm wood, and a very intermittent path brought us out opposite the side of the main buildings, at a spot where without much difficulty we could scramble across a ditch and through a break in the hedge on to a wide gravel surround. Opposite to us was a dilapidated stone portico which projected about six feet from a structure half of yellow brick and half of stucco. To our left we could see through a trellis fence into overgrown gardens; to our right was ample evidence of a rather better kept front lawn. The gravel path, almost twenty feet wide at the side of the house, appeared almost to encircle the building, and around to the left, tucked away at the rear, we could see small detached buildings which had probably once been stables and now seemed, from some very pronounced tyre treads in the soft surface, to be garages. Everything was still; in fact, it is the stillness I remember above everything. Although it must have been four o'clock by now, there was still no break in the heat, and as we waited in the ditch to see whether it was safe to explore further, the silence was almost eerie, though away in the right-hand distance we could see something that might have been an army vehicle approaching up the long front drive.

The house itself looked mainly eighteenth century, and of pretty undistinguished architecture. The older parts must have been nearer the centre and therefore hidden from us. The wing which jutted out in our direction might possibly have dated from the 1600s, though its decoration was on the scanty side and the whole was in a deplorable state of preservation. The damp-looking portico had a French door beneath it. Most of the other windows nearby were obscured by heavy velvet curtaining, but this one had been boarded up, quite roughly, with planks haphazardly nailed across it from side to side, as though the owners had left in a hurry and considered protection against vandals more important than preserving the woodwork. I noticed that the sun was setting away to the right, so that the portico faced roughly north and would never receive any natural warmth, a fact underlined by its damp and dismal condition.

I inspected Elkan's appearance. After our scramble over hills and through fields his uniform was in a sorrier state even than mine, and he was sweating unpleasantly. Woe

betide us if we were caught in this condition on the way back
to camp. 'If that really was an army car,' I said, 'we'd better
make ourselves scarce and find a back way home.'

He nodded reluctantly. 'This end doesn't seem to be used,
though. What a lovely spooky place! Let's have a butcher's
round the back.'

I shrugged my shoulders. We climbed out of the ditch,
tiptoed to our left and looked round the corner of the house.
About forty feet away was quite a sizeable rear wing in two
storeys. It was clearly well occupied, and to our horror by
army personnel! We glimpsed a WRAC corporal through
an upstairs window, and I caught the distant click of a
typewriter. I seemed to remember reading in Part One
Orders that some stately home had been taken over by
Southern Command Records Office, and this looked like it;
in which case any further trespassing by us would be
foolhardly in the extreme. I murmured as much to my
perspiring acquaintance.

'All right, we'll go, but there can't be any harm in a quick
peek through the window.' He darted towards the portico,
with me close behind, and applied his eye to the largest gap
between the planks. 'Ah,' he said, 'so that's why they
boarded it up.'

I peered through a knothole and saw what he meant. It
was a very large room, crammed from floor to ceiling with
antique furniture and bric à brac. Probably the entire valuable
contents of the house had been trundled into this disused wing
for storage. Refectory tables, escritoires, davenports, chests,
commodes and chairs of all kinds were prodigally displayed
before us and in many cases stacked atop each other: for the
hunter of old English furniture it was an Aladdin's cave.
'How much for the lot?' I asked frivolously.

There was no answer, so after a moment I turned to see
whether Elkan had heard me. He was still by my side, but
there was a strange startled expression on his face, and his

head was half tilted as though he were listening for something. His eyes bulged more than ever, and with his forehead glistening and his tunic unbuttoned he looked a sorry sight. 'Don't you hear it?' he asked.

'Hear what?'

'The drum!'

'The what?'

'I hear a drum – a rather tinny drum, beating repeatedly.'

'You're pulling my leg.'

'I wish I were. I don't like it.'

'Oh, come on. It must be the local boy scouts' band, though I can't hear it at all.'

'No, no, it's not that distant. Don't you understand? It's coming from inside this room!'

'But there's nobody inside, except probably a lot of mice.'

'I tell you I can hear it, getting closer. Listen, it's just inside the window . . .'

I can't adequately describe what happened next, nor indeed is it comfortable to recall it, even after the passage of thirty years and more. I looked back obligingly into the room, unable to see anything more than before, and instantly felt my back shiver at the onset of a tremendous gust of wind. The odd thing was, it didn't come at us from the side or the rear – and remember in any case my description of the remarkable stillness of the summer air that afternoon – but from above our heads, as though there were a wind machine concealed in the pillar cornices or, even more impossibly, in the great slab of stone which balanced on top of them. I seemed to be caught in a column of icy cold air which froze my veins from shoulder to toes, driving me into the ground. It was relentlessly fierce, and I thought afterwards that if I had not found the strength to run I would have been discovered dead in a heap on the step. I did run, and so did Elkan, and we were back in the ditch before we drew breath and looked at each other in abject terror. 'What the hell was that?' I asked.

His eyes were staring wider than ever, and his cheeks had an unhealthy red flush. Breathing heavily, he pulled at his shirt collar and sent a button flying away unheeded into the mud. 'The wind. You felt it too.'

'Of course I did. Why else were we running?'

'It was the drummer. The drummer sent it.'

'Oh, shut up about your confounded drum. Only you heard that.'

Through his gasps he managed a weak, open-mouthed smile. 'Then perhaps I am a medium after all. Perhaps you haven't the sensitivity.'

For some reason this galled me: with the arrogance of youth I felt reluctant to concede to him a power denied to me. I was of course quite happy about it afterwards, but at this moment I felt foolhardiness return as my panting subsided. 'Let's have another look,' I said.

Luckily for me, perhaps, as we were about to step out of the ditch an army car drove round from the front of the house and parked under a tree not ten feet from us. We shrank under a leafy hawthorn. Two second lieutenants got out and lit cigarettes, chatting about Ascot and Beaulieu in that airy empty-headed way possessed only by second lieutenants. Eventually one of them said, 'Oh, well,' and flicked his cigarette end, still lighted, right at our hiding place: I almost caught it in my mouth. The other stubbed his out in the gravel, and they sauntered away round the corner. We were about to emerge again, when another staff vehicle came round the corner, and then another. Soon the entire gravel area was filled with cars, presumably bringing guests for some official function, for two or three were limousines with chauffeurs in uniform. After our very hairy few moments under the portico, the atmosphere had been transformed with incredible swiftness into something very upperclass English, and there was no way we could reveal ourselves to these people without inviting the most regrettable consequences. Eventually I shrugged at Elkan, tapped my watch and, choosing a good moment, beckoned him to follow me. Within seconds we were lost in a tall crop, through which I cut a diagonal path until we could rejoin our original route.

We were in a deplorable state, mentally and physically, when we got back to camp. Luckily we were able to slip through a transport gate and reach our bunks without having to pass any properly dressed personnel; and a hot bath worked wonders, followed by a short session in the ironing room. When I got my trousers on again and brushed my hair it wanted only a quarter of an hour to supper, after which we had another boring dissertation to endure; so I stretched out on my bed to contemplate the afternoon's events and try to think of a rational explanation. I was interrupted by a tap on the door.

It was Elkan, smartened up like myself, but seeming mentally as disturbed and bewildered as he had been in the ditch. 'You're not playing tricks on me, are you?' he said plaintively.

'I assure you I'm far too tired. What tricks?'

'You give me your word you haven't a drum in here?'

'Absolutely not.'

He shook his head, then nodded it. 'Must be delayed shock. I can still hear that damned drum. Seems to be right on the other side of the wall.'

'Probably water pipes. There was some gurgling a few minutes back.'

'No, no, no. It's that blackamoor's drum, I tell you. You must have heard it. Say you did.' He was insistent, almost hysterical. I could see from the look in his eyes that he wasn't joking; indeed he had the appearance of a man who would never joke again. I got him to finish dressing and we went to eat. The fish was inedible, but there was plenty of drink available, especially after the lecture, and I deliberately got Elkan fairly squiffy before steering him back to his room around midnight. He seemed reasonably himself then, but at about three there he was again, tapping on my door. He didn't have to tell me what was wrong: he was shaking all over, and biting his fingernails: an abject sight. Eventually I put him into my bed and moved myself into his, leaving both doors propped open. I found his room no less comfortable and quiet than mine had been – not the slightest sound of a drum nor anything that could be mistaken for one – but within twenty minutes he was in the doorway again, looking like a ghost himself with a sheet trailing from his shoulder. At that time of night there was nothing I could suggest except that we share the same room, so we dragged a mattress round and got some sleep that way. He clearly didn't hear the drum when someone else was listening too, but you don't sleep in dormitories when you get to be a sergeant.

Throughout Sunday Elkan kept his haunted look, and the night was broken as before. On Monday morning, somewhat to my relief, we split up. I could see that Elkan was in mortal terror of returning to his unit at Netheravon, but there was nothing I could do except advise him to see his CO. I left him alone for a week, but on the following Monday I rang his mess in the evening, only to be told that he was in sick bay and not to be disturbed. When I rang again on the Friday, intending to pay a duty visit at the weekend, it was to hear that he'd been moved to Shaftesbury Military Hospital, by which I guessed that they were treating him as a mental case. As I hadn't been called in to give evidence, so to speak, I presumed he'd never described our adventure at Tidworth Hall.

Feeling inadvertently responsible for his plight, I cycled over on the Saturday, and found him with a group of apparent mental deficients, watching some sort of comedy

film. He was laughing in all the right places, but me he
didn't know at all. All the time he had his head on one side,
as though listening for something. Two weeks later his
parents had him transferred to some hospital nearer
London. I never contacted them. In fact, I never saw or
heard of him again. Callous of me, no doubt, but I was
afraid of . . . contamination. After all, of the two of us, it
might well have chanced to be me who was susceptible to
such influences. And Elkan only got what he so ardently
desired: proof that there are such things.

By the way, I looked up Squire Mompesson. He ended up
in an asylum too. Bedlam, as a matter of fact.

The Girl by the River

In retrospect I can't imagine why I thought I'd make a schoolmaster, but when I came out of the army in 1948 that's what I became for a couple of years, until the sight of small boys in the mass threatened to bring me out in hives. The fact was that I was scared of them, and they knew it. I think Mr Chips had the same feeling, but whereas he got over it, I never did, and as soon as I could get myself a job in advertising, I was off. As I could never maintain discipline even in the classroom, I particularly disliked having to go on summer camps and journeys, for on such occasions the agreeable tensions of rank had to be slackened to such a degree that some of the boys ended up thinking of the masters as their equals. I remember having to help escort twenty-five boys by bus and train as far as Rome. After two uncomfortable nights sitting up, the second of them on hard slatted seats, we had to change trains in Milan, and had actually done so when I remembered that my brief case containing all our passports was still on the first train, up in the luggage rack. We all hared back across the station, to find that the train had already been shunted into a siding; my Italian wasn't up to controlling the chaos which ensued. We got the passports and our party together again eventually, but the near disaster made us half a day late in Rome, and the worst thing was that I was never allowed to forget the catastrophe. For the rest of the journey I was inevitably known as Passport, which the ruder boys altered slightly, by the change of the first vowel and the omission of the 'R', into an even more opprobrious epithet. Naturally, it was the latter that stuck, and when back at school the headmaster heard it he demanded a full explanation. I suppose it sounds amusing now, but at the time I couldn't see the funny side of it.

The curious incident I am about to relate was also connected with a school trip, but one much nearer home. The boys had nothing to do with it really, except as part of the setting. We were at a so-called agricultural camp in Kirkham, on the Fylde, which is the stretch of rather flat agricultural land between what is now the M6 and the Blackpool coast. Those were the days when everybody was still supposed to be digging for Britain, and it was thought to be good for the souls of boys, if they have any, to become farmhands for a fortnight and earn ninepence an hour for stacking wheat sheaves or picking damsons. What the unions would say about it today I can't imagine. Two other masters brought the boys out by train from school, which was in the middle of Lancashire's industrial wasteland, but as I lived with my sisters near Preston, which was halfway to the campsite, I arranged to make my own way by cycle to the farm where we were to pitch tents. When I pedalled the ten miles or so on a Saturday morning the weather was glorious, but by the time I had sorted out one or two matters of administration there were lowering skies overhead, and memory tells me that it rained on and off for the entire fortnight. Before it set in the boys had dug latrine trenches, and erected the tents under supervision (not mine). There were eight of them to a round tent, sleeping toes to the pole. The two other masters and I had a tent to ourselves, which wasn't bad for space, though one of them smoked a foul pipe. Real comfort, of course, was out of the question: one simply put up with the circumstances in the rather forlorn hope that one was doing something useful, both for the national cause and for the mental and physical development of the boys. I heartily doubted it on both counts.

Since the boys already had me well under their thumb,

my attempts at supervision were quite ineffectual. To make matters worse, after two or three days the rain became so bad that our field was sodden and most of the tents under water. Something had to be done if we were not all to catch pneumonia; as it was, one of the boys was taken to the local hospital on suspicion. Luckily the farmer, Mr Shorrocks, had a disused block of pig styes, quite clean and covered by a high corrugated iron roof. Each stye was almost as big as a tent, and was divided from its neighbour by a low slate wall. Our decision to move in was followed by three solid days of drenching rain, so the difficulty was how to keep our young minds occupied and out of mischief. Success was achieved on the first point but not the second. I came into the styes rather quietly one afternoon and found a group of boys comfortably grouped on piles of straw, each with a pile of pennies, playing what looked suspiciously like pontoon. 'I hope,' I said firmly, 'that you boys are not gambling?' They looked up without any sign of guilt. 'Oh no, sir,' said one with a particularly cheeky face. 'We're just using the pennies as counters.' Collapse of stout party; end of discipline.

Well, like all bad things, the camp eventually came to an end, and we went home. As soon as I got back to my flat the sun began to shine, and did so almost unceasingly for the next month; one of life's smaller ironies. Anyway, I'm getting to my point, which is that on the night of my return home, which must have been towards the end of August, I had a very strange dream. I don't normally dream much, and I have been told that to do so is the sign of a romantic temperament, which I certainly don't possess. Although I am now perfectly happily married, I was at that time a contented bachelor, full of my own interests and somewhat suspicious of women. Probably a little scared of them too, which makes the dream even stranger.

It wasn't an erotic dream, don't think that: I've never

been prey to them. However, it was definitely shot through with a soft romantic glow, even the scenes in the camp; for that was where it started, in the place which had recently caused me so much discomfort. In my dream, which tended to melodramatic angles like those in some films I've seen, the camp was a wonderful sunlit place with a feeling of Turner or Van Gogh. I think the story started – for the dream indeed unfolded like a film, with scenes linked by what I think film-makers call dissolves – as the boys came home from their daily labours. There was an overhead view of them going into their tents, and then there was I with the other masters, getting dressed for the evening. (In some scenes it appeared that my own eyes took the place of the camera, but in others I was able to see myself as part of the action.) Thompson was complaining about being left on duty while we went off gallivanting: it must have been our night off. Baker offered me a lift in his car into Blackpool, but I said no thank you, as it was a truly glorious evening, with at least a couple of hours' sunshine to go, and I felt like taking my stick and having a really good walk round the locality, no doubt climaxing the evening with a pint of beer at some attractive hostelry. So there I was in the next sequence, following a signpost 'to Kirkham', tramping along woodland paths and coming out near the main street of the town, which then in reality boasted a unique feature in the shape of a cinema called the Co-op, the only picture house I know to be owned and operated by the Co-operative Society. I walked up the hill towards it, decided that the features on offer were of no appeal, and crossed the road towards a pair of open wrought-iron gates which a board proclaimed as leading into the public park. I remember seeing my shadow on the ground as I strolled through the entrance; as it was to my right, and very long, I suppose I must have been walking north, with sunset probably less than an hour away.

Just inside the gates was a smallish area of formal park with seats, a rockery, and I think a bowling green. No person was in sight. I chose the more easterly of two paths and passed between rhododendron bushes to a much less cultivated area, in fact not cultivated at all. It sloped steeply down over rough grass to a towpath bordering a limpid, slow-flowing river about twenty feet wide. (One person to whom I misguidedly recounted this dream told me that rivers always mean sex: I dispute this.) I sauntered, almost floated, down to the bank, feeling that all was for the best in the best of all possible worlds. The sun, low in the sky by now, turned the river into flowing gold, and almost blinded me when I looked west. Suddenly I noticed, near to where I was standing, an empty canoe, tethered lightly to a stump. I could have sworn that it had not been there when I first entered the scene, but there it was now, an irresistible invitation, like the cake that says 'EAT ME' in *Alice in Wonderland*. I think I remember looking guiltily up and down the bank, but before I really knew what I was doing I was in the canoe, paddling blissfully up river, or rather down, since I was heading into the sun and the coast is in that direction. The inevitably clumsy process of actually getting into the boat was somehow skated over: I was simply in it, with no effort required. I saw myself in a sequence of idyllic 'shots', rounding this and that bend, allowing myself to drift under trailing willows, dipping my fingers in the almost still water. Before long there came into view a rather charming stone bridge, and under it, on the right hand bank, a large mansion in what seemed to me a rather Spanish style, mostly brick but with decorated turrets. One of the latter had a feature most unusual in this country, a surmounting curtain wall with an open fixture for a huge bronze bell, which as I approached was being vigorously tolled. Scattered about the lawn were groups of young girls, from ten to late teenage, all in uniform dress; the phrase 'convent school' came into my mind. None of the girls took the slightest notice of my approach. Gradually they all obeyed the summons of the bell and went indoors, in chattering groups, with the exception of one older girl, who remained seated on a small jetty with her toes almost dangling in the water. I paddled near to her: still she did not look up. I spoke.

When I say I spoke, I don't remember actually hearing my voice, or seeing her lips move when she replied. Yet somehow we communicated. It was almost like telepathy; perhaps all dreams are like that. The gist of this unspoken conversation was that I asked her where I would come to if I went on paddling westward, and she said she didn't know. I asked whether she was a pupil at the school, and she said yes. At some point she looked rather longingly at the boat, then enquiringly at me, and it was borne on me that she had a most beautiful face, though the actual features never registered when I tried to recall them afterwards; it was like trying to describe an alabaster mask. I do remember that her eyes were big and round, and that there was an overwhelming sadness in her expression, as though she had been waiting a long time for something which she knew would never come. I asked her name, and she told me, but again I can't precisely remember it; I do know that it was something Latin and flowing, something which sounded wonderful when she said it; something like Francesca Bellini. (I suspect that I got Francesca from having recently seen the film *The Seventh Veil*, in which Francesca is the name of the concert pianist heroine; while on my ill-starred school trip to Rome I had become interested in the Bellini sculptures.)

Just as this curious non-conversation was coming to an awkward pause, the girl said, or implied, or whatever, how lovely it must be to be in a canoe on such a lovely evening. Naturally my reply was that she was very welcome to a little trip if she wouldn't get herself into trouble – or me, come to that – with the school authorities. She said that was all right, nobody would mind. The next 'scene' was the canoe gliding down the river, with us in it, back in the direction from which I had come. The girl had the front seat, so I could see only the back of her head, which she kept perfectly still. Her hair was long, and sleek, and clean. We arrived at the park, and again the clumsy business of getting out of the canoe was somehow skipped. There we were on the towpath, and I was grateful that no irate canoe owner was running up and down with a policeman in tow. I don't think we made any further conversation, only strolled around listening to the birdsong. I do remember that whereas I kept to the paths, she preferred the grass, not seeming to mind the dew collecting on her shoes. Suddenly, as the sun finally dipped behind a tall oak, she shivered; a breeze was blowing up along the river, and she was standing on the very edge of the towpath. I offered her my coat. 'No,' she said (and this time I remember seeing her lips move), 'no, I must go now.'

'Well, all right,' I replied. 'Back in the boat and I'll have you home in a jiffy.'

'No, you don't understand. I must go now. Right away. I have to leave you.'

I was perplexed. 'Don't be silly,' I said lightly, 'there's no quicker way you can go.'

Looking sadder than ever, she took a step backwards. Now, I've said she was right on the edge, and that step should have toppled her into the river. The strange thing was that it didn't, but by the time I realized she was still upright – though what if anything was she standing on? – I had made an instinctive leap forward to save her, nearly falling in myself. I'd never touched her before; and I didn't then. My hand went around her shoulder, then inwards to pull her back; instead of which it came back to me, right through her body . . .

I don't think I have ever been so astonished in my life, if dreams can be called life. I stood there gazing at my empty, open fingers, and through the spaces between I watched her eyes still fixed on me, as the rest of her slowly became invisible. Every inch of my skin tingled, and I know my mouth fell open in total bewilderment, as I'm sure yours would if someone you'd met was disintegrating before your eyes. It was rather like the Cheshire Cat, as her sad expression seemed to be there longer than anything else, but I wasn't looking for literary allusions just then. In fact, I was in a flat panic, darting here and there to see whether it might have been some trick of the light, calling her name as the twilight closed in and the mist slowly rose from the river. I could actually see myself doing this, for the 'camera' drew backwards and upwards away from me, as sometimes happens at the end of films, so that I became more and more insignificant and indeed hard to discern in the mist, before the scene faded out.

There was a coda before I woke up. I was in the tent next morning, pulling on my boots, as Baker wandered in with a newspaper. 'Even in this rural wonderland tragedy strikes,' he said. 'There was a girl drowned in the river last night.'

I looked up with a start and scrambled to my feet. 'Give me that,' I said roughly. And there was the headline for the final fade-out. Convent school . . . missing girl . . . body recovered. You won't need to guess whose picture I was gazing at.

Well, that was the end of my very strange dream, but not the end of my story. You see, it got on my nerves that I couldn't imagine what had provoked such a vivid fabrication in my mind, and indeed, in order to keep it vivid while I pondered over it, I jotted down all the details I could remember while they were still fresh. I even cycled back to Kirkham that very afternoon to see whether I could retrace the route I had taken in my dream, but it was such a

mixture of fact and fancy that I quickly gave up. Not only
was there no sign of a river for a convent school to be based
on, there were no park gates in the high street. The Co-op
Cinema was there, though, releasing a crowd of unruly kids
from a Saturday matinee. I gave up and went home.

The dream haunted me all through the winter. Not that I
experienced it again while asleep, but I simply couldn't get
it out of my mind while I was awake. It was April before I
had occasion to go near Kirkham again, and the reason was
a cycle trip to see a colleague in Knott End, a seaside
retirement village on the mouth of the Wyre, opposite
Fleetwood. The most obvious way was through Kirkham
itself: it didn't have a by-pass then, but the main road from
Preston boasted an excellent cycle track. Alternatively I
could strike north before Kirkham and take my chance
among an intricate lacework of narrow lanes. Then I
remembered. On my way to Kirkham for the camp I had
done just that, taking a detour to look at the reputedly
pretty village of West Willing. (There doesn't seem to be an
East Willing.) Something began to tick over at the back of
my mind, and I decided to go that way again. It was a
glorious day, and the ride was most enjoyable, but my mind
was on other matters. As soon as I got to West Willing I
knew I was on the right track, for the village has a river, a
very narrow one about twenty feet across, and right by the
bridge is a signpost pointing up a narrow lane and reading
'To Kirkham'. Why had the dream so completely driven
from my mind the fact that I had taken it the previous
August? Now I cycled slowly along it again, looking out for
clues. About a mile along was a bus stop, and under the tiny
shelter provided by a thoughtful local council was a small
frame for a 'What's On' poster, showing among other things
the current attractions at the Co-op Cinema in Kirkham. I
vaguely remember stopping to read a similar poster the
previous summer. And across the road, of course, were my

park gates, except that in reality they were locked and chained, with a faded sign which read: STRAFFORD HOUSE, MAIN ENTRANCE VIA WEST WILLING BRIDGE. Further along, the road began to twist and turn, and I could hear the sound of water. A sign reading 'Picnic Spot' led me through a car park down to a delightful bank where a small stream, about to link with the river, burbled merrily over a pebble bed. I tried to retrace my steps of the previous year, and knew what I would find: a spot below a weir, from which I could look westward under a stone road bridge to the far bank of the main water, on which stood, you will not be surprised to learn, my Spanish house, in the very aspect from which I had seen it in my dream. So fate had provided the explanation which my mind had unaccountably blanked out all these months. On my way to Kirkham that other Saturday, I had subconsciously registered signpost, cinema poster, gates, and this view, and my mind had later bent all these images, in their right order, to its curious will. It was not a full explanation, but it was better than nothing.

I still wondered, of course, whether the house might possibly be a school, and if so how I could possibly have known this from across a river at a distance of several hundred yards. Could I have seen girls on the lawns, and made the assumption? Perhaps, but dream and reality were now inextricably confused in my mind. There was one way in which the matter might be settled. With the help of my road map I made my way back to West Willing Bridge and charted a route to the road on which the house must clearly stand. There indeed it was, on the left, as I approached it half an hour later, almost but not quite unrecognizable from this angle (though as I expressed the thought to myself the inimitable bell turret came into view). A big blue board, its deep colour relieved by carefully painted letters in shining gold, proclaimed it as St Benedicta's College for Young

Ladies, which was curiously close to the impression given by my dream.

I stood there considering my next move, if any. The back of my neck prickled slightly, but that might have been a result of the unseasonally warm sunshine. I caught the eye of a gardener trimming the edges of the front lawn, and asked whether he could help me, explaining with some semblance of authority that I was an architectural student who would welcome a brief glimpse of the river side of this remarkable building. He looked a bit dubious at first, but eventually said that it should be all right, as full term hadn't started and there was nobody about except half a dozen permanent residents. He showed me a place to put my cycle, led me through a side gate and, richer by half a crown, left me alone. I wandered as in a dream through an arbour set out with garden tables, and came out on to the lawn. Just as I remembered, there was a slight slope down to the bank, and a central path from the house to the small jetty. On the jetty – and it was my fingers this time that went numb – a long-haired girl was sitting with her back to me, almost dangling her toes in the water. I felt short of breath, but could not prevent myself from approaching her. At one point my shoes crunched on the gravel, and the girl looked round enquiringly. I stopped dead in my tracks, in an attitude of total uncertainty. As I've made clear, the precise features of the girl in my dream were vague to me afterwards, so although I instantly seemed to recognize in this girl the same attitude and colouring, I couldn't be sure. But I had to say something, or my silence might frighten her.

'Francesca?' I said chokingly.

A shadow crossed her face, but she half smiled at me with an expression of weary patience. 'I'm afraid not,' she said. 'Francesca was my twin sister. She was drowned in the river last July.'

Hands with Long Fingers

I don't usually dream. What's more, until I met Paul Binet I had never in my life had an experience which might be considered supernatural. I took life as I found it; I enjoyed my work and my pleasure; I expected a scientific explanation for everything. Anything of value which I have accomplished has been in the way of shedding further light on obscure historical or literary events. I don't welcome mystery; I explain it away. In particular, I have exposed several frauds of a supposedly occult nature. Yet here I find myself setting down a series of events which defies rational analysis. Perhaps the very recapitulation of what happened, in chronological sequence, will help towards further clarification. But I suspect not.

When Emmanuel Hilary died in October, I was surprised to find myself invited by his son John to attend the funeral. Very surprised indeed. I knew the son only slightly. We were at Sidney Sussex together, though I think he was in fact a year my junior. At any rate we went to some of the same clubs. The father I knew not at all except from once attending his course of lectures on Italian architecture. John introduced us, and we had a drink together in the public house at the bottom of Mill Lane. In his last years old Emmanuel acquired the reputation of being a bit gaga. He squandered quite a lot of his considerable fortune on the restoration of a crumbling eighteenth-century villa near Florence. He died there. At the time I happened to be living in a rented cottage not far away, in a village on the slopes of Monte Morillo. I was researching a book on Cagliostro: not

really my line, but one must find a way of paying the
butcher's bills. When the invitation came, I hesitated for an
hour, then sent a note of acceptance. In the circumstances, a
refusal might have seemed discourteous. Besides, I felt
instinctively that there was something behind the invitation.
John must want to see me. Thirty years ago we had parted
in Cambridge without so much as a handshake. Our only
direct contact during the last decade was a club dinner after
my series of radio talks on the occult; but I remembered him
well as a man who did not suffer fools gladly, yet was himself
more devious than intelligent. In urging me to visit his
father's mansion he undoubtedly had some motive more
significant than wanting me to help eat up the baked meats
after sitting through a doleful church service in a faith that
wasn't mine.

The Villa Fabricotti was hidden from the road. However
much trouble Emmanuel had taken, its situation was such
that it could never suggest anything but damp and decay
unless the thick wood which surrounded it were cut down. It
was a rambling three-storey affair with some rococo
additions; the basic design was rather vaguely Baroque.
Some greenish creeper covered much of the outer wall and
almost all of the gatehouse. The inner grounds were an
unkempt wilderness of neglected fern and shrub. Hardly a
cheerful place to die in, I reflected as my elderly Fiat
ploughed its way along the muddy drive after a morning
storm. Although we were well into autumn the weather had
suddenly turned oppressive, and I noted with distaste almost
approaching alarm the presence of clouds of great heavy
insects, several of which crashed fatally into my windscreen,
leaving nasty grey smears. It was nearly noon; I was the last
to arrive. I noted with some amusement that the expectant
beneficiaries were all present although none of them lived
nearer than Westminster. They looked like people who
would take no chances.

John welcomed me with rather exaggerated bonhomie. It quickly turned out that one of his reasons for asking me was that he hoped I would join him and four others as pallbearers on the short procession to the local church and graveside. I nodded agreement, but thought he might have warned me: some people think they need only to have an idea to see it done. He introduced his wife Madeleine, a middle-aged charmer who looked well capable of getting her own way. Other so-called mourners included his elder sister Wanda and her husband Henry Marling, a beaky, avaricious looking pair. Then there was Reginald Bell, Emmanuel's other son-in-law via a daughter long deceased; and Eleanor Cavendish-Warren, some sort of cousin, who was clearly approaching her eighties.

We accomplished the business of the day as speedily as we could. A young male mute walked in front of the coffin, and all the women behind. Only the servants seemed genuinely moved; the family's tears were of the crocodile variety. Afterwards there was a buffet back at the villa, giving me a further chance to observe my fellow guests as they masticated their rather disgusting hot osso bucco and cold garlic sausage, followed by what seemed to be a bread pudding of extremely leaden texture. For me the coffee and strega were the only enjoyable part of the meal, and after that I was thinking of taking my leave when John, perhaps sensing this, came over to sit by me and offer another drink. Whatever else was in his mind couldn't seem to find expression, so to cover an awkward pause I asked:

'Who is the little man in black with the long hands and pale eyes?'

I gestured briefly at a sober figure dwarfed by the marble mantelpiece. He toyed solitarily with his coffee spoon. His well-cut coat was thigh-length and looked Edwardian; it was devoid of buttons or lapels. You couldn't help noticing his hands before anything else: perfectly formed, with elegant fingers, they seemed to have been borrowed from a man twice his size.

'That's Paul Binet. He sat at the back of the church.'

'Interesting-looking fellow. Is he French?'

'Half that and half Spanish, I think. He kind of goes with the house. Father found him a few years ago in New York, working in one of the museums, and took him on as a sort of librarian–companion. It seems he specializes in occult manuscripts, of which we now have quite a collection at the expense of the family fortunes. Mostly quite unreadable and unsaleable, I think. As a matter of fact, that was my main reason for asking you over.'

So it was out at last. I tried to look politely inquisitive.

'I have to go back to London in a couple of days, and I'm afraid business must go on even in the presence of death.' I mentally confirmed my previous impression of John as a sanctimonious hypocrite. 'After all, there are thousands of quite valuable books here, and I'm a complete Philistine. The family is rather afraid that Binet may try to get his hands on the choicest items, and I wondered whether . . . well, whether you'd be free to put some sort of valuation on them, give us a quick indication, anyway?' John was trying to smile. 'You know, tell us which ones to lock away.'

I raised an eyebrow non-committally. 'I *could* do that, I suppose.'

'I didn't want to offend you by offering a fee, though do say if you'd like one. I thought you might prefer to take your pick of the books, say five hundred quid's worth, or seven-fifty if you like. You might even enjoy yourself.'

I pursed my lips. 'It's an agreeable enough suggestion, and I'd be glad to spend a day or two at it. Especially with a bottle from your cellar to lay the dust at lunchtime. But what about Binet? Won't he resent my poaching on his territory?'

John instantly showed his true colours. 'Binet be damned. He's a servant in this house, and he'll do what he's told. The fact is, we none of us trust him. Maddy thinks he was trying to set the old man against us. However, it's over now, before any harm of that kind could be done. I've already seen the will, though we have to wait for the formal reading tomorrow.' He collected himself and looked a little sheepish. 'I say, I'm delighted you'll help us. Are you sure you wouldn't prefer a proper business arrangement?'

I shook my head. 'Your first suggestion will be fine, and I promise not to cheat. Five volumes of my choice, to a total not exceeding five hundred pounds.'

I came back next morning at ten, only to learn that the family lawyer had been delayed in Milan by some urgent court case, so the family mourners had to hang on and were clearly not happy about it. Nor was I, as it meant we'd all have to lunch together. John wasn't in, so the butler showed me straight to the library, a tall musty room with a richly ornamented ceiling. Its walls were crammed with decorated oak shelving, two banks of which projected into the centre to be joined by an ornamental arch. Left alone with a flask of coffee, I opened some windows and set to work. Of the seven thousand odd books in the room, I quickly calculated that more than half were too modern to have any significant value; so I noted the position of the rest and got busy on them. Despite a certain orderliness – in some sections the Dewey system had been adopted – some sections seemed very curiously classified. Suddenly my attention was drawn by three bulky unabridged copies of Frazer's *The Golden Bough*, in different ornamental editions. I stepped into the alcove which housed them, and found myself surrounded by a vast number of volumes on the occult, constituting in total so great a proportion of the library as to overbalance it completely. They ranged from paper-covered how-to-do-it manuals of conjuring tricks to a few privately-printed volumes of black magic rituals, including an item which totally took my breath away, a complete seventeenth-century rubric for the black mass. There were books about spirit-raising, zombies and voodoo, human sacrifice, witchcraft through the ages, and every other aspect of the supernatural you might think of in a nightmare. An odd collection indeed to find in the house of a man just buried, who presumably might have gleaned from his library enough skills to transcend the barrier of death.

My attention was suddenly distracted by a light slapping or clapping noise. I was so concealed by the alcove that I might have been hiding there. I stepped out to find Binet standing at one of the open windows which surveyed the terrace. He had his long tapering hands half stretched out before him, almost as though he was applauding. I couldn't see any sense in the action at first, then I realized what he was doing. I have mentioned the very furry insects which banged and squashed themselves against the windscreen of my car on my first arrival. It seemed now that there was a small swarm of them outside the window, and Binet was catching them in his hands! Not killing them with a clap, but capturing them in his deft long fingers, cupping them carefully one at a time, and transferring them to a kind of glass case which stood on a nearby desk, opening and closing it while he inserted the struggling insect with a stylish flick of his supple fingers. As I moved closer I could see fluttering inside the case half a dozen of the unpleasant creatures, and a couple more dead on the bottom. Suddenly he became aware of my presence and was so startled that he let his last captive free. It flew off into a dark green bush.

'What on earth do you want those things for?' I asked almost involuntarily.

His eyes rolled a little, his mouth opened silently, and he shook his head from side to side. 'It is nothing,' he murmured. 'An experiment, only an experiment. And you?

You were . . . looking for something?'

Something about the way he looked up at me suggested a dog which knows it is about to be beaten; something else suggested a dangerous animal about to spring in its own defence. In that second Binet's whole personality seemed to be exposed. I knew that I could never forget the slightly hunched shoulders, the crew cut hair, the sallow complexion, the suspicion of an accent in his otherwise impeccable English diction. I judged him to be in his mid-forties, though there were aspects which might have made him twenty years younger or ten years older. I was repelled by the hatred which clearly seethed in his pale eyes. Yet I had no doubt whatever that he had cared more than any member of the family for the well being of old Emmanuel. He had that distrust of outsiders which is the hallmark of the perfect servant. Blood may be thicker than water, but love is thicker than either, and devotion to duty is a kind of love. So I admired him; yet there was something unsettling about him. I feared him; yet I understood him. The truth is perhaps that I instinctively sensed between us a kind of empathy despite the fact that it would have been difficult to find two human beings more outwardly different. I stress the word empathy rather than sympathy. My feeling was only that somehow Binet and I were on the same plane. We would understand each other yet not necessarily agree. This feeling of mine, after only a few seconds of conversation, seems more than a little related to the curious events which followed.

I quickly discovered that even though John may have mentioned my likely presence in the library, he had not explained it. Privately cursing my college friend, I spun Binet a yarn about John's wanting to make use of the presence of an alleged expert to give a general view on the interest of the collection. Binet listened attentively but was clearly not convinced. He shrugged politely at my apology for trespassing on his preserves, and finally shook his head.

'It is not your fault. Not at all. I am aware that they do not trust me.' His eyes opened wider in private amusement, and the pupils gleamed. 'But they may find that there is a small surprise waiting for them. And then the world will know who Emmanuel really trusted.'

There seemed no answer to so naïve a threat. The words had been delivered lightly, yet they chilled and silenced me. I thought afterwards that perhaps he had not intended me to hear them. Perhaps the truth was that he did not care whether I heard them or not. Abruptly he turned from me and left the room, making no more noise than the breeze which whistled outside among the cypresses. As the door closed behind him, my eyes fell to the strange little glass case in which a few insects still struggled while five now lay dead. I forced myself to examine the species more closely. Horrible things they were, something over an inch long, with long jointed flea-like legs, a furry abdomen and wavering antennae. What could be Binet's purpose in collecting such revolting objects? Deciding that more prolonged study of them would spoil my appetite for lunch, I made to return to my task. As I did so, my hand touched a book which was lying open on the corner of Binet's desk. It was in French. The title was *La Transférence du Mort*.

The funeral had been on a Wednesday. I worked on the library throughout Thursday and the first part of Friday. It was towards lunchtime on that day that the bombshell dropped. I was aware that the lawyer from Milan had arrived, and that he was in conclave with the family. It had just occurred to me to wonder whether the will had contained any surprises when I heard the scrape of several chairs on the parquet floor upstairs. As I crossed the hall with the intention of washing my hands and taking a stroll before lunch, John came running down the staircase in an excess of bad temper. His face was like a thunderstorm. He had to say something as I innocently confronted him. What he said was: 'Binet's got it! The whole damn lot! May the old man rot in hell!'

I never sought the whys and wherefores of the business. There was no putting up with the gloomy vindictiveness of the family any more than with the gleeful triumph of Binet. As I packed up, taking with me only two books instead of the five agreed, John told me merely that two wills had been found. The first gave the house to John and divided the fortune fairly evenly between him and the rest of the family, with a decent but not overwhelming bequest for Binet. The second and later document, lodged with the lawyer only weeks before the old man's death, left everything, apart from small gifts and charitable donations, unconditionally to Binet. Not only did the family fail to get what they expected; none of them was even mentioned.

For the next month or more my literary researches took me only briefly to London; then I was off again to Liechtenstein, San Marino, and finally Copenhagen. Occasional phone calls to friends kept me up with what was happening in the Binet affair. Predictably, the will was being contested by the family on the grounds that the old man was of unsound mind when he made it. I passed through Florence in early December, and once drove past the old house, but it seemed empty, though the old padre whom I met in the street told me that so far as he knew Binet was still in residence. Just in time for Christmas I flew home. Among the letters awaiting me was a note from John to let me know that the second will had been successfully revoked, and that Binet had been given notice to quit.

It was during that night that the dream came to me. I would have attributed it to tiredness, over-eating or incipient influenza had it not been so very vivid, like a beautifully photographed film. It began with Binet's face, in what I suppose I have to call close-up. Heavily shadowed, malign, evil. He was saying something which I could not quite catch, but then the 'camera' drew back and there was I, with my back to it, listening to him. We were in the library of the Villa Fabricotti, standing near his desk by the window. He wore what appeared to be the same black suit, the one with no lapels, and rather to my surprise he seemed to be drunk. With the curious certainty of dreamers I ascribed his condition, for some unknown reason, to the effects of calvados. Some of the shelves were empty, but the occult section was undiminished. Most of the furniture was thick with dust. Even in my dream the atmosphere was unbearably claustrophobic: I longed to get out into the fresh air. A small bed in the corner had been slept in but not made up.

'You live very simply,' I said, my voice echoing around the room.

Now I could hear him. 'Simply, my friend?' he hissed. 'It is the others who are simple. Binet won before, and he will win again. You know my plan. Now I shall carry it out!'

'Plan?' I said vaguely. 'What plan do you mean?' But he had already turned away to the desk, and when he faced me again his hands held the wooden box with glass panels in which I had seen him trap the grey insects. I took a step backwards in revulsion, but it was full of the damned things still.

'I shall show you, my friend,' said Binet almost maniacally, 'what good friends these creatures are, how they help to ensure that justice is done. The Hilarys think they have won, but my reach is longer than they can imagine. Watch!'

I can't remember exactly how he did it without freeing all the insects, but suddenly he selected one and held it by the wings, struggling between the fingers of his left hand. A truly monstrous sight in the precise detail now afforded to me. With his free hand Binet drew from some part of his clothing a long pin.

'What the devil . . .' I exclaimed.

Binet smiled, almost sweetly. 'Precisely,' he said, driving the pin through the body of the insect, which reacted violently before shuddering into lifelessness. 'You see before you the remains of Mr John Hilary!'

I was truly shocked. 'You raving lunatic!' I said viciously.

Binet grinned foolishly at me, sweat standing out on his forehead as he held aloft on its pin his little victim. 'We shall see,' he murmured with a sudden appearance of exhaustion. 'And now, my friend, I think you had better leave . . .'

Suddenly I was running in fear down the overgrown drive, and behind me I heard insane, helpless, convulsive laughter which I knew to be Binet's. In my mind's eye I saw him opening a drawer in which, carefully laid out on white silk, were six small circles of coloured material, edged with darker thread. On one of these he laid the insect he had killed, and closed the drawer. Superimposed on this image there faded in an old-fashioned newsboy walking quickly through the streets, waving at passers-by and shouting: 'JOHN HILARY DEAD! JOHN HILARY DEAD!'

I woke up at this point, and hurried for a bath as hot as I could stand it. Anything to wipe away the memory of that dream. I took my long-suffering wife, who had by agreement retired before my midnight arrival, a cup of tea. She promised breakfast in thirty minutes. Meanwhile, still obsessed by the dream, I felt that I must try to contact John Hilary and see that he was in good health. It worried me that much. I had his Haywards Heath number in my book, and dialled it twice, but there was no reply. I looked up the London phone book but there were five John Hilarys. By the time breakfast was ready I was feeling somewhat calmer, but as my wife poured the tea she remarked, after asking about my trip home:

'By the way, didn't you say something last time you were home about meeting some people called Hilary? John and Madeleine?'

I nearly burned my mouth on the tea. 'Yes, I went to his father's funeral. What about them?'

'I'm sorry to say they were killed in an air crash. It was in yesterday's paper. I kept it for you.'

I grabbed the newspaper with an apparent rudeness which astonished my wife. There indeed were their names, among thirty-eight victims of the Paris air crash I'd heard about, with enough further detail to identify them beyond doubt.

All shocks fade. I had ceased to think very much about the event, and had almost forgotten my dream, when in mid-January I noticed in the *Times* obituaries the rather unusual name of Eleanor Cavendish-Warren. There was no doubt that she was the Hilary I had met; though seventy-eight, she had died suddenly and unaccountably while wintering on Cap Ferrat. Later in the month I read casually of a fatal car accident involving one Henry Marling and his wife. It took me a whole afternoon to remember where I had heard the name before. I felt like a man trapped in a recurring nightmare. Of all the beneficiaries under old Emmanuel's will, only one was still alive: Reginald Bell. I had to warn him, yet I knew almost nothing about him. Remembering, I thought, his saying that he was an architect, I finally tracked him down to an office in the city. His secretary when she answered was reserved, sorrowful, and proper. She was sorry to tell me that only two days ago her employer had succumbed to a heart attack while holidaying on a Nile cruise.

I was afraid to go back to Florence. I was afraid of meeting Binet. It was the end of May before I made the journey, on account of a final piece of research which could only be achieved there. My wife came with me: not exactly for protection, but because I didn't want even to think about my previous visit. On arrival, however, the city and countryside seemed so serene that my fears vanished, and two days later I was recklessly driving along the main street of Monte Pareto, approaching the gateway to the Villa Fabricotti. My sensitive stomach rumbled distinctly as I pulled up near a sign informing me that the place was to let or for sale.

I asked some nearby workmen if they knew what had happened to Paul Binet. Yes, they said, he was dead. Found in the grounds on the morning he was due to pack up and go. Stiff as a board, with a purple face and a terrible expression on it. They didn't know what happened to the books, but a lot of the articles from the house, apart from the very valuable ones which had been taken away, had been put up by the lawyers for sale through a local merchant.

I found the shop without difficulty, and wandered uneasily around it. I recognized odd pieces of occasional furniture, including a wrought-iron standard lamp which had been in the hall. I was about to leave when in a corner, resting on the second shelf of a whatnot, I glimpsed an object which riveted me to the spot. Despite my revulsion I had to walk over and pick it up. It was a glass dome about six inches high, and its contents had last been seen in my dream. Sticking up from the base on a wire frame were arranged what might have been six tiny, grotesque dolls. They wore gaily coloured capes, and looked as though they were about to play ring-a-ring-a-roses. At first and even second glance it was possible not to notice that the dolls were really insects.

The Viaduct

I was walking back one evening from a party on a two-hundred-foot yacht in Monte Carlo's fashionable harbour. An Italian millionaire's yacht. I was, really. I had never met the millionaire, and he had no conception of my existence, but a business friend had had an invitation and took me along instead of standing me dinner. My friend didn't seem to know any of the other guests, and the host didn't even bother to turn up, and although from the outside the boat, or is it a ship at that length, looked very nice indeed, on the inside despite its fifteen staterooms it had all the beguiling ambience of a public lavatory.

The guests were a cosmopolitan crowd numbering seventy or eighty, and few of them seemed to know each other either, though all happily drank large quantities of the absent host's wine and consumed as many as they could grab of the fifteen or so supper courses, not to mention handfuls of Havana cigars. At about midnight my friend did discover someone he wanted to do business with, and this seemed a decent point at which to take my own leave, on the grounds that my bare little blue and cream room in Loew's Hotel was cooler and fresher and quieter than the boat; and had a bed in it.

Although Loew's overhangs the sea – indeed the concrete pillars which support it are being alarmingly undercut by the Mediterranean – it is not an attractive construction. In recent years Prince Rainier has allowed his fairy tale kingdom to be overrun by speculators anxious to make a quick million or two by running up cheap concrete high rises of the most appalling taste, colour and design. From most of them you can't even see the sea, much less get at it. Loew's itself has no beach and can be reached on foot from the port only through a long concrete tunnel of entirely unaesthetic dimensions, at the far end of which the hotel may be approached by pedestrians via a chill set of spiral concrete steps. As I neared these, a massive uniformed fellow clattered down the last flight to the pavement, holding before him a much smaller, stockier man by the collar; holding him what's more at arm's length so that the small man's flailing arms had no chance whatever of landing a blow. It didn't seem an equal match, so in the most foolhardy (and uncharacteristic) fashion I ran forward and yelled something inappropriate like 'Oi,' at which the big one looked at me rather sheepishly, dropped the little one into a heap on the pavement, shrugged his shoulders and marched off up the steps again.

The little man wasn't hurt: as much damage had been done to his dignity as to his shirt. But his high forehead had somehow scraped the concrete and a little blood was oozing. His English was about as good as my French, which is to say that we didn't understand each other very well, but I made him gather that if he would accompany me up to my room I would happily wash off any stray dirt from the wound and dress it as best I could. He concurred readily enough, and on the way began to tell me (I think) what a poor fellow he was and how ashamed he felt of his prowess, or lack of same. His name, it seemed, was Vincent Bejard – pronounced in the French way, of course – and he was an assistant customs officer. (At this point I wished momentarily that I hadn't interfered.) To cut a long story short, his wife – they lived in Menton up the coast – had admitted to him an affair with another man, a doorman at Loew's and well suited to the job since he was the big bruiser I had just sent packing. Having pondered the problem for several days, Vincent had that night been trying, in vain of course, to teach the interloper a lesson, but his pleas had rolled like water off a duck's back, and the threat of force had merely amused the offender to the extent I had witnessed, i.e. ignominious removal of Vincent from the premises. Now there was nothing for Vincent to do but go home and throw himself on his wife's mercy: it was an embarrassing prospect, but he assured me that he was quite unable to live without her, that she was the only woman in the world for him, and that without her support he might as well be dead. There aren't many useful arguments one can muster with a person of such decided views, and so I simply smiled and looked sympathetic and bought him a drink, making sure to get him out of the hotel by a side door so that he wouldn't bump into his dreaded rival again.

I might have forgotten all about Vincent, but during the following week I settled temporarily in a flat and set about the business which had brought me down to Monaco. This involved a weekly trip thirty miles east to San Remo, and rather than endure repeatedly the painful negotiation of the narrow coastal route I elected to start by making the multi-hairpin ascent to Roquebrune for the sake of a smooth high-speed drive along the new autoroute with its dazzling succession of tunnels and viaducts which have made the drive from Nice to Genoa one of the most spectacular in the world. On my first trip as I emerged from a long tunnel into the exceptionally wide gap north of Ventimiglia on the Italian border, I saw ahead of me the French customs post, which is actually situated on a tall viaduct, above a verdant scene so casually cultivated and haphazardly industrialized that you immediately sense the lazy Italian influence succeeding the tidy French. The motorway sloped down gently towards the green customs cabins, and as I approached one of them I instantly recognized the portly uniformed figure beside it as belonging to Vincent. He knew me at once, and didn't even bother to recite the usual customs formalities; instead he asked whether I had time for a drink and insisted on my parking so that he could buy me one in the customs officers' tiny canteen, not much bigger than the kitchen of a normal British semi. Here I enjoyed a Ricard on ice while gazing out over the distant sea; the opposite view showed the Alpes Maritimes rising steeply into their snow caps. I complimented him on his choice of post; he wagged his head from side to side and said mournfully that I should try it when the wind blew from the north. I asked him how things were at home, and he said 'pas mal' in that tone which unmistakably means that they couldn't be much worse. He thanked me repeatedly for my small kindness, and insisted it was a debt he would repay. On the way back to my car he introduced me to some of his comrades and told them with a wink not to be too suspicious of me if they saw me coming through again, even if I was wearing five watches on each wrist. We bade each other a cheery farewell and promised to repeat the encounter.

In a sense we did, for each week of the next half dozen I managed to see Vincent for at least a wave and a nod, even if he did not personally pass me through. On a couple of occasions I thought he looked a little doleful, but on the others he readily managed his shy smile, and once joked about his increasing girth. Only last week I gave him a piece of paper with my address and telephone number scribbled on it, and told him to ring me when he came to Monte Carlo again. He said he certainly would. So nothing prepared me for what happened.

It happened today, this morning. I am writing it down exactly as it took place in case I don't believe it tomorrow. I was not on my usual errand. It was a blithe February day, and I had promised a pleasantly-disposed colleague a drive north through Sospel to Col de Turini, where at six thousand feet, with a bit of luck, we could enjoy a sunny al fresco lunch amid the snow, while watching skiers come down the mountain and rejoin the queue for the chair lift. Ventimiglia seemed the best starting point, so as usual I took the autoroute at Roquebrune and sped cheerfully through the tunnels at seventy. Halfway along, my friend reminded me that there was a customs go-slow that day and we might be held up. Cursing myself for having forgotten, I applied the brake as we emerged from the tunnel and saw that, sure enough, the approach to the customs post below was thronged with more vehicles than one usually sees there even at the height of summer. 'We're here for the best part of an hour,' I sighed, choosing the right-hand queue as offering the best view as well as being one of the shortest. Hardly had I settled into place, however, than I was astonished to see Vincent walking towards me from the direction of the canteen, with a look of unmistakable horror on his face. He was waving at me vehemently, beckoning me out of the lane on to the hard shoulder, which had as usual been left clear of vehicles. Glancing at my companion, who did not seem to have noticed, I started the engine, turned the wheels, and just managed to clear myself from the bumpers of the car in front. More than a little bemused, I followed Vincent's gestured instructions, parking myself within inches of the thick steel protection rail, a point from which my passenger had a dizzy view of the valley below. Braking firmly, I climbed out of the car to see what the fuss was all about. Vincent seemed to have disappeared, but just as I glanced back at the queue of vehicles a dirty old truck emerged from the tunnel with the driver waving frantically from the wheel. Clearly out of control, the vehicle accelerated helplessly down the slope and ran smack into the vehicle directly in front of what thirty seconds previously had been my place. The truck driver went straight through the windscreen and was taken to hospital in a very distressing condition; a woman in the car in front has a dislocated neck and may not live.

Vincent was not to be found again. I mentioned my astonishment at seeing him in the first place; this stemmed from a telephone call I had received yesterday from his colleague, who had discovered my scrap of paper in Vincent's drawer at the customs post. Vincent's wife had finally and irrevocably left him for the doorman; and so, ten minutes after reporting for duty, he had thrown himself off the high viaduct, near the point at which he so briefly rematerialized this morning to ensure my safety and thus repay his debt.

Lady of the Midnight Sun

Donald Tomson was a bachelor by inclination, an infrequent pursuer of women. As he grew to accept middle age he found that he liked his own company best, and had a partiality for holidays in seaside resorts out of season. Here at some modest board residence he would enjoy the full attention of the kitchen and restaurant staff, after days enjoyably spent pottering around antique stalls, briskly striding along lonely beaches, or making discriminate purchases at gents' outfitters or furniture emporia, which often had the sales cards out to make way for next season's stock.

Mr Little's Bookshop, his premises in Ripon were called, though Mr Little had been dead for many years even before Donald took over. His antiquarian business had distinct international connections; however, he was seldom called upon to travel abroad at anyone else's expense, and he was reluctant to do so upon his own. It was thus with a sense of mounting excitement that he watched the days on his calendar diminish in number before his scheduled departure for Iceland. Here he was to be the United Kingdom representative at a five-day convention of bookish delegates invited by the Scandinavian countries. They were to exchange opinions and exhibit their wares, thus hopefully stimulating their mutual trade. Only recently there had come into Donald's hands two copies of the Icelandic sagas in the original language – Njal's and Egil's – which looked old enough and sufficiently well illustrated to have some considerable value for anybody who could read the text. In Reykjavik, he might hope for a handsome profit. Further more, since the Icelanders were reported to be voracious readers of works in English, he hoped he might come upon a collection or two which he could buy cheap and sell, on his return, very dear.

The flight from Glasgow was punctual and surprisingly crowded, depositing him at Keflavik airport shortly before midnight. Except for a couple of very occasional acquaintances he expected to know none of the other delegates, and an agreeable sense of adventure engulfed him as he stepped into the open air to be confronted by a red ball of sun which would never that night – for this was July – sink below the watery horizon. Enquiry as to the cost of a taxi into Reykjavik taught him a sharp lesson about Iceland's galloping inflation, so he ran for a bus, which efficiently deposited him some forty minutes later by the pier outside the Hotel Borg, after a drive through a landscape strangely consisting of endless eerie expanses of black lava crust, broken only by a few distant geyser spouts.

Though his room at the Borg – an odd little turret it was, seemingly built on as an afterthought at the end of the top storey – proved comfortable enough, Donald managed regrettably little sleep during what was left of the night. To him a constantly open window was not merely desirable but necessary; yet if he allowed the air thus to circulate he found himself staring even through closed lids into that incredibly fiery sun, which hung over the coastline like a pantomime backcloth. If on the other hand he closed the black velour drapes he felt too breathless to sleep, especially since the highly sulphurous smell of the local tapwater strongly communicated itself under the closed door of the bathroom. At about five he gave in to the need for darkness, and lapsed finally into a doze. His alarm ringing at eight was distinctly unwelcome, the more so since he had been experiencing a curious dream, or nightmare, concerning some indefinable influence which came seeping at him through the featureless velour with which he had blotted out the actual landscape. Something quite evil, he thought, vaguely annoyed to have awakened without remembering more about it. Well, the only influence now was a thin but brilliant shaft of sunshine striking at him through a jagged tear in the curtains. Staggering sleepily, he drew these back to reveal a scene which, with its dull concrete houses and corrugated iron roofs, would have seemed disappointingly English suburban had it not been fringed by exhilarating views of lochs, islets, and faraway volcanic mountains which were still snow-capped and would presumably remain so throughout the summer. Donald was pleased, incidentally, to find that his room led to a little semi-circular balcony, as did all the others on this level; they were separated from each other by low hedges of some unfamiliar but thickly-sprouting northern bush. Its supple branches had formed around the wrought-iron fence, which was broken by a little gate presently encircled by barbed wire, the intention of which was presumably to prevent unwelcome socializing. Donald wondered whether he would have time for much sitting out there in the sun, whether indeed the climate would be sufficiently benign for such a pastime, even in the high season. He concluded rather quickly that even though the opportunity might present itself, he would probably refrain from taking advantage of it. Out there he felt curiously – what was the word? – vulnerable.

After a hurried Icelandic breakfast of cheese slices and brown bread he determined on a morning's exploration of the city, since his conference was to begin with a lunchtime assembly. He was disappointed to find most of Reykjavik bearing a distinct resemblance to the outskirts of Nottingham or Leeds. Its situation, on a long flat tongue of land jutting out to sea, was perfectly delightful, but the city had spread so untidily that once you were walking in it the sea seemed almost irrelevant unless some long cinder-scattered avenue happened to bring you to the hard-working harbour. The quaint old Nordic kingdom he had envisioned was replaced by a somewhat horrendous reality of featureless dwellings, cheap restaurants and overheated shops in which stylelessly shaggy woollen garments were sold by assistants who spoke rather better English than he did himself. Over a coffee in a serve-yourself establishment called Nessie (apparently in honour of the Loch Ness monster), he was informed by a cheerful local journalist that the old medieval buildings, being of wood, had gradually collapsed; even their site had been gradually abandoned, since a new modern Reykjavik was arising some two miles away, and he was warned that the proud and independent Icelanders would not appreciate jokes about it. As an antiquarian he was urged to visit the medieval sod houses which had been preserved on a distant hill, but time did not permit this. A somewhat depressing morning was however much improved when on his way to the meeting place, a converted school, he found a tiny second-hand bookshop from which he carried away, for the equivalent of three pounds, a first edition of Auden and MacNiece's *Letters from Iceland*, which he could easily sell at home for twenty-five. The afternoon was even better: he sold his sagas for an amount almost beyond the dreams of avarice.

That evening, replete with superficial conversation and chastened by the chill night wind which permeated the city, he decided to retire early without dinner, a procedure which he frequently found to be restorative. He hoped that the day-long filling of his lungs with semi-arctic air would induce sleep despite the problem of the curtains, but as an extra precaution at seven-thirty he swallowed an anti-histamine pill which would probably make him tired as well as easing his breathing, which was frequently affected by a touch of sinusitis. He would have been in bed before eight had not a knock at his door introduced three fellow delegates with a bottle of the lethal form of local schnapps known as Black Death. They insisted on his partaking of their discovery, and since he was unused to spirits he had sipped his way through two glasses of it before he began to realize its extreme potency. His tendency next morning, therefore, was to blame the drink for what subsequently happened. Perhaps he was right. The fact was that just as soon as he had closed the door on his friends, with protestations of extreme tiredness, he fell upon his bed in a most pleasant state of euphoria. It seemed to him that he had remained entirely clear-headed, yet he remembered seriously wondering where he might cheaply acquire a pair of seven-league boots which would enable him effortlessly to ascend the jagged range of mountains on the skyline. Below his window a fair proportion of Reykjavik's one hundred thousand inhabitants seemed to be driving madly from hither to thither and back, and the muted cacophony of brake and klaxon made an acceptably soporific background for his deepening unconsciousness.

At midnight, almost exactly, he awoke with that familiar choking feeling which meant that the drapes would have to be opened, sun or no sun. As he stumbled out of bed with half-closed eyes, he grimaced at the bad taste left in his mouth by the schnapps; but his self-disapproval at this was forgotten at his sudden realization that the drapes were not closed after all and that the sky was not dark, though the sun had momentarily retreated behind a thick blanket of cloud. The effect of this was to flood the balconies with a strangely opalescent light, reminiscent of the doom-laden period before a thunderstorm; a light, he remembered thinking, which might have proved stimulating to Edgar Allan Poe at the height of his creative period. The air now seemed unusually mild for the middle of the night, and had acquired a sweetness which had nothing to do with the normally all-pervading sulphur.

Standing at the open French window, Donald realized with a start that he was in his pyjamas and that someone else was out there, not on his balcony but on the next one. It was a woman. His normal instinct would have been to dash for cover at once, or at least to grab for his dressing gown; but in his present mildly drugged state he stayed where he was with a fair assumption of nonchalance and what he recalled later as a mild and uncharacteristic interest in how so piquant a situation might develop. He thought at first that the woman had not even seen him. She was standing at her balcony rail, gazing out to sea, her brown-blonde hair catching and reflecting what light there was, her half profile outlined against an ice-cap some twenty miles away. Her nose was aquiline, her eyes blue, her face an epitome of cold Nordic beauty. Though Donald made no sound, she turned very slowly towards him, and immediately, despite his limited experience of women, he sensed fire beneath the ice. He saw that she wore a medieval-looking evening dress in a glittery silken material mainly composed of blues and greens; there was a headband too, of similar stuff, and over her left breast a-large brooch in the form of a decorated ram's horn, its twists gleaming with inlaid jewels.

Donald never made out how the lady suddenly contrived to be standing on *his* balcony rather than her own, or how without introducing themselves they seemed to be in such indisputable spiritual communion. It was as though they knew each other too well to need conversation: just looking at her filled Donald with the stuff of a hundred romances, with stories of trolls and witches and Viking chieftains pillaging fishing villages, of mountain streams and hard winters and virgin forests and unending summer nights. The spirit of medieval Nordic romance filled his soul. Bodily communion followed hard upon; the lady would brook no resistance. With a simple movement she stood before him naked, and he realized with a sudden shock that he was in the same state. (Had he been in the same state all along? Had he imagined his pyjamas?) There was a hungry yet satisfied look in her eyes as she bore him backwards on to the soft duvet-covered bed. He took the woman's part, being too weak to insist, lying on his back as she flowed over him like warm spring water and seemed delightfully to fill every crevice in his body.

The alarm woke him at seven-thirty, but he was unusually slow about his toilet. Midway through shaving, the incidents of the night infiltrated his memory. For some minutes he stood immovable on the bath mat. It was simply impossible for him to decide whether the thing had really happened, or whether it had been generated in sleep by a combination of Fabahystin and Black Death. He puzzled about it over breakfast. He puzzled about it with dismay. He knew for certain that he had been sexually aroused during the night, but then he had been abstemious of late, so that was natural. He went out on to his balcony and glanced discreetly over the shrubs: there was no sign of life in the next room, the French window of which looked as though it could have been closed for a week or a month. His hand fell, and something pricked his finger. He looked down in surprise at the barbed wire still twisted round the little wrought-iron gate to prevent its use.

Rather than risk the possibility – a remote one – of meeting the lady in the restaurant, he ordered breakfast in his room, and afterwards hurried out of the hotel by a side entrance to hail a taxi. As the morning wore on, and trading proved brisk, he almost forgot his curious adventure, or at least pushed it to the back of his mind. This was the official bring-and-buy day, and he was able to make several most interesting exchanges. His trip was proving more rewarding in this respect than he had imagined. Once there popped into his mind the thought that books were more sensuous and more satisfying than women, but this was promptly replaced by a vision of the strange lady with her lips half-open, her eyes gazing into his, and her jewelled ram's head dazzling his vision. Perplexity suffused him. How could he have imagined such detail? He who knew nothing of Icelandic myth? How, having conjured it up in his sleep, could he remember it so precisely next day? Every stitch of golden embroidery round her collar was visible to him, and the metallic blues and greens of her dress made his head swim.

After the entirely white lunch which had been provided – boiled fish, mashed potatoes, and rice pudding – a strong drink at cocktail time seemed a good idea. An official cocktail party had in fact been arranged, with a speech by the mayor in the municipal art gallery, and at five-fifteen the unresisting delegates were taken there by bus. The gallery was an abysmal concrete bunker, and the mayor's speech a formality in unintelligible English; but Donald glimpsed one or two pictures which took the corner of his eye. He was pleased when, conversation having become general, the lady organizer of the book market, a modestly attractive person in her thirties, took him by the arm and offered to show him some of the other rooms. He found himself instinctively comparing her with the lady on the balcony. This one was quiet and shrewd, an organizer and a feminist; that one had cared for nothing but the pleasures of the flesh. This one at least he knew was real. She led him through various galleries, talking of business and teaching him to pronounce her jaw-breaking Icelandic name. It was not until they were almost back in the main concourse that Donald suddenly found himself deprived of breath. There before him, framed in gilt and bathed in a discreet spotlight, was a full-length oil portrait of the lady of his uncomfortably abandoned dream. If it *was* a dream. There in obstinately tangible detail were the blue-green dress, the ram's horn brooch, the gold embroidered headband, the come-hither look in the eyes.

The astonishment on his face was such that an explanation had to be offered. It was that he thought he had possibly seen the painting before. Who was the subject?

His Icelandic friend shrugged, smiled, and pointed to the little title card in two languages. Donald read aloud: 'Frydda, Princess of the Goths'. He managed a smile at last, to mask his confusion. 'I suppose she's a character from the sagas, in which case I could hardly have known her. She must look like someone else.'

His friend chuckled meaningfully. 'Yes, she is from the sagas, from Bjorn's as a matter of fact. She came with the invaders, and is supposed to have had an insatiable sexual appetite. The story was that no man, once she took a fancy to him, could ever escape her, even in death.' Donald uneasily pulled at his collar. 'But in fact, although you couldn't very well have known Frydda, you could easily, if you had been to Reykjavik before, have known the subject of the painting, which was done about seven years ago. You see, she was the wife of the manager of the Hotel Borg.'

'Oh, really? The Borg? The Borg where I'm staying?'

His friend nodded and blushed charmingly as she continued. 'They say that like Frydda she had quite an appetite. It amused her, because of Frydda's reputation, to dress up in that costume. She had the brooch made from an old engraving. The man who painted the picture was her last lover. He used to book into the hotel, into the little turret room at the end of the top storey, and she would come to him in the night when the coast was clear. Unfortunately her judgement was a bit erratic. One night her husband came in, found the lovers in bed together, and shot them both dead.'

The Moving Rocks

He felt eccentric. He felt ecstatic. In a lost corner of America, probably thirty miles from the nearest human being, there lay on his back, on a caked and crazed surface of yellow mud, an Englishman of forty who was fulfilling a sudden urge to demonstrate an affinity with the good earth. From an unbroken azure sky the sun blazed down upon him, but it was an unexpectedly kindly sun, its fierceness tempered by the pure and rarefied air of a desert valley which had not yet been polluted by modern man. His arms stretched out languorously, almost of their own accord. Each fist clenched one of the knobbly pebbles he had picked up from the selection of thousands which surrounded him, strange shiny little black stones like lumps of polished charcoal, scattered randomly over the vast flat surface of the playa. Breathing deeply, and smiling to himself at the sheer absurdity of the scene he must present to any passing bird, Nicholas dozed . . .

Very few people have actually died in Death Valley. Some nearly did, but that was because they failed to treat the geography with that respect which must be due to such a grotesquely desolate place. Even respectful people grew careless sometimes, especially since 1933 when the valley was opened up as a National Monument and the advertised ranger patrols lulled into a false sense of security some wanderers who failed to realize how seldom the green official vehicles strayed from the shiny new blacktops. The place was named by a party of forty-niners who, through ignorance or sheer cussedness, left their slow-moving wagon train on the Nevada side and tried in vain to find their own short cut to the Pacific shores. They could not have guessed from their sketchy maps that the lie of the Sierra Nevada and its sister ranges would be so horrifically against them. Only the slowest progress could they make, up and down endless slopes of soft shale and mud. Finally their wagons were stranded for five weeks on the salty rubble of this particularly deep and inhospitable trench in the planet's crust. Stuck below sea level in hot sand, they found themselves hemmed in before and behind by snow-capped mountains over ten thousand feet high. There was no vegetation to speak of, only brackish water to drink, and the temperature even at night seldom fell in summer below a hundred degrees. Eventually they found a laborious way out, but by then one of their number had perished, so it would not be surprising if, as the legend says, they really did look back, from the head of what came to be known as Townes Pass, and say: 'Goodbye, Death Valley!'

More than a hundred and thirty years later, every fall, admirers still congregate in their thousands round valley campfires to celebrate the hardy spirit of those pioneers, and to enjoy that unique exhilaration of loneliness and grandeur which so many deserts provide. They come in campers and light aircraft, on motor cycles and on horseback, and in thousands of cars from shiny new Cadillacs to battered old Volkswagens. Yet even at its most crowded the valley remains the property of nature and not man, a seemingly endless tract where it is easy to be alone. The visitors swarm principally around the campsites and the two hotel complexes which constitute the only outposts of modern comfort in this bleak but beautiful landscape. Christmastime finds every room filled, and in April the visitors come again in case there has been enough winter rain to tempt out the wild flowers. But at the end of April both hotels close their main facilities because the heat grows too oppressive to be fun for most people. And this was the middle of May.

Nicholas Kentish had always had a vague hankering for deserts. He knew not why: perhaps they were in his blood. After all, although his surname stressed his entirely English paternal origins, he must carry in his genes some influence from that great-great-grandmother whose still-extant childhood photograph showed her to be the daughter of a moustachioed rancher in Elko, Nevada. Elko was a place Nicholas had never managed to visit, for it was well off the main air routes and had no connection with the movie business which provided his bread and butter. But for twelve years now he had been making an annual pilgrimage to Los Angeles, and it did not take him long to discover the comparative proximity of Death Valley, which he remembered principally as the setting for the final combat in Von Stroheim's silent classic *Greed*. (Nicholas was a movie buff as well as a movie buyer, a round peg in a round hole.) He added a long weekend to his second visit to California, and by leaving the hotel before dawn in a hired Mustang he accomplished his solo excursion to the awesomely-named resort, via California City and Red Mountain and Trona, in little more than five hours. His great joy on arrival was to lean back outside his Stovepipe Wells bungalow with his feet up on the hitching rail, watching the sun come up over the grapevines. Just like Henry Fonda in *My Darling Clementine*.

The brittle, rather transitory society of Hollywood and its environs seemed on his next trip more than a little lacking after the natural majesty he had so briefly surveyed. His business friends, who seldom strayed from their swimming pools, were he found still curious about his mysterious weekend, which some suspected he had actually spent in the arms of a blonde in Santa Barbara. Was Death Valley so wonderful a place? Really? In that case, next time he planned to go, perhaps he would take them along. They'd like to go with someone who knew it. He smiled to himself, and said since it was really just up the road, he'd be happy to give them notes so that they could explore for themselves at any time they pleased; but they preferred to wait for him. And so, on almost every succeeding trip he found himself acting the part of desert courier. He came to know the unchanging valley in most of its moods, even including the occasional sandstorm or deluge, and he never found it in the least boring. The interest of some of his friends was undoubtedly superficial, but none of them failed to be ardent in their apparent enthusiasm, and there had been many happy, tiring days. He remembered walking on the Panamint Desert with Jackie and Madeleine and Bill; picnicking in the sand dunes with the Pages and the Lazaruses; concluding a deal with Charlie in the Furnace Creek bar; careering through Bloody Gap with Neville and Irving and George; breakfasting in the Exchange Club at Beatty with Tim and Mark and Ray and the other Bill; enjoying the reaction of Alan and Jeremy to the moonscapes of Zabriskie Point; and doing all these things again with a dozen other people. They all told their friends that if they were ever thinking of going to Death Valley, there was one Englishman from whom they should seek advice.

But now, for the first time in ten years, he was here entirely alone. It hadn't been easy, but he had managed it. He wanted to know some of the sights more intimately than was possible with a crowd, to stay at each just as long as he liked, to have a few new ones entirely to himself. Furthermore, and for the very first time, he had been able to hire a sturdy four-wheel drive, which would make some of the obscurer trails more safely accessible. His exhilaration at the last thought was not untinged with fear, for being most unmechanically minded he would in a sense have preferred the kind of safety which comes with numbers. Best in fact to have one vehicle following another, just in case of accidents. Still, now that he was here, nothing could prevent him from finding the Racetrack. And if that seems an unlikely desert venue, let it be explained that within the National Monument the name has become attached to a remote oval-shaped dry lake surrounded by mountains. On its flat surface Indians may or may not have raced horses, but what was indisputably true, though never observed, was the fact of quite large rocks apparently dragging themselves across the hard mud by supernatural agency. Or perhaps 'unexplained' would be a better adjective for the long straight or zigzag tracks which had baffled scientists for a generation and more. They could scarcely be made while the surface was bone dry and unyielding, which was most of the time; yet when it was slick after rain, where were the tell-tale extra tracks which must have been made by men or animals moving them? The best explanation yet hazarded was wind, wind of hurricane force which might just possibly whip along the valley once in a blue moon and propel even rocks this size along an iced but still muddy surface. It was a tall story, but Death Valley was full of incredible things. And Nicholas would enjoy sizing up the evidence and making his own judgement.

It was evening when he unpacked, at Furnace Creek this time. He retired early, drunk already on desert air but looking forward eagerly to three full days in the valley. He spent the first renewing his acquaintance with familiar sights, with Twenty Mule Team Canyon and Dante's View and the Devil's Golfcourse, finishing with a glorious solitary hike up Golden Canyon to Zabriskie Point, where a surprised and solitary tourist needed little encouragement to drive a mile or two out of his way in order to return Nicholas to his car. For the third day he planned a careful exploration of a ghost town named Rhyolite, now numbering six residents compared with the ten thousand counted in 1907, when an abundant discovery of ore caused the institution of two railway stations, three hotels, two newspapers and a sixty-thousand-dollar bank. Finally there would be a triumphant drive down the twenty-mile length of Titus Canyon, carved in prehistoric times by water out of the mountain rock. But the second day was to be the pièce de resistance. He was at the door of the visitor centre when the ranger opened it just before nine. A visit to the Racetrack involved a fifty-mile drive to the north, followed by a wide lefthand U-turn and then thirty miles back south, more or less, along a narrow parallel valley behind the Cottonwoods. What he needed to know was, could he return by continuing on that trail through vaguely mapped former settlements like Goldbelt and Hidden Valley? If so, he would emerge in fifteen or so miles on the hardtop near Panamint Springs, from which the road to his hotel was quick and easy.

The rather corpulent ranger sucked hard on his teeth. 'Well, I'd say not,' he finally pronounced. 'Not unless you was with *me*. That ain't so much one trail as a jumble of 'em, and even if they're not deep in sand it takes a keen eye to spot the right one. Yep, I'd say they's just about the worst trails in the whole valley.'

'They're marked on my map.'

'That may be, but if you try 'em on your own, as sure as eggs is eggs we'll have to spend the evening coming out to find you. That might be right embarrassing for all concerned, and besides, you'd have a real bad time sitting out there, wondering if we was coming. Mighty spooky out there in the dark, with only the coyotes and burros for company. They come out at night, you see. No, I'd say go out to the Racetrack, even if yours is the only wheels on the road. It's safe enough. But when you're through enjoying yourself, you double back the way you came, by Teakettle Junction. It all looks different on the way home, so you won't be bored. You've checked your water and your spare tyre and your jack?'

'Sure.' Nicholas, disappointed and yet seeing the sense of

the argument, smiled at his own modest lapse into the vernacular.

'And you'll be sure to report here when you get back?'

'Don't worry, I will.'

'Uh-huh.' The ranger was scribbling notes on his pad. 'Okay. So you'll be stopping at Scotty's for gas and water. Drinking water too, don't forget that. I'll give you ninety minutes to get there, and an hour for seeing the sights, and another hour to the Racetrack.'

'That enough? I thought it was a rough road.'

'A little dusty is all. We keep it bulldozed. An hour at the Racetrack, tops, and two hours back. Maybe a little more, but I expect you'll put your foot down. Six-and-a-half hours altogether; say seven for good measure. That gets you back there by four. If you have to change a tyre, say five. We close five-thirty. If you ain't here by then, I guess we come looking for you. But don't let us have to if you can help it.'

'I won't. And thanks. I feel reassured.'

'That's what we're here for. If you're running late, there's a phone at Ubehebe, and here's what you dial.' He handed over a card. 'I'll just take the number of your vehicle.'

It was a long time since Nicholas had been so fussed over, and he was enjoying it. He shook hands with the ranger, then turned for one last question.

'What about the moving rocks?'

'What about 'em?'

'Have you seen them? Do they really move?'

The ranger sighed. 'Oh, I've seen 'em, and yes they do, but what makes 'em move I *couldn't* say. Used to think it might be tourists playing tricks, but if it is, they sure found a crafty way of doing it.'

Nicholas made good time: the roads were empty. On the drive north he averaged sixty and saw only four other vehicles. Scotty's Castle, the eccentric Utopia of a reclusive millionaire and his prospector friend, is an ugly Spanish-style mansion located several miles up a canyon and quite a height above the valley floor, of which it commands only a partial and oblique view. Unimpressed, Nicholas avoided the house tour, bought a packed lunch and some bottled water, checked his gas and oil, and spent twenty minutes stretched out on a wall in full reach of the dry and invigorating sun. After this respite he consumed an ice cream, then thoroughly enjoyed the fast seven-mile drive to the Ubehebe volcano, a breathtakingly deep black crater nearly a mile wide, with a flash of orange at the bottom of the cup. On a previous visit he had not cared for the cinder dust blown about by the wind, but today the air was still and he made a grim survey for miles in every direction of the harsh undulating ground, black with lava debris. From the eastern rim of the volcano he looked down at last with a sigh on the single-armed signpost which pointed away from the blacktop into a depressingly featureless valley; below it was a red-edged board warning that the trip to the Racetrack and back involved fifty-seven miles of rough riding. The sun was passing behind a cloud, and Nicholas shivered slightly. If Indians made a living in this desolate terrain, they must have been pretty hardy people. Mysterious folk, Indians; they gave nothing away. Nicholas had never been able to feel sympathy for them, always rooting in movies for the cowboys to win. There was a family story, not documented, that his great-grandfather, the son of the lady in the picture, had treated his Indians badly and driven them one winter off his property. Many of them had died, and it was said that the rancher had been reprimanded in the local courts; but he had not been sentenced, and Nicholas was glad. If he ever got to Elko he would try to look up the true facts in the newspaper files, if they existed still after a hundred years. But the main reason, he knew, why he would probably never go to Elko was that he might not like what he read. Still, what were a few Indians?

The unmetalled road which unrolled before him was much smoother than he expected, and he had time to daydream as he passed hundreds of flowering cacti, followed by a patch thick with joshua trees. He dreamed on the whole, rather dismayingly, of menacing things, of lynchings and of animal traps and of dying men crawling across the desert floor in search of water. At one point he fancied he saw a long line of Indians, classically silhouetted along the crest of a low hill, but they were only tree stumps. He could not imagine what was depressing his imagination on an occasion when it should have been most excited. After some miles the valley widened and he felt better; perhaps he had been attacked by a form of claustrophobia. Now the soft ashy mountains gave way to more solid and stratified forms which at certain salient points had weathered into a kind of menagerie: Nicholas clearly made out an owl, an elephant, a ram's head and a crouching lion, all shadow-shaped by the noonday sun. The road ran for a while along a central ridge, which stopped suddenly at the point called Teakettle Junction, where indistinct trails ran off to the left and a weatherbeaten signpost was festooned with ancient pieces of camping equipment. Here the main track dropped suddenly, and Nicholas could see that some ten miles ahead, away and below, range after range of close-packed hills closed it off at the far end. In the enormous natural cup thus formed lay the splendour of the Racetrack, its flat yellow mud playa instantly captivating the eye, and seeming perhaps even brighter than it was because of the contrast with the dark surrounding hills. The ordinary tourist guide books offered little explanation of this geographical phenomenon; but Nicholas had a superior one which described the mud as an agglomeration of vast quantities of dust and shale which at some prehistoric time were blown off the mountains, stripping them bare, and settled a thousand feet deep in what was once a melodramatically steep valley. Towards the end nearest to Nicholas, black fingers of pointed rock broke through the yellow surface in a formation popularly known as the Grandstand. They were the tips of a short irregular mountain range which originally sat in the now subterranean valley. Nicholas parked and gazed. It was a simple enough scene in primary colours, but he had seen nothing like it before, and in the bright sunlight it seemed both beautiful and sinister, like a detail from a surrealist work by Salvador Dali. In its way it was quite perfect, an overwhelming testament to the majesty of God. But God was not always merciful: he had forgotten to provide water.

The road ran down by the western side of the dry lake. Nicholas took it slowly, enjoying every moment. He stopped when he first drew level with the playa, and again opposite the Grandstand. On the way back he would walk over to it and take photographs; a pity there would be no human figure for reference. Well, he could certainly manage without company: for the next hour, this place was to be his alone. But as he started up the engine again, he saw that it wasn't. From the south end, one small vehicle was making its way towards him and raising one hell of a lot of dust. Well, with luck it would pass and be gone. But how was it to pass? Bulldozers had clearly been along quite recently to increase the depth of the roadside ditch intended to prevent visitors from driving on to the playa. In the process, part of the road had disappeared, and it was now barely single track. There must be a passing place; and indeed, halfway along Nicholas found a small lay-by which even included an information board from which all information had been torn away. Nicholas shrugged and waited. The approaching vehicle turned out to be an extremely dusty and battered old pick-up, which as it came nearer made a worrying clatter; Nicholas would have been horrified at the thought of straying so far from the hardtop in so inadequate a vehicle. The sole occupant clearly had no such qualms. As he drew level he gave a cheery grin and turned off his ignition. The old truck hiccuped into silence, and Nicholas had to smile to himself as he waved back. Being film-oriented, he had sometimes described 'a Walter Brennan type' in the hope of quickly conveying his meaning. Brennan was a character actor who, whenever he felt the need of another Academy Award to add to his collection, took his teeth out, grew a three-day stubble, and assumed the appearance of a western hayseed. This old fellow was Brennan to the life, and certainly to the teeth, or lack of them. He even had an unlit cob pipe in the corner of his mouth, and his first word was 'Howdy'. It was a scene from a movie.

'First time here?' asked the old man.

'It is indeed, and I'm overwhelmed. It's all so magnificent.'

'Dunno about that. Hell of a place in the winter when the wind gets up, they say. Not that I know anybody who's been here in the winter. Not since the time of the Indians.'

'The Indians who were supposed to race horses?'

'Maybe. No, maybe not. Them Indians must have been later. I was thinking of the Indians who lived here, in the village. If you call it living. Pretty hard land to live off. Guess they didn't know no better. They was just a little lost tribe, you see, driven down from the north. Somewhere in Nevada.'

Nicholas shivered. 'And where was the village?'

The old man jerked a finger behind him. 'You're practically standing on it. Well, maybe a mile back, towards the south end. This yellow stuff, you see, that's all fill.'

'I know, it blew off the mountain.'

'Yep, but when the Indians came the valley was quite a bit deeper. They'd no way of knowing it was all filling in, slowly but surely. Then one night, maybe a hundred and some odd years ago, there was a kind of earthquake, 'bout the same time old Ubehebe last popped. Maybe it was more of a landslide: I only know what my grandpappy used to tell me. Anyway, one night this whole mountain just fell into the valley and crumbled to nothing, right on top of them Indians. This used to be quite a regular road then, from Big Pine to Skidoo, but it wasn't till more'n a week later that folks found out what had happened. They say there was still weeping and wailing coming from under the grit, but they never did find no corpses to bury. And nobody ever lived in this valley after that. They said it was cursed.'

Nicholas felt saddened: his exhilaration was gone again. 'Who was your granddaddy, who told you all this?'

The old man had remembered his pipe, and lit it noisily. 'If you go down the West Side Road, south of Furnace Creek, you'll find his grave. Shorty Harris, a single blanket jackass prospector, that's what it says. He roamed these valleys all his life. Knew the Indians too, what was left of 'em. All gone to Vegas now. None even in Shoshone, and that was named after 'em. Just some dead ones under this mud. Buried alive, most of 'em. The thing Indians fear most.'

'Not only the Indians.' Seeking an end to the conversation, Nicholas made to turn on the ignition, then remembered his last question. 'I came to see the moving rocks. Where are they?'

'You're heading for 'em. All down the south end, over where the main settlement was. You'll find plenty.'

'And what does make them move?'

The old man shrugged. 'You tell me. Old Shorty, he used to say it was them dead Indians still trying to talk, cut off in their prime and hopping mad about it, not ready yet to go to the happy hunting grounds. He used to sit here sometimes, on one of them rocks, and talk back.'

'A kind of poltergeist activity.' Nicholas knew when he said it that he was talking to himself.

'I dunno what that is, but I do know nobody believed old Shorty, and that made him as mad as the Indians. Took to drinking after that; then nobody believed him at all.'

'Not even you?'

'Well, I was too young to count. I can see him now, though, the first time he brought me here. Kind of scared me, it did. Nothing happened while I was watching, but he told me about a time when he was standing out there and all the rocks started inching towards him from every which way. He was so frightened he cut and run . . . but after that, he said, he got to find some sort of comfort up here in this lonely place. You can understand that, maybe. Solitary man, trekking up and down these valleys looking for gold that wasn't there. Nice to think somebody's there to talk to, under the earth, even if they don't always answer back.'

'And you never saw anything?'

'Depends what you mean. I see what everybody else can see, like tracks with no rocks, and tracks that start out in the middle of the lake. How'd a big rock get out there in the first place?'

'Wind?'

'Wind my ass. Shorty said he once saw a couple of rocks the size of a man's head flying through the air, and one of them turned straight at him and whistled past his ear. That day there weren't no wind at all.'

Nicholas finally turned on the ignition. 'Sounds as though the spirits were unfriendly after all.'

The old man followed suit. 'Temperamental like other folks, I guess. Well, I'm off to my little store at Lathrop Wells. My rocks are the kind you cut open and polish and sell. Call in next time you're through.'

Nicholas watched the truck labour up the hill, dwindling quickly to the size of a pinhead. Finally its exhaust disappeared over the brow at Teakettle Junction, and he was alone. Suddenly he found himself shivering again, despite the heat around him: the reason was that he had allowed the shadow from the western mountains to creep around until he was sitting in a long arm of it. He addressed himself to the empty valley ahead, and cruised down the trail until the lake began to round off and bright yellow gave way to dull green. Here the trail deteriorated badly, and a turning point had been bulldozed into the soft earth. As Nicholas clambered out and looked back along the immense valley, there was not a whisper of wind. The four-mile stretch of caked yellow mud half-blinded him with its brilliance, and the Grandstand poked out from it like the fingers of a giant hand. Should he walk up to it from here? He would like to, but there and back was probably a six-mile jaunt and he might dry out: there was only a quart of water left in his bottle. No, the Grandstand would be a stop on the way back, prefaced by a short circular tour of the south end.

Taking a swig of water from his container, Nicholas leaped blithely across the ditch on to the playa, showing an agility he had not suspected in himself. It must be the air, the glorious clean, warm, dry air, as refreshing and invigorating as a sauna bath. He felt ten feet tall and ready for anything. The valley was a wonderful discovery: next year he would bring his friends here as a special treat. The women probably wouldn't like it, for it wasn't exactly pretty, more stark and awe-inspiring, with grey hills showing only a few patches of acid green where desert moss or tumbleweed had found a hold. In the occasional outcrops he could still find the faces of animals: here a gorilla, there an ostrich. But no Indians. He took a deep breath and began to skip along the even surface, something he had probably not done for twenty years. The hard mud, split and cracked a million times into miniature crazy paving, was as springy as a ballroom floor, bouncing him into the air. He tried his voice against the opposite mountain, raising a splendid echo. Briefly he pirouetted around on his toes like a ballet dancer. He did a few deep breathing exercises to limber himself up. The unaccountable sadness was gone: he couldn't remember when he felt so well. And now for the moving rocks.

At first he had not noticed them; he even forgot momentarily that he was looking for them. But here they were all right, perhaps not quite so big nor so many as he expected, but undeniably present, scattered randomly across the broad yellow surface. Hundreds of them he saw, mostly too small to leave any track; but at least a score of those which had were too big, it seemed to him, to have been moved by the power of a single unaided human being. Yet moved they had been, for there behind them, an inch or so deep in the hard mud, were tracks four and five hundred feet long, some straight, some angular and some tortuously circular. At one point half a dozen of them came close enough together on the sun-hardened surface to look like some form of maze. Yet there was not a single foot or tyre print: quite clearly the boulders had moved without either human or mechanical assistance. It was a splendid mystery, and a continuing one, for some of the tracks had faded while others looked quite fresh. A little breathless, and obeying an irresistible impulse to be as close as he could get to this mystical ground, Nicholas lay down on his back and stretched out his hands, laying them palms down on the warm surface. This was his domain. Like the first astronauts on the moon, he claimed it. But for whom? For Great Britain seemed absurd. Why not for himself? Sleepily he said aloud: 'I claim this land for Nicholas Kentish . . .' An unexpected breeze seemed to whisper in reply. He stretched, and each hand came into contact with a small knobbly pebble which felt cool to the touch. He clenched one in each fist and closed his eyes blissfully. He slept.

Nicholas woke up uncomfortably. Even before opening his eyes he knew that he should have felt delightfully rested, and that he did not. He felt like Gulliver stranded on the beach of Lilliput, tied down by a thousand miniature ropes. Like Dorian Gray he was suddenly an old and disgusting organism, his youth and vigour long vanished. There was arthritic cramp in his legs, and the sun hurt his eyes. He scrambled to his feet with difficulty. His hands hurt: it was those damned pebbles he had picked up: they were burning his palms. Now that was really silly. He groaned and covered his eyes. He must have lain there too long and got a bad touch of the sun. It was certainly much cooler. How long had he been there? He glanced at his watch. Two hours? It seemed impossible, yet when he double-checked, the hands still said three-fifteen. He would have to hurry if the rangers were not to waste their time sending out a search party: he might just make it back in time. He'd certainly had the best of the sun: his face might be dried and stretched by its rays, but the sky had now clouded over, and the previously admired beauty of the valley was far less striking. If he had come to it now it would have seemed a chill and unlovable place, not worth the trip since the colour contrast between the hills and the playa was far less marked. Everything seemed to have blended into a uniform greyness, yet there were no definable mist banks or patches. It was just one great grey mist, and he was part of it. He shook his head and arms in an attempt to limber up, but all his limbs were useless, like jelly: it was as though his energy and strength had been drained away into the ground. He needed water, and that was in the car, which seemed to be the best part of a mile away. He'd have a job to make it. Idiot. It really was foolish to venture into deserts on one's own.

As he took his first step towards the car he remembered the dream. As is so often the case with dreams, from possessing his whole being it had dwindled on waking to a fancy instantly forgotten. But it hadn't been a pleasant dream, that he knew, and now as the details came flooding back he shuddered in the clammy heat. It had begun with the fact of his lying there on his back, and then becoming conscious of a slow, deeply rumbling earth tremor which had caused him, in his dream, to sit up and look about him, only to find the flat yellow desert surface sluggishly coming to the boil, like porridge. The heat from this activity was oddly enough only a little greater than had been the case in reality: it was like sitting in a warm bath. He looked up at the mountains and realized that they were shimmering and crumbling too, dissolving away with the awful inevitability of a film disaster shown in slow motion. Great boulders rolled down the heaving masses on to the playa, but this mattered scarcely at all to Nicholas, who was sinking inch by inch into the soft yellow mud and lethargically accepting the process, almost enjoying it as dreamers will. Enjoying it, that is, until he sensed that he was not so much sinking as being pulled; pulled by unseen hands reaching out of the mud and grasping him by the knee, the thigh, the waist. Meanwhile from every side he heard voices, voices murmuring in a foreign tongue. Soon only his head and hands were visible, his hands grasping at nothing; panic would have set in had he not been too busy when his head went under in preventing himself from choking on yellow dust. He did not choke. He found himself in some indefinable subterranean place, a place full of inscrutable dark-skinned people who ranged themselves around him, silently accusing. Trapped, he looked from one to another of them, but he found no mercy in their gaze. At length, the one most directly facing him gave a nod to someone over Nicholas' shoulder. Nicholas spun around to see approaching him a massive Indian whom he knew, with that instant recognition common to all dreams, to be his executioner . . .

Nicholas shuddered. That was all. The dream was over: he had woken up. He patted the buttoned pockets of his safari jacket to ensure that his wallet and papers were still in place, and realized as he did so that he was still holding the small stones, and that they were not merely warm but hot to his palms. He dropped them with an involuntary movement of revulsion, and noticed that they sank instantly into the pale earth, leaving not a trace of their passage. How could that be? His eyes told him that the mud was caked and hard. Was he still dreaming? Surely not, but he was tired and feeble: he needed to rest. Just a few steps away was a boulder big enough to sit on. Like the others, it had left a track, but this track was nothing like straight, more of a giant doodle. Furthermore, as Nicholas now realized in slow horror, not only was the curving track clearly fresh, but the rock was still moving, ploughing its way through the mud like a weary hippopotamus. He leaped back from it with a cry. If he was dreaming again, this dream was not to be shaken off. All around him, he realized with horror, the rocks were moving again, moving in irregular curves and zigzags. Then, even as he watched it, he saw one rise from the playa surface and hurtle through the air, missing him by a yard and landing with a dull thud on the surface behind him. Three hundred pounds of solid rock, flying through the air? It was not to be borne. Yet between him and his car there was now a virtual cloud of small rocks, hovering and buzzing like a cloud of midges, deliberately arranging themselves, it seemed, so that he couldn't get through. He had no possible protection against them, or against the other larger masses which now rose menacingly from the mud as though held in invisible giant hands. All he could do was run in the opposite direction, into the open centre of the Racetrack, as far as he could get from the rocks and from the mountains which had produced them. But he had not the energy to get up speed. Stumbling along in helpless fear and terror, he totally failed despite backward glances to observe one large boulder which rose from the ground as he passed it and seemed to watch his progress as though taking aim. Then it came through the air after him like a Spitfire after a

Messerschmidt, and as he glanced over his shoulder in abject fear and exhaustion, it caught up with him.

They found him there before the sun was gone. They found him spreadeagled on the yellow mud floor. He was quite cold.

'It's a mystery,' said the chief ranger. 'If he fell and hit his head on a rock, where's the damned rock? Nearest one is a hundred feet away. Besides, look at his toe prints on the surface. He was running, running for his life.'

'But from what?'

The ranger sighed as he gazed around the now sinister valley. 'I don't suppose we'll ever know, any more than we'll find out what caused them burns on his hands. Aint nobody else's prints here, but ours, that's for sure.' He gazed at the pilot, whose only answer was a slight shiver. 'Come on, let's get him into the chopper.'

Within minutes the flying machine had disappeared into the gathering dusk. The silent rocks did not move again, but as the day's heat gave way to evening chill a few of them cracked, and a passer-by might even have taken the sound for conversation.

Demon

Warburton had been observing me narrowly since the port came round, clearly deciding whether or not I would make a worthy recipient for the problem he wished to unload. Now he said abruptly: 'Have you ever heard of people being killed by having pins stuck into their wax images?'

It was a bit of a lurch from our previous topic, and it made me sit up and take notice. I never knew Warburton very well, and hadn't seen him for thirty years when he turned up unexpectedly at an old boys' dinner. After an adventurous youth, it seemed he had spent years on a Northumberland police force, then made something of a mark at Scotland Yard before settling into his own business in the West Country. He claimed to have been mayor of Barnstaple at the age of forty, and nobody disputed this. I don't think anybody cared. He rather latched on to me at the dinner because I was the only exact contemporary he could find. I didn't mind that, but I thought he did rather too much jovial heckling during my toast to the school, which is after all a rather serious moment. Nor did he stand to attention during the rendering of 'Forty Years On'. I remembered not caring much for Warburton as a member of my form. A bit of a bully he was, used to paralyse people temporarily by kneeing them hard in the side of the thigh, and roar with laughter as they hobbled away. However, time wounds all heels (as Groucho Marx once said) and I saw no reason now to resist Warburton's social advances. In fact, when he subsequently invited me to dinner at his exclusive club in Jermyn Street I accepted with pleasure, as it seemed likely to make an agreeable adventure of the mind, sitting over a balloon or two of old brandy and trying to relocate with a man who'd been absent from one's life for all that time, gauging how our experiences of life had moulded us in different ways. In fact both the meal and the reminiscences were disappointing, for although Warburton could tell tallish tales of Tierra del Fuego and Siberia and the Colorado river, the years past forty had merely turned him into a reactionary and given him a sizeable paunch. All his interest now flowed from the importance of his present post as Chief Constable of Berkshire, one which had until his sudden question seemed unlikely to spin off an array of irresistible stories.

In answer to his enquiry, I asked lightly: 'Wax images? Is that the latest crime wave your forces are putting down?'

'Oh, hardly. But I expect you've heard of the practice?'

'Only among the lunatic fringe. I believe it used to be quite fashionable for African witch doctors.'

'Not exclusively. I've seen a lot of odd things in my time. I've personally come into contact with more than a few white-skinned witches, and I've no doubt at all that such things work sometimes, though in most cases by suggestion on a terrified victim rather than by any occult means. I mean, if you know somebody's doing it to you, and they even tell you the time in advance, that could put you into a highly nervous state, and you might even die right on cue of a heart attack.'

'I concede that possibility. But I take it you were about to develop the theme.'

'Yes, by asking whether you think it might work even better if you used human flesh instead of wax.'

'You mean . . . no, I don't know *what* you mean.'

'Then let me explain over another glass of Hine Antique. Yes, I insist. You see, this story came my way officially, yet so far as I can see there's no official explanation possible. I mean, the victim had no idea it was going to happen. Couldn't have had.'

'It was a murder case?'

'No, it never got to that, not that anybody could prove. At the beginning it was just GBH – grievous bodily harm. In our neck of the woods it caused a mild sensation, but I don't suppose you, being a Londoner, ever heard of it at all. It came up in court nearly a year ago. I should tell you by way of preface that I found myself some while back on the board of a private psychiatric hospital out our way. It was called Ravenstone. Still is. I have nothing at all to do with the running of the place: just a case of rubber stamping the super's decisions every quarter. But of course I tried to take a general interest, and that way a lot of rumours came to my ears. Attached to the main clinic was a nurses' home for male and female students. These young people were on a three-year course, and after their training some stayed on, while the rest found themselves pretty well qualified for jobs elsewhere. Most of what they did as students was practice rather than theory, working on the wards under supervision. So Ravenstone in effect got free nurses in return for a modest amount of tuition by a few permanent senior people.

'Well, some of the rumours, as you might expect, concerned the extra-curricular behaviour of these students, who were a very mixed bunch, many of them hailing from what in better days we used to call the colonies. Multi-racial, in other words, and none the worse for that so far as nursing goes; but I'm old-fashioned enough to be against sexual misalliances for all sorts of reasons. The group I'm talking about, eighteen of them, all came in together with an exception which I'll mention later. All through their first year nothing untoward happened, except . . . wait a minute, you didn't get that brandy.'

I stirred languorously in my leather armchair. I had

nothing to do for the rest of the evening but listen to a good story, and this was the one that Warburton told me.

Rupert Griffin was a handsome young man by any black standard. No doubt most Caucasians would have found his features strangely elongated, the lips too full, the back of the skull too protruberant; but he was catnip to women of all colours, and he knew it. He was also, to begin with, an extremely efficient nurse and an assiduous student. The patients adored him because of his native confidence, his gentle hands, and his ready smile: whatever he did for them they felt instinctively was the right thing. Sadly, although Rupert was a very good natural actor, this self-confidence did not extend to himself. He was born in Africa, and his own parents never spoke English. They were killed in his infancy during an uprising, and he was brought up by missionaries who were later able to arrange for him a modest education, and a home with foster parents, in England. He repaid his white benefactors with constant demonstrations of affection, but nothing they did for him could entirely eradicate his African origins. These showed up in a constant desire to spend his spare time with his own kind and to study his ancestral beliefs; in a love of strenuous dancing and sport (he excelled at most forms of physical activity, including ju jitsu); in a violent temper; in a tendency to superstition; and in a fear and awe of death which had to be judged morbid in one so young. All these things were brought out in cross-examination at the trial: the prosecuting counsel said he was so obsessed by Africa, and so guilty at having left it, that it was a pity he didn't go back there before the trouble started. It was also said, by those who didn't like him, that when he looked at you with his unblinking saucer-like eyes, it was as though the devil were penetrating your soul and taking possession of it. Warburton, who saw him only a couple of times before he stood in the dock, considered him as one of those people born to cause trouble, though not necessarily by their own wish. He was a natural catalyst, a demonic force best avoided by those seeking peace of mind.

The inclination of most of the female student nurses was different. By all accounts they threw themselves at him with no sense of danger to come. Leaders among these would-be sacrificial victims were three white girls, which no hospital observer seemed to think amiss: how modern we are, said Warburton. Nor was any criticism heard of the hospital authorities for turning a blind eye to the known fact that a student in this mixed block seldom spent every night of the week in his own bed. There seems to have been no thought that such goings-on might be bad for discipline. Anyway, things worked themselves out to a point: within a month or so, two of Rupert's three followers were nursing their wounded pride, and the third had virtually moved in with him, though in that crowded cubicle how they found room to make tea, let alone love, was beyond Warburton's comprehension.

The chosen young lady was Sylvia Benson. She came of a good family, the jerseys and pearls set, with a couple of honourables in one branch, and the whiteness of her skin contrasted most strikingly with the complexion of her intended, who was as black as the proverbial ace of spades. They were inseparable in public as well as in private, and their unanimity of opinion on any given subject became very boring. In some desperate last-minute attempt to back-pedal, urged no doubt by Sylvia's family, the hospital administrator tried to break them up by staggering their shifts, but this obvious device only made them more ardent. Then Sylvia's father abandoned pretence, came down to see her, and raised merry hell. He withdrew Sylvia from the hospital – just blew in one day in his white Mercedes and took her away virtually by force: it turned out that she wasn't quite eighteen. Even so, it did seem dangerously high-handed in this day and age. Heaven knows what Rupert might have done to the colonel, but matters were taken out of his hands, for two days after her enforced return home Sylvia swallowed an overdose of her mother's tranquillizers and lay for a fortnight at death's door.

She recovered, and the family was scared enough to allow her to come back to Ravenstone, but for a time at least she was a changed girl. It came out later that she'd been expecting Rupert's child – how careless these sophisticated young people can be! – but as a result of the suicide attempt she had lost it. Her return to Ravenstone was something of a puzzler because she had written to Rupert beforehand to tell him that her feelings had changed, that all was now over between them. Rupert seems to have taken this decision reasonably well, perhaps because at the time he was developing an interest, along with another male nurse called Frank Best, in one of these new so-called religions called Matasi, which was supposed to bring peace to the soul but which turned out to be little more than a form of voodoo with pretensions. Best, a half caste, was later found to have in his room a cupboard converted into a kind of altar, stocked with all kinds of obscene rubbish: Warburton remembered being shown an object consisting of a bird's body carved in wood, with the head and claws from a real cockerel. God knows what they got up to: Warburton thought it better not to enquire, and the prosecution found it largely irrelevant. Concurrent with this new interest Rupert acquired yet another girl friend, a black nurse called Dorothy Shay. Perhaps she was too willing, for he seems to have used her with some scorn, and she doesn't figure much in the story except that her presence stirred up some jealous feelings in Sylvia, whose feelings changed yet again. Pretty soon Rupert seems to have been bedding both of them pretty regularly, clearly imagining that neither cared about the other.

How they managed to work amid all this tension, Warburton couldn't guess, but they did, for there was nothing in their monthly reports to show dissatisfaction, and it took another year, almost, for things to come to a head. Gradually Dorothy faded obligingly out of the contest, and it was generally accepted that the Rupert–Sylvia thing was very much on again as a permanency. Only this time things didn't run smoothly. Various witnesses could testify to undignified arguments between them, sometimes culminating in minor violence. At one point it became Rupert's turn to stage a suicide: he threatened to cut his own throat, and actually stood up there and then and hacked at it with a penknife, but the wound was only superficial. He had a strong sense of melodrama. The incident brought Sylvia to heel for a while, but before long her father came back into the picture, because Rupert started writing him impertinent letters accusing him of turning his daughter's mind away from Rupert, whereas in fact the colonel would have been down at Ravenstone a long time before if he'd had the slightest inkling of what was going on: he'd accepted Sylvia's word after her suicide attempt that she and Rupert were through. Well, the super had to carpet Rupert about the letters, which were full of threats and mumbo-jumbo. The boy lost his temper and put some sort of silly curse on Sylvia's father there and then. That was his undoing: the super realized a little belatedly that Rupert might not be stable enough to make a reliable psychiatric nurse, and the boy's course was abruptly terminated. He left the hospital without a reference, and moved into a flat in Battersea.

Earning almost nothing for the next few months, he seems to have got into all kinds of money trouble, though he managed to escape the attention of the police. He did have a car for a while, but soon lost it through non-payment of instalments. But he always found the railway fare out to the hospital at weekends, partly to carry on his Matasi rituals with Frank Best, and partly to go for long walks with Sylvia, inevitably finishing up in her room for the night. Supervision was clearly non-existent, and he was very lucky that nobody ratted on him to the authorities. The other girls sometimes kept cave, in fact: they were a misguidedly romantic lot. The discarded Dorothy Shay even did his hair once a month, regarding herself as his best platonic friend even though she'd been out of the running for a long time. Oddly enough Sylvia, according to her own later testimony, was now trying to steer Rupert back towards Dorothy. She herself had finally come to see him as an overwhelming but hopefully temporary passion; she was getting her bearings again, probably preparing instinctively to shed her youthful follies and take her place in the society in which she'd been brought up. He on the other hand had by now selected her as his bride in Matasi; you'll pardon me if I don't go into detail, because Warburton hadn't boned up on that side of things except to know that the ceremony involved an animal sacrifice.

On the near-fatal Saturday Rupert turned up in the afternoon as usual and found Sylvia trying to make excuses, saying she hadn't expected him that week and had a dinner date at eight with some girl friends. Before long, over a cup of tea in her room, Dorothy rather spitefully told Rupert what was really going on; Sylvia, who apparently never had a steady boy friend before Rupert, had now unexpectedly picked up with a young doctor who divided his time between Ravenstone and another local hospital, and her dinner date that evening was with him. At five-thirty or so Rupert, risking expulsion, sat down in the staff canteen next to Sylvia, his eyes blazing like a demon in fury. She promptly walked out but a scene was unavoidable. He caught up with her in the corridor outside her room, where most of her friends could hear their angry discussion. She said she wanted them to stay friends, but the grand amour

was over and he'd better get used to the fact. He said that
she couldn't think of such a thing, as their union had long
since been ordained by Matasi, and to break it would go
against nature and cause their mutual destruction – by
supernatural violence. She told him not to be an idiot. He
slapped her face hard and stormed off, just as two orderlies
turned up, having been sent by the super to eject him from
the premises. He eluded them nimbly enough and hid in
Dorothy's room, which was on a different floor. Here,
trembling from head to foot, he asked for stationery, and
wrote two letters. One he addressed to Frank Best, the other,
oddly, to Dorothy herself. Sealing them both, he asked her
to deliver Best's not before half past seven, and to open hers
at the same time. He then said he was going to Best's room
for a Matasi service, kissed Dorothy on the forehead, and
left. She testified that he seemed quite composed: it wasn't
until an hour later, just before seven, that she noticed the
absence of a sharp-pointed kitchen knife which she always
kept on the sink.

Dorothy was perhaps not too bright, but she sat on the
bed and pondered about the significance of the knife and the
letters, until at about seven-fifteen she determined to open
the envelope addressed to herself. The contents alarmed her
without being explicit, and she immediately ran over to
consult with Best, who said that Rupert had left him five
minutes earlier. Dorothy told him about the row with
Sylvia, and urged him to open his letter, which he did. It
was in the so-called Matasi language and translated roughly
as follows:

My teacher, I leave my soul in your hands. The wheel of
death turns, and brings life in Matasi. My love and I will
lie together in purgatory, and all will be for good.

Well, young Best was sensible enough to decide that all was

decidedly not for good, and at the hearing later he said how he regretted ever having got mixed up with Matasi, which he described as one of those post-adolescent delusions. He wanted to dash off there and then to save whatever dreadful situation was developing, but as a result of a recently broken ankle he had to wear a leg brace which took a minute or two to fit, so he sent Dorothy off ahead to warn Sylvia, which was an odd situation since the two girls, not unnaturally, hadn't been on speaking terms for months. Sylvia's room was on the second floor of the hostel. The breathless Dorothy got to the top of the stairs and skidded to a halt to find Sylvia walking along the corridor, clearly wondering what the devil Dorothy was doing there. Dorothy turned away embarrassed, but glad to see that Sylvia was alone and in good order; Sylvia ignored her and walked into her own room. What neither of them knew was that Rupert was inside waiting for her.

What happened next took only a matter of seconds. Sylvia told Rupert to get out, adding that there was a bitch up the corridor waiting for him, something she clearly thought was true. Rupert said he'd never loved anyone but her, and didn't intend them to be separated. Sylvia said he'd have to put up with it. Without further ado he stabbed her, several times, with Dorothy's knife. Naturally she screamed, and half a dozen people came running in, with Dorothy at the head of the queue and the limping Frank at the tail. They were just in time to watch the half-demented Rupert have another shot at cutting his own throat. Actually both sets of wounds were fairly half-hearted, but there was plenty of blood, especially along the corridor when Rupert ran out yelling suicidal curses. He was stopped in the grounds, and both he and Sylvia were taken to hospital, where the police interviewed them. Sylvia didn't want to press charges, which shows either stupidity or a remarkably generous nature. Of course she had no option, as whether they called it grievous bodily harm or wounding with intent there was a stiff penalty involved. Rupert claimed temporary amnesia, so there had to be a trial, but by the time the defence had failed to make the slightest dent in the testimony of the prosecution witnesses, who included Dorothy and Frank as well as Sylvia, it was agreed to cut short the general waste of public time and money by persuading Rupert to plead guilty to a lesser indictment, that of unlawful wounding. He got three years for that.

'Agatha Christie,' I said, 'would doubtless have found all this an interesting basis for a murder mystery, with Sylvia, who couldn't possibly have done it, revealed on the last page as the scheming villainess; but haven't we strayed rather far from your introduction?'

'What introduction? Oh, the wax images. I was coming to that. You see, when sentence was pronounced Rupert, who'd been very calm throughout the case and even exchanged smiles with some of his former friends in the witness stand, erupted again, and screamed at the judge that the trial was against the laws of Matasi and that if he couldn't have Sylvia then nobody else would, that their souls were already joined and that in Matasi they were one person. He was lucky not to have another six months added on; instead the judge made a firm order for psychiatric treatment. From prison Rupert sent Sylvia a stream of threatening letters which were all returned, mostly unopened, by her father; they all finished with declarations of his undying love, his sorrow that both of them must shortly die, and his conviction that they would meet again in another life. The letters and envelopes were all decorated with Matasi slogans. Part of his treatment, meanwhile, was occupational therapy which included the making of plaster cast statuettes, but he was taken off that when the guards found him repeatedly stabbing at the wax moulds. During the next month or two his guards noticed him passing the time in his cell doing some form of ritual exercise which he said was yoga. There was nothing in the rules against that, so they didn't interfere, especially as they couldn't understand what he was muttering to himself. What they failed to spot was that one day he managed to abstract a fairly sharp knife from the leather workshop, and that evening at ten o'clock there came from his cell a stream of maniacal chanting in a language the guards couldn't understand, followed by a sharp agonized cry. By the time the door was opened, he was dying, stabbed through the heart.'

'And?' I said expectantly, recognizing a cliffhanger when I heard one.

'And: in the very same moment, forty miles away at a dance, Sylvia Benson dropped dead of an apparent heart attack. The coroner's post mortem could find no good reason at all for such a shocking thing to happen. Apart from the stab scars, which had almost healed, she'd always been a perfectly healthy girl.'

The House on the Cliff

Percival Gotobed had no aversion to women. Nor were they essential to his happiness. In his distant youth he had enjoyed several reasonably passionate affairs, though he found in every case that boredom crept in after a few short weeks of ardour, and he was always glad when they ended. Now in latish middle age he was enjoying a prolonged Victorian-style bachelorhood, with vintage port, small but expensive cigars, quilted smoking jackets and twinges of arthritis. His extremely well furnished rooms topped a solid Edwardian block in the Cromwell Road, on the more fashionable side of Hammersmith. Here he invited his many friends to dine, and at their premises he was invited to dine in his turn. They all talked a great deal. Professionally he had been for many years, and by choice, librarian of one of the most exclusive London clubs. He loved books with a passion which was not mitigated as the years went by, nor in this field of activity did even a suspicion of boredom creep in. He found however that the remuneration available to librarians was insufficient for maintaining himself in the style to which he dearly wished to become accustomed. For the last few years he had therefore sought means of augmenting his income. Half a dozen articles on light literary topics, submitted to magazines ranging from *Country Life* to *Men Only*, made him known to the half-dozen editors who matter. His somewhat roguish biography of Jerome K. Jerome was surprisingly well received: surprisingly to him, that is, for in truth he underestimated his ability to write in a pleasingly urbane style which readers of all heights of brow could understand and enjoy. Percival had happily struck a light literary vein which he could go on mining until the end of his days.

This pleasing situation developed beyond all expectation on the eve of his fifty-fifth birthday. Percival was asked one day at a cocktail party whether he would consent to appear on a bookish television programme in order to expand his views, recently published in the *Sunday Times* colour supplement, on the sexual philosophy of W. Somerset Maugham as expressed in his stories of the far east. He accepted with alacrity. The programme itself passed without public comment of any kind, but Percival felt he had made a small personal mark, and was not altogether surprised when the producer asked for more of the same. By the end of the year Percival had become the BBC's tame literary expert, the person trotted out whenever a commonsense but erudite view is required. He promptly wrote for BBC Publications a moderately successful paperback called *Books and the Common Reader*; and from this limited eminence it was but a short step to participation in a weekly television panel game. Here he was fortunate to be offered regular appearances in a frivolity called *Ghosts*, based on a misleadingly-titled test of wit once popular in our public schools. One begins with two letters handed out by the master of ceremonies. To these, at beginning or end, one must add a letter of one's choice to produce a sequence which might plausibly form part of a dictionary word. If one is challenged by the next in line, the word has to be given; if it cannot be given, one loses a point. The adding of letters continues until someone gives up, which also causes the loss of a point. At every third mark against one, one must answer a complex question of literary origin, and failure here causes further blemishes on one's scutcheon. There are no points for winning: the winner is the person with the fewest mistakes. In this respect Percival became within weeks something of a national celebrity, for he went through his first seven-week season without a single point against him. When one added to this achievement a mildly waspish on-screen personality which sometimes showed itself in testiness to his fellow-players, the English at large warmed to him as they had warmed to no one since the loss of the far more irascible Gilbert Harding in the early fifties.

Though now tending to portliness, Percival was a neat little man: neat in thought and knowledge, neat in clothing (shoes from McAfee's, cuff links from Asprey's), almost excessively neat in his lifestyle. What he most enjoyed was neither the work nor the fame, but the return each evening to his richly-furnished, womb-like apartment with its familiar bachelor pleasures. The antique Armagnac swirled around the cut glass ship's decanter; the mild but satisfying Villiger cigars which filled the room with aromatic powder blue smoke; the pneumatic recliner chair to which had been added a special table arm in case he wished to write while recumbent; the video cassette player through which he could revisit a selection of his favourite old films; and of course his three thousand favourite books, which overflowed irresistibly from their perfectly ordered shelves, constructed in solid oak at considerable cost, to Percival's own design. He could afford to spend whatever he liked on his own comfort and pleasure. Extra sources of income presented themselves daily, from invitations to open bazaars to the sale of review copies to the bald and bearded bookseller round the corner.

Percival sometimes felt himself misplaced in an urban twentieth-century milieu, and sighed frequently for the more elegant past. There was no decorative object in his apartment which suggested a date later than 1900. The plumbing and electrical fittings on the other hand were as modern as possible, for being a devotee of comfort he recalled from his reading of *Lost Horizon* that the monks of Shangri-La took care to have baths of delicate green porcelain shipped in from Akron, Ohio. By blinking a blind eye to such practical exceptions, he could preserve the impression of nineteenth-century gentility whenever he chose or was able to stay in his apartment. When Mammon forced him out into the Chiswick High Road, however, it was a different matter. London's main western artery can never have been a thing of wonder or beauty, but by the nineteen-eighties it had become shoddy in the extreme, a wide stream of noise and billboards and crumbling stucco, polluted by exhaust fumes and pierced by the shriek of brakes. When he complained petulantly about the constant deterioration in his city environment, friends advised Percival that he should invest portions of his considerable earnings in a distant property of his own, situated in some rural or seaside village, a sequestered place of mental refreshment and of peace, an enviable retreat in which by judicious arrangement he might arrange to spend up to half his many remaining days. Any suggestion that his friends, in making such suggestions to Percival, wished to see less of him, would be uncharitable; and he personally thought it a splendid idea. A solitary Shangri-La with himself as both Conway and High Lama! All great writers had lorded it over such a place; why had he not thought of it before? But where to find his English Utopia? In these littered times every city or town Percival visited was a disappointment, a maze of concrete and one-way systems, full of hamburger restaurants and the same shopping arcades and discount stores as were so avoidable everywhere else. Most coastal resorts were even worse, and could be depressingly derelict in winter months; yet he thought he would prefer to be near the sea. He would not fear the heartless monster, but challenge it. It would only be difficult to choose a maritime community large enough to be civilized all the year round but small enough to avoid summer invasion by hordes of ice-cream-eating, motor-biking tourists.

At length the BBC inadvertently came to his rescue by suggesting a series of radio talks in which, with his well-known and dearly-loved grumpishness, he would revisit haunts of his youth and find them wanting. *Letters From Britain*, it was to be called, in playfully obvious imitation of Mr Cooke's subtler *Letter From America*. The selection of places was to be entirely Percival's, the only condition that there must be some genuine nostalgia to be demonstrated. The list was not difficult to compose, for in his youth he had bicycled widely and been less difficult to please. Eastbourne, with its antiquarian bookshops in the shadow of Beachy Head. Mallaig, near which he spent a year at a naval station which he now knew to be totally demolished; that would be a splendid scene to describe, and he could bring in the Loch Morar monster as well. Scourie in Scotland's further north, where the diabolically twisting old road, a memory to be taken to one's grave, with its humps and drops and one-in-three hills, had been modernized by civil servants into something quite anonymous and forgettable: he could have a go at *them*. Haworth, on the Yorkshire moors, with its spirited Brontë industry and Wuthering Heights nearby. Douglas in the Isle of Man, where he had spent many a childhood holiday, rattling along the clifftop tramway to Port Soderick, listening to nigger minstrels on Douglas Head, and rolling pennies at Onchan. Aldeburgh, with its air of east-facing melancholy and its associations with M. R. James and Benjamin Britten. Alston, the highest village in England; Castle Combe, supposedly the prettiest. Harlech, with its splendid castle receding further and further from the sea. Sidmouth, where he once spent the hottest day he could remember, surveying the sleepy resort from its quiet high cliffs. Whitby, where no restaurant could serve him local lobster because the entire catch had gone to London hotels. It was a perfect dream of an idea which could clearly continue just as long as Percival desired. Guide books were provided, first class tickets were arranged, four star hotels were booked (two nights at each stop, with a car to meet him off the night train in Inverness and then to stay with him until he was deposited back in Hammersmith West nearly four weeks later). It sounded like the sort of holiday he had often dreamed of and been unable to afford; and at the end of it he would be five thousand pounds the richer. Life simply could not better be.

And so he gleefully travelled nearly two thousand miles and filled a stiff-backed exercise book with notes. His final port of call was Sidmouth, on the south coast of Devon, and on arrival he realized at once that he had found the ideal spot for his new home. The compact little town centre seemed to have changed not a jot in the thirty years which had passed since his last visit. Nestling in a wide old river valley, between two sizeable cliffs of red Devon rock, it now spread further back into the countryside than he would have liked, and the access roads were so tortuous as to provoke regular traffic jams; but the short promenade still had no shops on it, the fishermen still sold their catch at the east end, and the narrow shopping streets still boasted pleasant antique shops, cafés serving cream teas, and a gentleman's outfitter which appeared to have changed neither its stock nor its staff since 1935. Finally, Percival noted that the average age of the inhabitants seemed reassuringly high: no teenage hobbledehoys were likely to disturb the even tenor of any days he spent in this community. Here a gentleman, comfortably off, might inspirationally discern the promised land, yet be close enough to Sodom and Gomorrah for practical commercial purposes.

It would obviously be idiotic to propose living half the year at the seaside and not find a domicile within sight and sound of the sea. One should in fact seem to command it, by living in a house right above the beach, rather than way back on the hill where one would need a telescope to know what was going on in the bay. In accepting this view of the matter, Percival's choice was virtually limited to six dramatically located dwellings, and he could see all of them from his front room at the Belmont, which maintained a discreet lawn between itself and the promenade. Five of the houses were just to the right of the hotel, at the town's western extremity, built apparently on a long low rock which climbed right out of the beach to a height of fifteen feet or more, where it formed promenade level. Though partially terraced, as though for protection against storms, the houses were of individual design, one with a thatch, and most agreeably disposed. Unfortunately, none appeared to be for sale. Moreover, Percival's ardour was somewhat quenched when a storm did blow up in the April night and breakfasters next morning were treated to the spectacle, no doubt rare, of waves dashing themselves against the rock and over the roofs of the idyllic houses. Percival's disappointed eye wandered to the opposite and eastern end of the promenade where, at a level considerably higher and thus safer, a single plot appeared to have been cut into the sloping cliff in order to accommodate one secluded house. Only the upper storey was visible because of a high ridge which rose from the clifftop on the town side, and Percival could not tell what state the structure was in, but – his heart quickened – there was something on the cliff path which looked very much like a For Sale sign. As soon as the rain stopped he donned his Inverness cape, grasped his Malacca cane, and trotted intently towards the solitary building, leaning into the wind and holding his deerstalker cap on his head. At the fish market he made a fresh appraisal. The chief disadvantage of the place began to be obvious, namely the lack of any but pedestrian access. A capacious car park lay behind the fish stalls, but from there it would be a walk across the footbridge and up quite a steep winding tarmac path for a hundred yards or more. The house itself was passed only by the spectacular footpath which steeply ascended the cliff, reducing itself from tarmac to gravel at a point immediately past the wrought-iron gate of which the words *Spindletop House* were an integral part. Metal windows suggested the late thirties as the time of the house's construction, and the rock into which it was set had probably yielded the red sandstone of which it was built. Alas, it was in what might charitably be called a state of some disrepair. This seemed to Percival quite inexplicable when he took stock of the view it commanded from its high position, higher than any other house around. There was a perfectly splendid view to the west, of the cliffs near Otterton; the owner, moreover, would have the entire east cliff as his back garden, maintained at no charge by the local authority.

The firm of house agents named on the sign, nearly illegible from long exposure to the damp south wind, had offices sandwiched between Woolworth's and Mrs Grundy's Tea Shoppe. 'So,' said Percival easily as he strode into the room, 'what's the story about the house on the east cliff? How long has it been empty, for a start?'

The round-eyed, dyspeptic-looking person sipping tea, named by a prism on his desk as Mr John Cook, was startled by this brisk approach and choked slightly on a tealeaf. Sitting up, he touched his tie, stroked the back of his gleaming pate and decided to be honest. 'Er, rather more than twelve months, dear sir,' he said carefully. 'To be frank, we haven't found it an easy sale.'

'Not surprising if you let it go to rack and ruin,' said Percival with the cheerful firmness of one making a negotiating point. 'Who got permission to cut into the cliff and build a house there in the first place? How many town clerks did he have to bribe?'

Mr Cook permitted himself a conspiratorial smile. 'The original developer was himself a town clerk, sir. He never got to live in the house, though. Died suddenly while it was still being built.'

'The wages of sin?'

'Very possibly, very possibly,' said Mr Cook in a tone which suggested that he didn't quite see the joke. 'Anyway, if I didn't tell you, you would quickly find out for yourself that the unfortunate incident, after the building of the house itself had caused quite a bit of argy bargy, cast something of a jinx on the place. For a while nobody wanted it at all, especially as the finer points of the interior were never quite finished as planned, and then the war came and it would appear we filled it up all right with people who didn't much care where they lived so long as it was away from the blitz. In those days, the shortage of petrol meant that the lack of a garage didn't matter.'

'Quite.'

'After the war the hoodoo was forgotten and letting was easier, though most of the retired people who came here didn't relish that little climb. It's steeper than you think.'

Percival nodded. 'I've just tried it.'

'Well, I've had to do it quite a number of times, and it takes the wind out of me, especially when you have to contend with an easterly gale as well.'

'You've shown a few people round, then?'

'Oh, the last lot only a month ago. But there are reasons they didn't take to it, which you'll see for yourself if I show you over.'

'Then please do,' said Percival, who had remained standing throughout the interview, 'for I like the location very much indeed. From what you say it should be cheap, and I'm not short of a few bob for any necessary renovations.'

Fifteen minutes later the padlock and chain had been removed, and Spindletop House lay open for inspection. Percival emitted a sound of disgust as he stepped into the hall. 'What a foul smell. Do you bury the bodies under the floor boards?'

Mr Cook smiled at this sally. 'I'm afraid the house was never properly damp-coursed, and unless you're prepared to have that done I couldn't recommend your living here permanently. It'll get better if we leave the front door open for a while. I'm afraid the original architect took insufficient note of an underground stream which trickles through the cliff, rather too close to the foundations for comfort, and the damp has got worse over the years.'

Percival shrugged. 'If damp's all it is, and it can be cured, and the foundations are sound, then say no more except to knock another couple of thousand off the price. Who's the seller, by the way?'

'Until recently, the widow of the original owner, a Mr Franklin. She had dreams of coming back here and would only lease, but she died just a few weeks ago at ninety, after years in a local nursing home, and I know her daughter could be persuaded to part with the freehold.'

'I suppose she knows something we don't. Perhaps the house is about to slide into the sea?'

'There's absolutely no question of that,' said Mr Cook, pursing his lips. 'We had the property surveyed six years ago. It's firmly ledged on a rock nearly ten feet below floor level. Yes, they excavated all that way, back in the thirties.'

'1937, I'll wager,' said Percival. 'The windows and the half-flat roof give it away.'

'Mr Franklin intended that for sunbathing.'

'And what happened to the rubble?'

Mr Cook shook his head. 'It forms a rather curiously shaped undercliff on the beach below. My word, they would never allow such a thing today.'

The exploration began, and Percival was surprised that there was so little of interest to see: building had simply stopped short before the rooms were personalized. It was a much smaller house than he had thought, which only meant that it would be easier to handle. Downstairs there was one very agreeable L-shaped room with inglenook fireplace; from it, French doors opened on to a small stone-laid terrace with a view straight out to sea. Kitchen, small study (also with sea view), cloakroom and hall completed the ground floor. Quite a handsome plain staircase led in three flights up to a small landing forming three sides of a square: from this, box room and bathroom faced north, and on the seaward side two quite splendid bedrooms with corner windows commanded south-east and south-west views. Both rooms gave via single glass doors on to an all-round wooden balcony divided by a trellis. The drop from it, to the rocks below, was quite vertiginous. From the rail one seemed to command the scene as a conductor does an orchestra: the cliffs, the sea, Dawlish across the bay, and Sidmouth snug in its narrow valley below.

'You see,' murmured Mr Cook in Percival's ear after a suitable interval,' there was no way to get the full view from the lower level without excavating the protective ridge. Upstairs is the real glory of this house; upstairs is surely where the owner must spend most of his time. You can imagine the impact on a clear summer's day.'

Percival could indeed. 'Heaven,' he said. 'I'll take it, Mr Cook. That's if you make me an offer I can't refuse. And subject to contract, of course.'

Mr Cook sighed and began to rub his hands as though in invisible soapy water. 'I feel sure there could be no argument over price, and as an estate agent I am of course delighted that you are interested. As a considerate human being, however, I cannot allow you to proceed without telling you the rest of the house's history.'

'Don't say,' cried Percival intuitively, 'that a place as modern as this is haunted?' He sat expectantly on the wood-slatted seat below the balcony rail.

Mr Cook raised his eyes to heaven. 'I wish there were some other way of putting it. Mind you, I can confirm nothing from my own personal experience. It may very well be that it's just a local legend which arose because the house started off so badly and was then empty for such long periods. But the fact is that only ten years ago it did have a most undesirable tenant, a Mrs Crawley. The name would mean nothing to you, nor indeed did it to anyone here. She rented the house from my predecessor and said it was for the summer. But she stayed, two years altogether, not seeming to mind the problems, though of course in those days it hadn't deteriorated quite so badly. A lot of rumours quickly grew up about her, because she lived alone and made no effort to join in the life of the town. But she did befriend some of the local teenagers; ran a sort of club for them, which was most unsuitable as she was well past forty and it ill behove her to carry on like a sixteen-year-old even though her looks were still very striking. I arrived during that period and saw her several times. Handsome creature she was, with long black hair and big dark eyes under curving eyebrows. The thing that spoiled her was a cruel downward turning mouth and an air of, oh, I don't know, no more than arrogance perhaps.'

'What was her first name?' asked Percival.

'Oddly enough she made a condition of the lease that it wouldn't be reported, but it was Constance.'

'Constance Crawley. It rings a bell somewhere. I'm something of a student of criminology, and . . .'

'Why yes, but we didn't find out till much later, you see. The poisoning case: her husband, the Whitstable doctor, back in the sixties. She was clearly suspected, but there was no evidence.'

'I remember. She was having an affair then with a boy half her age. And wasn't there something about voodoo practices?'

'I honestly can't recall that. Anyway, before long there were complaints about what was going on at the old house on Saturday nights, though it's so sheltered from prying eyes that I don't see how anyone could know unless they used a telescope, which knowing this town they probably did. What was clear from the noise was that she had some of the teenagers up there and they were playing what would now be called disco music. Oh, and for some reason she had a searchlight fixed up on this balcony; it used to annoy people when she roved it along the promenade after midnight.'

'So what happened?' Percival was becoming impatient.

'Well, one Saturday night, or rather Sunday morning, one of the teenagers, a particularly bad hat who'd already been in trouble with the law, fell from the rail here and was smashed to death on the rocks below.' Mr Cook touched the old dull-coloured wood, and Percival could not refrain from shivering. 'There was even more bad feeling after that as you can imagine, even though the coroner had to bring in a verdict of accident, but Mrs Crawley was exonerated from all blame – there was testimony that she'd been in the kitchen at the time – and despite the funny looks she got she stayed on, though the Saturday parties did stop and if the young people continued to visit Spindletop House they did so very discreetly.'

'One at a time?'

'Very possibly. Mrs Crawley herself was seen in the street more often, almost flaunting herself in the public eye, as though to show her contempt for the gossips. There was some talk of getting up a petition to terminate her lease under some ancient morality by-law but it didn't happen because one Sunday morning she too was found dead on the rocks. Naked under a black silk dressing gown.'

'Foul play?'

'Everybody wondered, of course, but this time there was no evidence whatever. Nobody was known to have been in the house the previous evening. So it was brought in as accident again. And since that time there haven't been any long-term tenants for Spindletop House. Nobody in fact stayed more than a month, even when they'd taken longer leases and couldn't get their money back. And one night, oddly enough on the anniversary of Mrs Crawley's death, a freak storm blew up that actually smashed a few windows, and one or two incredibly high waves got in and soaked the place. We went in and patched things up, but we never got the floors really dry even with blow-heaters, especially with the moisture seeping up from the cliff underneath. The old widow wouldn't pay for any major repair, and frankly I thought that in due course we'd probably have to pull it down, but it hasn't got any worse the last year or so, and if you really want to, I think you're in time to save it. There are a couple of good firms here I could recommend to do the work. The thing I'd really want to warn you about is that if you, as another single person and a stranger, move in, you're bound to meet with some suspicion from the locals unless you take great pains to allay it. It's only natural, you see: the known facts have already been embroidered into legends, and there are plenty of people who will tell you that they have seen Mrs Crawley on moonlit nights between this house and the footbridge below.'

'Naked, of course, under her black silk dressing gown.' Percival's mind was silently ticking over. A haunted house! There was a thought for his adoring public; their tart-tongued idol sharing a house with a ghost! He remembered, he thought, that Alexander Woollcott's reputation across America had soared when he began to be preoccupied by unsolved real-life mysteries; and look how Edgar Lustgarten's career had thrived when he appointed himself the nation's connoisseur of crime. Ghost-hunting, at the very least, would be a useful extra string in Percival Gotobed's bow, and if he could start himself off with a story bound to bring headlines in the *Sun* and *Mirror*, his reputation in the field would be established at a stroke. 'Supposing,' he said, 'we brought the whole thing out into the open?'

Mr Cook looked slightly bewildered.

'Supposing,' Percival continued, 'we made a public story, a national press lead, out of the house being occupied again? That must seem farfetched to you, Mr Cook, as you may not have recognized me, but I do have some small reputation as a television personality. I expect I may be known to half the population of Sidmouth.' He chuckled. 'Television does reach here, doesn't it?'

Mr Cook smiled deferentially. 'The hills interfere with reception sometimes, but yes it does. And of course I recognized you, but I thought you were . . . incognito?'

'I can't afford to be incognito. Can we talk to the editor of your local paper?'

This was easily and quickly arranged. Graham Figgis was somewhere in his late forties. He smoked too much because he was more than a little bored with life on the *Sidmouth Courier*, which came out on Saturdays only and seldom had a headline worthy of the name: he remembered with a frequent wince a recent issue in which he had been reduced to 'DOGS FIGHT ON BEACH: HONITON VETS TO RESCUE'. He willingly met with Mr Cook and Mr Gotobed that evening in the bar of the Who'd a Tho't It (another splendid subject for me, thought Percival: pub names) and Figgis sensed the story before it was properly put to him. 'You really intend to buy the house?' he asked.

'Only if I can be guaranteed that it won't make me an outcast in my newly-adopted environment. Only if the paper will help me give it a clean bill of health. In return for which I have the power to make Sidmouth pre-eminent among British watering places.'

'Some of us would say it is already,' smiled Figgis without sarcasm. 'But I accept your point: a little publicity is sometimes good for the soul. What's your idea, then? Spend the night there on your own, I suppose, all locked in and with nobody near enough to hear you scream?'

Percival was slightly dashed but tried not to show it. 'I don't see why not,' he said. 'Before it's done up, I mean. This week, if you like. Providing Mr Cook and I can come to a financial arrangement.'

Figgis drew heavily on a cheap cigar, and coughed sepulchrally. 'It's always been a good story,' he said, 'providing the central figure's well enough known, and of course you are. What's that game you play on the telly, *Ghosts*? Not a bad link-up, that. Fleet Street would probably go for it. Do you believe in ghosts, by the way?'

Percival smirked. 'Why don't we say that I keep an open mind?'

Figgis was making shorthand notes. 'The *Courier* would fix you up with the necessities. All you'd need would be a camp bed with a mattress and a sleeping bag, plus some form of portable heating if the power doesn't work.'

'It does work,' said Mr Cook slightly peevishly.

An hour later, Mr Cook called on Mr Figgis to announce that an accommodation had been reached between Mr Gotobed and the owner of Spindletop House, so that the experiment could take place on the following evening. All that remained was for Mr Figgis to book a photographer and ensure that he would be in time to capture plenty of space in the Saturday nationals as well as dominating his own paper. 'They'll queue up for it,' he assured Percival, 'and you and I will go fifty fifty on the profit.'

How the details were worked out is immaterial: suffice it to say that they were. On the following morning Percival completed the programme which had brought him to Sidmouth, and sent his crew packing. In the afternoon a little party of people trudged up the east cliff path, and

Percival was photographed in every possible pose outside Spindletop House, including a shot taken from the beach with Percival leaning over the west balcony. The sun was theoretically in a perfect position for that one, but to Figgis' photographer it seemed to be playing funny tricks. He had difficulty focusing on Percival, seeming always to see two figures, one behind the other. Deciding to say nothing about it in view of the large quantities of barley wine he had consumed the previous evening, he took an extra shot for safety and departed about his business.

The three jovial conspirators met again that evening for a slap-up dinner at the Belmont. Percival gladly played host – the modest cost would slip unnoticed into his BBC expense account – and at eleven went to his room to pick up a grip already packed with towel and toothbrush and a few books. Shortly after this, they solemnly set off on their short walk along the cold and deserted promenade, at the far end of which the photographer waited in a car to take the last few atmospheric flash shots, including one of Percival in the open front doorway and another at the French doors of the living room, with moon and sea behind him to outline his rounded and recognizable figure. As an added touch of showmanship, a heavy hook and eye had been screwed into the outside front door and jamb, and as the oak closed behind his cheerful keepers Percival waited in the dark hall to hear them forcing the metal shut and applying a seal. One photograph of that, a final chorus of farewells, and they were away, their footsteps dying out almost at once because of the ridge. He was alone until eight in the morning, and it was not yet midnight. Nor, he realized suddenly with a pang, was there a means of escape, should one be required: the north windows opened only as small casements, and the only way to the beach was from the balcony via an old wooden staircase too much of which had rotted away to make it more than a desperate possibility. Even if he accidentally started a fire, he was trapped. Extreme care must and would be taken.

During the first quarter-hour of silence, Percival felt rather more alone than he had expected, but the sensation gradually wore off and left him only mildly excited by his unusual circumstances. The wiring system had proved to be more or less in order, so that although no room had a lampshade and not all of them bulbs, he was able to generate as much dim light as he could possibly need for the hour or so during which he planned to be awake. He did so, by turning on every working switch in the house, and getting a mild shock from the one on the landing, the bulb of which promptly spurted into darkness. As the hall light had no bulb at all, this left the stairway a very gloomy place indeed, but the bedroom lights, hurriedly switched on, cast along the landing a dim glow which would have to suffice. Percival retreated to the kitchen, in which cubicle he decanted a cup of steaming decaffeinated coffee from the thermos thoughtfully provided by the hotel. As he did so, he noted the distant howl of wind from over the bleak and silvery sea. Only persons with a penchant for melodrama would think of this as anything but a summer residence, he decided as he sauntered back into the sitting room. Here, sitting in a camp chair with his belongings on a low table at his side and a rickety old standard lamp at his rear, he put two full spoonsful of sugar into the cup and stirred the liquid vigorously. Since childhood he had had a sweet tooth which an adult tendency to flab had caused him to restrain, but this was no night to be worrying about calories.

When the beverage was consumed, he looked round for further occupation. It occurred to him to check that the phone worked, though there wasn't much he could do about the matter if it didn't. He picked up the receiver and found it strangely satisfying to listen to the dialling tone. He replaced the instrument, then picked it up and listened again. It was a friendly note, full of lively anticipation and vigorous self-confidence; however, he couldn't go on listening to it all night. One thing he could do was try to relieve this damned smell of damp and must. He brought out from his grip a scented aerosol purchased for the very purpose, and sprayed it determinedly around him.

It was annoying that he still felt so wide awake. He stood, performed exercises, sang a little, made yet another inspection which was quickly completed. All was securely fastened, at least against intruders of flesh and blood. As soon as the thought crossed his mind, Percival wished he could send it back. To console himself he chuckled aloud at nothing in particular, and to show his strength slightly opened a casement of the living room's north window, allowing a little fresh air to mingle with the fetid stuff. The old one-bar electric fire was still warming up creakily, and a larger area of its reflector was pitted with corrosion than was able to shine with the brilliance originally intended. He blew away some matted cobweb from the shadeless frame of the lamp standard, and turned the switch: it seemed to work best in some intermediate position which was difficult to gauge and almost impossible to maintain, for every movement of his weight on the floor boards seemed to lose him the light. He finally settled the standard on a part of the floor not affected by his chair, and draped an old rag over the frame so as to make the dim light somewhat directional; then he sat carefully in the chair so that he had the light over his right shoulder. Now however he was irritated to find within his view the single unadorned light bulb which hung desolately from the ceiling socket. Always believing that directly visible sources of light were bad for the eyes, Percival leaped up to switch it off, leaving the room illuminated only by the curiously draped standard lamp, which was practical and even romantic in a funny sort of way but left disturbing great patches of shadow. So what, he would be asleep soon: the camp bed in the corner already seemed most inviting, but there was no light socket near it and he wanted to read for a while first. Before he returned to his seat, however, his eye was caught by white patches in the lower part of the oak-and-plywood panelling which ran around the lower part of the room, patches which seemed to have been thrown up into contrast by the now limited lighting. On closer inspection he recognized the patches as damp, undoubtedly rising from the foundations: in some parts, especially near the windows, a sinister white efflorescence was standing away from the wood like a crystalline fungus. Percival crouched to examine a particularly large patch, and promptly stood up again. Was that some kind of singing he could hear? A woman's voice, distantly crooning some folk song? It couldn't possibly be the sea, as it was coming from the opposite direction, through the open casement from the clifftop. He visualized the kind of creature who might be singing out there in the dark, and shivered; but then he laughed to himself and remembered something Cook had said about strange noises caused by wind in the telephone wires. He crossed the room and listened at the landward window before closing it, but all was now still – and black. The earthen ridge might clearly afford some protection from the wind and from prying eyes, but how depressing it was! At night, *anything* might be hiding in its shadow.

Percival stood quietly for a moment in the empty room. He would have liked to hear the singing again, just to be sure what it was. For no other reason, for he disliked woman's voices at the best of times, and this was not the best of times. It had been an eerie, nagging sound, the kind to put one's teeth on edge or send a goose scurrying across one's grave. Choose another metaphor, *quick*: like a slowed-down version of the pop music one hears today in all but the very best restaurants; enough to drive one to drink. The thought of drink finally brought a smile to Percival's lips, for he remembered a certain well-filled flask which currently reposed in his overnight bag, but should not stay there for long. A quarter of a bottle of whisky it contained: not an excessive amount, but certainly sufficient to ensure a good night's sleep, if consumed deliberately and appreciatively over the next hour or two while Mr Gotobed sampled some of his favourite books. He settled into the audibly protesting chair, and reached into the grip to remind himself what old and valued friends he had brought along as companions to share this nocturnal adventure. *Three Men in a Boat*: perhaps a shade too light to absorb his interest at the moment, apart from that sudden bit about the floating corpse, which he certainly didn't want to chance upon. *The Ghost Stories of an Antiquary*: now, why on earth had he brought that? Sheer unconscious bravado, he supposed: though for all he knew, fictional ghosts might scare off the real ones, if any. So perhaps later on (and perhaps not). *The Casebook of Sherlock Holmes*: yes, that would do very well. Not the best of Holmes, but quite satisfactory for the occasion. He poured himself a generous drink and settled down comfortably with *The Three Garridebs*, smiling knowingly to himself at its shameless borrowings from *The Red Headed League* and *The Stockbroker's Clerk*. Well, thought Percival, they say there are only six possible plots in the whole of literature, so out of sixty stories three rather alike isn't bad; and the Garrideb yarn he found delightful in detail if unpersuasive as a narrative.

Ten or fifteen minutes later, as he was nearing the arrest of Killer Evans, the light began flickering again, and as he was cursing the faulty switch, it went out altogether, which he didn't like at all. 'Damn!' he said aloud. The thin moonlight offered a wisp of illumination, and revealed a striking seascape, but he was in no mood for aesthetics. He stretched his right hand back over his shoulder to the place where he knew the switch to be, and indeed found it at once. But before he could turn the little metal tag, horror of horrors, what felt like icy human fingers closed softly over his. He thought afterwards that there were three of them, perhaps including a thumb, and at the moment they crossed his own a voice seemed to murmur in his ear. What the words were, he had no way of telling, for even as they were spoken he was leaping, almost flying, in one effortless action out of the chair towards the main wall switch. The entire room was now drably but safely illuminated, and he could see for certain that he was the only personage in it: not even a twist of grey smoke shared his solitude. His heart was beating fast, nevertheless, as he went back to the standard lamp and did what was necessary to return it to reliable life. Having done so, he moved his entire sitting area into a corner, first checking that the panels around it were solid. He then stood for a minute and lit a cigar, but found the taste curiously unpleasant and extinguished it. Whisky still tasted right, however: that was reassuring. He wondered for a moment whether Cook or Figgis were playing tricks, but discounted the possibility; and no one else but the photographer even knew the circumstances of his vigil, as the hotel had merely understood that he would be out all night. No, the prankster was clearly his own vivid imagination. The uncanny pressure on his fingers must have resulted from some kind of numbness: he had been leaning rather heavily on that elbow while reading. What about the voice, though? Fear may have drowned out the words, but he could still bring back the timbre, and he shuddered at the thought. It was no idle question to ask himself whether it had been the same as the singing voice he had heard from his stooped position by the panelling; on reflection, he thought the two were indeed compatible, and the decision chilled him. He said aloud: 'Go away!' This was just in *case* a ghost existed. Not that he admitted the possibility. And if it did, what harm could it do? It was one's own startled reaction to such things which might bring on a heart attack, or a stroke, or madness. If one were properly prepared for the event, what one should offer was a very firm instruction to leave; or perhaps a welcome if one felt in a mood to expand one's horizons. It didn't really matter providing one showed the ghost who was boss: then it could haunt all it wished.

Despite these comforting thoughts, when he sat down again he found himself deflected from Sherlock Holmes by consideration of what the notorious Mrs Crawley, a former tenant of Spindletop House, might have looked like. He remembered Cook's description of the dark hair, the cruel mouth, the black clothes. To these facets his imagination was able to add scarlet lipstick, a studded waist belt, white but slightly crooked teeth, and green fingernails, while her long hair flowed to one side, like seaweed under water. Her eyes, too, were strange: they seemed to fix one hypnotically from a long distance. Now, why and how should he get such a vivid impression of someone long dead, someone he'd never met? It was almost as though he could see her in the shadows, in the room; as though she had mysteriously returned to the house and were willing him towards her. Had there been a newspaper picture of her? He couldn't remember. In fact, he couldn't remember much about today, or rather yesterday, for midnight had long gone. Only now was real. The little dim pool of light around him seemed to grow brighter, and everything else correspondingly darker; the walls and windows seemed much further away, as though the reaching of them would involve an arduous journey. A slow mysterious tiredness now fell over him in waves; yet it required no effort at all for him to rise to his feet, as he now did without knowing the reason for his action. He almost floated, as though held above the ground by an invisible giant. Blank-eyed he was, and he knew it; afraid, he was no more. In some fashion he stepped, or glided, out of the pool of light into the darkly shadowed hall, where sufficient illumination was now inexplicably afforded for his attention to be arrested by the stained glass panel in the front door. It couldn't be the moon, for the moon was on the seaward side of the house, and the porch light, he dimly remembered, had been broken. What kind of coloured shield was this? Three ravens? Or were they vultures? And diagonally below, what looked like three daggers. Nothing he could remember from his slight acquaintance with heraldry; but how strange that he hadn't noticed the illuminated casement before, or the motto which was ribboned under it. *Tenebras Mareque Amo*: that should surely mean, I love the darkness and the sea. Well, she would, of course. For the sea was pure and the darkness so soft and comforting, like the black folds of the dress of that lady who had now emerged fully formed from his imagination and was standing to his left, at the first bend of the stairs. She raised a hand: that was his summons. It was his time: for she was his, and he was hers, and that was the way it had been planned. They were to be one: she was the woman for whom he had waited all these years, the woman for whom his blood now pounded in his loins. He mounted the stairs slowly and effortlessly: she had no difficulty whatever in ascending them backwards, without any displacement of her billowing dress. Soon they had reached the landing, their eyes fixed on each other, and she was still beckoning as she retreated towards the south-west bedroom, the one which by day had had the most sensational view. As he reached the room he saw that the balcony door was open behind his sensual mistress, and the old tattered rags which had once been curtains waved angrily in the night breeze. What was there about this woman that was so desirable? Wickedness, perhaps; she had the abandon, the wilfulness, the sex of ten. Why had he not realized this great gap in his happiness? Well, he would have it now. He lusted after this woman as he had lusted after no other in his life: wild erotic thoughts raced through his brain, none of them seeming impossible of fulfilment. Now he found himself stepping on to the balcony, his ears assailed and half deafened by the surge of the sea below. And the woman was within his reach. She was murmuring in his ear. (Yes, it had indeed been her voice all along!) Her breath was hot against his cheek. Still he could not quite interpret her message. He had to pass some simple test, that was it, and she would be his. Fly, perhaps, from the balcony to those rocky beaches below. Well, that must be easy, especially if she would fly with him, and show him how. Together they would soar like birds on the night wind above this private country of theirs, to which no one should be admitted save their devoted followers. She faced him now, hovering in the air above the dark rocks. Her grey lips parted in a slow smile, and he felt on his forehead the touch of her tongue. He took another confident step, and held out his hands for assistance. He stood on his toes, and leaned forward.

Promptly at eight, as was arranged, Mr Figgis and his photographer watched Mr Cook break the seal on the front door (snap), remove the hook from the eye (snap), and knock. It seemed at once that there would be no answer. 'Must be sound asleep,' said Mr Cook after ten seconds or so. 'Not much of a story if he is,' responded Figgis. 'Have to fake it.' Another half-minute went by before he added: 'Why not use your key?' 'Of course,' said Mr Cook obligingly, inserting it into the lock and turning. And as the door opened, there in the dark hall they saw the figure of Percival Gotobed, blinking at the light and looking uncharacteristically bewildered.

'Good morning,' said Mr Cook roguishly. 'I think we overslept: it must have been an uneventful night after all.'

It seemed to Figgis that his star looked very shaken. 'Bit of a strain, was it?' he asked. 'Well, it's over now, and all plain sailing. Just come outside so that we can take our shots and go, then we'll postpone the interview till lunch. By the way, the *Express* are very hot on the story: a big offer for your polished-up version, I'd say. The one with the jokes.'

Percival seemed to sigh. Then, as the others stepped back, he moved forward into the morning air, which was filled with birdsong.

Mr Cook was a little late for lunch at the Belmont, and was surprised to find no sign of the others at the bar. However, before he could enquire of the barman, Figgis entered the room, huffing and puffing and looking quite alarmed. 'Have you seen him?' he cried.

'Seen? Who?'

'Why, Gotobed, of course. Do you know he never came back to the hotel?'

'What?'

'Why we left him up there alone I'll never know. What did he say to you?'

'Why, I can't quite remember. It was more an impression I got that having only just woken up, he wanted time to compose his thoughts. Perhaps to absorb the atmosphere of the house in the early morning. It was such a glorious day. I just said he should close the door behind him when he did leave.'

'Well, he didn't. When I didn't find him here twenty minutes ago I ran up to Spindletop and the door was still open. His things are still there, but of the man himself there's absolutely no sign. I looked all over. His chauffeur doesn't know anything either, and he's getting impatient about the journey back to London.'

'How very strange.'

'Yes, and now I'm going to tell you something stranger.

How many photographs did my man take outside the house this morning?'

'Four, I think. One with us on each side, the others with him alone.'

'Absolutely right. Well, half an hour ago I got these prints. There's a good one of you and me standing a little apart with a blank space between us, and on the others there's nobody, just the open door. Gotobed isn't on any of them!'

It was ten days later that Figgis took a walk on the beach with his spaniel. Since the Gotobed excitement, which was only just beginning to fade from the nationals, he had avoided the east cliff, previously one of his favourite haunts. Today marked the first time he felt strong enough to chide himself for being so lily-livered. The sensation-loving national pressmen had all gone back where they belonged. Figgis was once again cock of his own midden instead of a perplexed witness, whose story was not universally believed. As he progressed along the level beach towards the huge rock on which Spindletop House stood, he deliberately turned his eyes seaward, but when he drew level with it, curiosity got the better of him. With a distinct effort he slowly rotated his head to the left, then up the cliff to the solid little pink house which, with its projecting upper balconies shadowing the rest, looked from this angle singularly like a vulture about to take flight. The morning sun shone straight into his eyes; but surely that was a human figure standing with an air of triumph at the rail of the west balcony? A female figure dressed in black, with long dark hair streaming in the breeze? Standing there with his back to the bubbling surf, craning his neck and shading his eyes in a desperate hope of confirming the evidence of his senses, Figgis felt suddenly transfixed by some nameless evil. But the spell, if spell there was, was shattered when a second figure moved out suddenly from behind the first and took its place at the rail – a figure whose uniquely portly silhouette fixed it immediately as that of Percival Gotobed. It was at this point that Figgis, his nerves already tattered, ran screaming in panic back along the lonely seashore, his dog yapping at his heels, neither of them stopping to take breath until they reached the safety of the High Street. For Figgis three days previously had stood in silent witness on the high Cobb at Lyme Regis, when the broken body of Percival Gotobed was retrieved with difficulty and danger from the angry sea which at low tide had cast it out upon an inshore rock.

The Ghost of Sherlock Holmes

At the time of its solution, the murder at Birchington Manor caused the merest ripple of comment in the press, and is certainly not looked upon by criminologists as one of the classic cases of English detection. The fact that an unsympathetic killer had confessed was accepted by press and public without further question. I smile to myself: there would have been rather more excitement if the steps leading to that confession had been documented. The truth is that this sordid attempt to outwit the law was revealed to the police only through the acute and unexpected observations of a friend of mine who happened to be on the spot when the murder took place. He never again showed the slightest aptitude for such deductions, and the reader must decide for himself whether there was anything paranormal in what took place.

I am a doctor, and I was once a police doctor, but it took me less than a year in that calling to decide that I would prefer to assist the innocent than to conduct post mortems on the victims of violence, who all too often (in our bigger cities at all events) come themselves from the violent edges of society. Before I was forty, therefore, I found myself a cosy country practice in that part of Surrey from which my wife and I hailed, and settled down to enjoy my modest domestic comforts while doing my best for a derided but not undeserving section of mankind, the middle classes.

One of the permanently respected arrangements between Mildred and myself was that I should be allowed six or seven bachelor weekends a year. The chief reason for this was that although many mutual friends were welcomed to our house, very often for weeks at a time, there were a couple of my old comrades whom Mildred simply couldn't stand. One of them was this fellow Gelding, Nathaniel Gelding, whom I'd known quite slightly at college from belonging to the same societies; we bumped into each other again fifteeen years later when we were called to serve on the same jury, and after that we met quite frequently, as it turned out that we had secondary interests in common: the music of Saint-Saëns, the books of Robert Louis Stevenson, the stories of Sherlock Holmes and his imitators, and the architecture of country churches (though I never shared his passion for brass rubbing, a singularly useless occupation). He persuaded me to join the Bath Club in Brook Street, alas now gone; here we both pretended we belonged to a more leisurely age, thoroughly enjoying our occasional lunches of cold game pie and salad, washed down by a pleasant Niersteiner and followed by that succulent rice pudding of which the club was justly proud.

Gelding on first appearance might have seemed as bad a joke as his name. Though technically he was not bad looking, there was about him an emasculated quality, a dried and tentative air, as though he were forever silently apologizing for his presence. All our women friends who met him said he gave them the shivers. I suppose they instinctively recognized and resented the fact that he posed no sexual threat to them, though I'm sure he didn't feel strongly enough about the matter to be either misogynic or actively homosexual. He was an old-fashioned neutral, a Victorian archetype who might have been labelled 'kind uncle' or 'friend of the family', though to be honest he was so unworldly that any advice he might have given, even to a small child, would almost certainly have proved worthless. At his least effectual he was reminiscent of Mr Padge in *The Diary of a Nobody*, whose only conversation was to say 'that's right' to everything while occupying the most comfortable chair by the fire. Gelding had eyes of so pale a blue that they hardly registered; his mouse-coloured hair was springy but uninteresting; he moved silently, in a slightly stooping posture which Mildred characterized as 'creepy'. I liked him, I suppose, because I could dominate him. I was bluff and blustery, and he always took the path of least resistance. He needed me to make decisions, and I needed him, or someone like him, to calm me down. For whatever reason, we both thoroughly enjoyed our infrequent reunions.

At the time I am describing, Gelding kept a rather poky secondhand bookshop (he called it 'antiquarian') in Marlow, and lived alone above the premises. To my mind his stock was far too limited to be interesting, and he seldom seemed to sell anything, perhaps because any likely volume which came in was promptly spirited away to Gelding's own groaning shelves in the roughly converted attic. I once followed him up there, and it was the only time I ever saw him enthusiastic, his whole face illuminated as he fondled a first edition of *Old Mortality*. I suppose he was the same age as me, knocking fifty, but in his case it didn't matter at all; in Shaw's phrase, he was a man whom age cannot wither because he has never bloomed.

Gelding didn't much care for leaving his shop during the working week until he came across a bibliophilic Marlovian whom he came to trust with it on the occasional Saturday out of season. The weekend I now describe was just such an occasion, for we had decided on two full days of pottering about Sussex. Nothing was planned, but the centrepoint would be Saturday dinner with more than enough wine. Gelding didn't sleep much, and was outside my house promptly at six-thirty: by arrangement he didn't knock, for fear of waking Mildred. I crept out, and we transferred his belongings to my Hillman, which is a bit roomier than his old Morris. By nine we had marvelled at the view from Box Hill, descended, and climbed again to Coldharbour, where the tower touches the thousand foot mark and is said to cover the corpse of its donor, buried upside down. We had peered through the doors of the still closed antique shops of Forest Row; and we were preparing to ransack the bookshops of Lewes, which seemed to me even drearier than Gelding's own. He didn't say much – he never did – but I knew he was quietly enjoying himself, especially when we hit upon preparations for a church bazaar, where upon production of his trade card we were allowed to make purchases from one or two interesting lots as they came in. It was a glorious spring day, the countryside was at its best, and we were free as middle-aged birds. By noon we had found the Long Man at Wilmington, which is not a pub but an ancient chalk figure on the hillside. We gazed at it from the abbey car park while consuming the coffee, slab cake and tinned salmon sandwiches which Gelding had insisted on bringing with him. (I wish he wouldn't: newsprint tends to come off on moist bread, and he doesn't seem to have heard of greaseproof paper or tinfoil.) Then from Polegate, on the fringes of Eastbourne, we found on the map an interesting-looking side road which meandered towards the coast at Birling Gap. We took it at once, for every Sherlockian must assume from the stories that this is the precise area to which the great detective retired to keep bees; and by some mischance neither Gelding nor I had previously explored it. Though Gelding was a passive member of the Sherlock Holmes Society of London, he had been ill with gastric influenza at the time of the only excursion to the area since his membership commenced; and I had little patience with the society's playful pretences that Holmes really lived and that Conan Doyle was merely his literary agent. I was interested simply to explore the setting which the author had used, and to see how far if at all he had altered it for the stories.

The narrow lane quickly left suburbia behind and led us

past stonefaced old houses. Between them we could glimpse untrammelled stretches of countryside. At a hamlet called Javington there was an attractive old pub, The Hungry Man; we noted it as a possibility for the night. Then the country broadened out into the wide valley of Friston Forest, its fertile meadows giving place gradually to neat arrangements of young trees. After a glimpse of a most interesting private estate on the right we came to a T-junction and were confronted by the old church of Alfriston, which we naturally inspected (and pronounced satisfactory). Less than half a mile to the east, passing two fingerposts reading EAST DEAN VILLAGE ONLY, we turned right into the coast road to Birling Gap and Beachy Head.

The Gap is a drab disappointment. The only aspect from which it can possibly look attractive is seaward: I can quite imagine that from a passing ship its little collection of buildings at the top of a chalk cliff may seem both quaint and intriguing, especially as it is roughly central to the Seven Sisters. By land it offers a very different ambience. The road at this point comes within a hundred yards of the cliff edge, and one drives into an unpaved car park, finding oneself surrounded by derelict cottages, ramshackle summer bungalows, and a self-styled hotel built in the worst holiday camp tradition, giving the appearance of having escaped the attention of paintbrushes since the restrictions of World War Two. Some buildings may have fallen into the sea as the result of erosion; certainly the cliff path referred to in *The Lion's Mane* is nowhere in evidence, but it may have existed only in Conan Doyle's imagination. Instead, a wooden staircase, built in a square spiral and encased in a heavy metal frame, leads unaesthetically down to a lonely beach which is both stony and full of tar. Come again, said a sign outside a 'café', which was offering revoltingly greasy hamburgers. Not if we can help it, we told ourselves.

It was now two-fifteen, nearly closing time in that part of

the country, and we both suddenly fancied half a pint of bitter and a reliable sausage roll. Eastward stretched the wild expanses of Beachy Head, with Eastbourne itself five miles away; but less than a mile to the north was East Dean, the village we had by-passed. As I hastily retraced our tyre tracks, I clearly sensed that Gelding was even more abstracted than usual. Twice he failed to reply to remarks of mine, and I found his eyes fixed on the high chalky ground above the village to our left. He responded with enthusiasm however when a left fork shortly revealed to us a charming village rather like an illustration from an Enid Blyton book. Cosier than a Cotswold showplace, East Dean spread itself around an irregular square lawn on a slope, with little restaurants cutely called Grimaldi and Grimaldi Too; at the low corner was a straggling half-timbered inn called The Tiger, with elderly inhabitants snoozing outside it in the fitful sun. Inside it was all black beams and horse brasses and darts, a pub from the kind of old British movie where the village folk gather to resist threats of invasion by Germans or flying saucers, or simpler threats of interference in local pleasures by London bureaucrats. After a quick pint of some dark brew called Old Rowley we felt ready either for action or for sleep. We determined on a thorough exploration of this unexpectedly delightful community. I levered open the heavy oak door to let Gelding through, but he stood there in the doorway as though frozen to the spot. 'Look up there!' he cried. 'The man on the tor.'

I remembered *The Hound of the Baskervilles* well enough: the phrase uttered by Gelding is a chapter-heading in it. Sherlock Holmes, supposed to be back in Baker Street, is glimpsed by Watson against a Dartmoor moonscape, silhouetted on the crest of a granite outcrop. Gelding's gaze now was fixed on the lofty swelling ground, between the hamlet and the sea, which had previously taken his attention: unspoiled grassland rose majestically behind the white cottages, protecting them even from the sound of the waves. Indeed a man *was* silhouetted up there, a man with a walking stick, though to me he seemed to disappear almost immediately over the hill in the direction of the cliff edge. He was a good mile away, in my judgement, and I sensed nothing eerie about him. But clearly Gelding did, for he stood transfixed by some emotion which might have been shock, disbelief, or merely surprise. I muttered something about Old Rowley being stronger than either of us thought, and led him unresisting in the direction of the village church, with its pivot gate and its modern organ arch, erected in sorrow by the mother of a local lad killed in a motor cycle accident. Gelding nodded silently at everything, but I knew that he was only going through the motions. The one interesting remark he made was that he felt he'd been there before, but we were both pretty sure that he couldn't have, otherwise he'd have remembered the occasion.

As we left the church it was Gelding who led the way. I had no idea of our destination, not that it mattered. Up a short hill and along an impressive street called Wentway, where the richer residents seemed to live; between two luxurious houses; down through a hollow, up through a bramble-filled gap to the open cliff beyond; high above the distant waves, along the merest track, deeply breathing the ozone and sweating in the sun, leaving the derelict buildings of Birling Gap a mile to our left. I realized that we were now somewhere near the spot where the distant silhouetted figure had been, and for the life of me I couldn't see why that was important enough to get so hot and dusty, not to say scratched by thistles and gorse. At one point my companion called ahead as though to some other wayfarer, and although when I first looked up I thought I did see a man, possibly the same man as before, I was half-blinded by the sun and by the time I had put on my dark glasses there was nobody to be seen, not a single person to share our enjoyment of the views from this magnificent stretch of cliff. Gelding was sprinting, or at any rate moving with most unaccustomed alacrity; but suddenly he stopped and pointed. Ahead of us in the unbroken greensward, perhaps a hundred yards from the cliff edge, was a natural hollow about a hundred feet across, and sheltered in it was what might once have been a most attractive cottage, a unique weekend retreat for those of solitary inclination. It was falling apart now, its wooden frame showing in many places through broken stucco, and it couldn't have been lived in, at a guess, for twenty years. It seemed a crying shame, for I was instantly attracted to the location, which wasn't so far from the main road after all, for on the far side I could see a track clearly leading towards Alfriston. As we stepped into the hollow the sea breeze ceased to ruffle our hair: the place was a positive sun trap. We could now see that the building was in total rack and ruin. Half the roof had fallen in, the windows had predictably been vandalized, and only a gap in the remains of the front fence indicated the original where-abouts of a gate. A seven-foot post still stood there with a cross bar which looked as though it had once held what the Americans call a shingle. I hunted around in the long grass until I found a broken board. The inscription on it was still legible. BEEKEEPER'S COTTAGE.

Gelding, slightly breathless, managed one of his rare smiles. 'You must admit,' he said, speaking faster than usual, 'that if this really is Sherlock Holmes' old cottage, he himself couldn't have found it any faster with so few clues.'

'I don't know, he must have come along the main road instead of tearing himself to bits on those brambles. But you weren't looking for it. Were you?'

'I was looking for something, I can't quite tell you what. But it does make sense that Holmes would have lived up here, away from the hurly burly. It's absolutely in character, and this declivity must have been perfect for bees. Look, there's the remains of a hive over there.'

'Mm. The only thing you haven't considered is that Sherlock Holmes never existed at all, except in the mind of his creator. And it would be going a bit far even for you to suggest that Conan Doyle bought this cottage so that a fictional character could live in it.'

'If he was never alive, then who is the man we saw up here an hour ago? The man I've been following?'

The question took my breath away, especially as it was delivered with a most uncharacteristic fire in Gelding's eye, a kind of light of triumph. Never in my life had I seen him in this mood. I tried, rather less than successfully, to pass the thing off with a chuckle. 'Perhaps the house is somebody's seventy-year-old joke,' I said. 'Or perhaps some manic Sherlockian lived here and fancied himself a reincarnation of the master.'

Gelding shrugged and turned away, but I sensed an element of 'wait and see' in his attitude. For a few minutes I began to think that if we encountered the elusive solitary walker on his return journey, he really might turn out to be Sherlock Holmes; climatically it was one of those magical afternoons on which anything could happen. But the rest of our walk, though invigorating, proved uneventful. We trotted along the clifftop until we were in sight of Seaford, then turned back, keeping as close to the crumbling white edge as we dared. We sat for a while and gazed out to sea, feeling like Churchill willing the Nazis not to invade, and it was nearer six than five when we stumbled down the last few feet of the bramble track into East Dean and rested against our car. The Tiger had just re-opened, and looked inviting; we were too tired to go on, so why not stay there if we could? Yes, we could, said mine host: he had a choice of three rooms available. They proved to be spartan, with a communal bathroom, but we booked two of them just the same, and performed our evening ablutions with an emotion amounting almost to glee. Very soon after, we did more than justice to a home-made steak pudding followed by some good crusty cheese; a bottle of St Emilion was washed down after a suitable interval by a friendly armagnac. Gelding seemed to have relaxed very considerably, though once or twice I fancied on his face a look of surprise, as though he saw someone at the window. At about nine-thirty I ordered another round and intended it to be the last, for my copy of *Idle Thoughts of an Idle Fellow* was calling from my bedside table; but just as the drinks arrived, the main door of the pub opened to admit two well-dressed burly men as middle-aged as ourselves, and I recognized one of them instantly. It was George Fitch, who in my time with the force had been an inspector but was now, I thought I'd heard, superintendent. He shook hands warmly and introduced the other chap as Colonel Aspinall, chief constable of the county and a personal friend with whom he was staying the weekend. We all sat down for another hour of drinking, during which time Gelding made mention – it was almost his first remark – of the curiously named old cottage we'd found on the cliff. The chief constable said that this particular village wasn't his local beat, but he understood a great many of the old decaying properties on the cliff needed clearing away. 'We'll see about it next November fifth,' he said cheerfully. Gelding went on to ask whether Sherlock Holmes was much revered in the district, and whether there was a local branch of the Sherlock Holmes Society, but Aspinall seemed to have little idea what he was on about, and I tried to change the conversation before my friend made a complete ass of himself. I told Gelding on the way upstairs that if he would shut up about Sherlock Holmes, I would promise not to mention that I saw a reincarnation of Julius Caesar.

Even including the pleasant interruption we were in bed

by eleven – Gelding seemed particularly tired – but we did promise to take lunch the next day with the chief constable at his house on the other side of Eastbourne. Nobody expected that we would in fact meet before breakfast, but at seven A.M. a grim-faced Fitch was knocking on the inn door and asking for me. The services of a police doctor were required, and my being in the district was fortuitous. There had been a crime of violence at a house up the road. Would I come?

There is really no way for a professional to refuse such a request, though I quickly consulted Gelding, for after all the delay would detract from his weekend as much as from mine. He nodded thoughtfully, looking absurd in his old-fashioned nightshirt. Then he said yes, by all means, and might he come along rather than wait alone at the inn? I replied that I was sure nobody would mind; but I watched with some apprehension as Gelding's eyes turned slowly from me to gaze through the window up to the high cliff. And this time – it gave me quite a shock – there really was the solid figure of a man up there. A man who seemed from his attitude to be standing very still and looking down straight at us. And he was still there, apparently immovable, when we left the inn.

Ten minutes later, having had no breakfast except a glass of water, we had driven four miles towards Seaford and were entering the gates of Birchington Manor, a portland stone pile in the worst kind of Victorian Gothic, with a town hall aura and a dejected looking central portico. There were probably half a dozen bedrooms, no more; what I couldn't understand was why the original planners had chosen a site with so little sense of the sea, which reverberated against the cliffs no more than half a mile away. The house lay down a slope, and behind it, some four hundred yards away, ran a stream which presumably formed the rear boundary. There was a small wood on the left, and on the right some higher ground which, partly hedged off, seemed to be used for growing vegetables; a tattered scarecrow stood guard over this section. Only the upper floors of the house were at road level, an arrangement I have never liked and certainly would not choose for any house of my own.

'It's murder, I'm afraid,' Fitch had said on the way. 'No doubt about it. The local police are here, but they're going to need Scotland Yard, especially as their key man's on holiday. The chief constable's very shocked. He knew the old boy quite well and was a fairly frequent dinner guest. Marcus Leonard, you know, the paper manufacturer.' I nodded as though I knew, but I'd never heard of the man, and nor I swear had Gelding. 'In his mid-seventies, but pretty chipper by all accounts and a thoroughly nice old boy who did a lot of charity work, as well as still dabbling in the affairs of the family firm. For the last seven years, since his wife died, he lived in this house with one old resident servant – who's been taken to the hospital with shock. So has the nephew, Charles Franklin, who acted as the old boy's secretary and will come into most of his money. It seems that last night the two of them came back from the Eastbourne theatre soon after midnight, having stopped for supper after the show. The servant had been told before they left to go to bed as his usual time, so Franklin went forward to unlock the front door before returning to help his uncle out of the car. But as soon as he opened the door he realized that he'd disturbed burglars. He says there were at least three of them, and he's given descriptions of two. They grabbed him, bundled him into a walk-in hallrobe, and turned the key. Then the old man started to shout, no doubt wondering why he'd been left, and Franklin heard them go out to the car. Old Marcus, stupidly enough, I suppose, kept calling feebly for help, and the burglars were heard to drag him into the house. Then there was a kind of light thud and no more shouting. Franklin said everything went very quiet, as though the burglars were suddenly shocked by what they'd done. When conversation resumed it was in such low tones that Franklin couldn't catch the words. Then there were footsteps in the hall, and a squeak as the door opened. Faintly in the distance, a couple of minutes later, he heard a car start up. He spent about five hours in the cupboard before managing to unscrew the hinges with a penknife. He found his uncle dead on the study carpet, and rang for help at once. The old servant was still asleep.'

'Tragic,' I said as we climbed out of the car. 'It's crimes like this which make me think we should bring back capital punishment. Those burglars should be hanged.'

Gelding gave me a curiously sharp look. Curious for him, I mean, for he wasn't normally given to sharpness of any kind. 'Data,' he said. 'We must wait for the data. It is a capital mistake to theorize without data.'

We moved into the gloomy house. Halfway along the panelled hall with its marble floor, I noticed a door off its hinges, leaning uselessly against the wall; then we turned into the first room on the right, a heavily furnished library or study which was just too big to be cosy. Carved walnut was the predominating feature. The floor was covered by an enormous Turkish rug, and on it, a sorry sight, was the stiffened body of Marcus Leonard. His wizened mouth having fallen open in an expression of dismay, he looked more like ninety than seventy. The white hair on one side of the head was scarlet with blood which had run all over his face from a temple wound which at his age must have caused instantaneous death. I knelt helplessly by the body. It was a different challenge from my accustomed measles and nervous tension, but I remembered my old skills and did my work quickly and, I hope, efficiently. Everything seemed to fit in with what we had heard, and after a few minutes I sat at a side table to scribble my report. Meanwhile other police officials, including a fingerprint man, were positively milling about the room, which was gloomily lit by the rays of a watery morning sun. The fact that it was Sunday only made the scene more depressing. Gelding had quietly taken a seat by the door, and I motioned to him that I wouldn't be long. He nodded, put his hands together as though in prayer, and pursed his mouth on his fingertips.

Fitch thanked me when I handed him the paper bearing my scribbled report, and said he was sure the murderous thieves wouldn't get far, as the local police were checking all ports.

'Did they take much?' I asked.

'Not enough to justify murder, not that anything ever does. Some pretty good silver and some Chinese bronzes, that seems to be about it. Old Marcus' gold watch was gone too, and his cuff links. Looks as though they just grabbed what they could see. Yet they must have planned the job carefully, for they wore gloves; our chaps can't find any strange fingerprints at all; and Franklin remembers gloves on one of them; grey, he thinks. But why didn't they take the Daimler? Franklin obviously left the keys in it, and there isn't any shortage of garages that would have done a quick disguise job for them. I mean, it was just sitting there. If it wasn't for the missing silver I'd almost suspect young Franklin. But he *was* locked in the hallrobe for five hours.'

'Not necessarily,' said Gelding in a distantly dreamy voice. We turned in surprise at the interruption: he was gazing straight ahead of him, his hands lightly resting on the arms of his carver chair, his shadowed face given a golden profile by the morning sun. 'I have examined the cupboard,' he added. 'The damage is equally consistent with its having been taken off its hinges first and the lock turned afterwards.'

'Mm,' said Fitch. 'Do you know, I hadn't got round to thinking of that, but of course it could have happened that way. It's just more likely to have been the other. And if

Franklin was lying, surely he'd have thought up a more airtight tale.'

'I haven't met the gentleman,' said Gelding, 'but he may be a student of criminology. Perhaps he knows that the more difficult alibis to break are the simple ones with a modicum of doubt about them. The ones where the detective in charge has his suspicions but can't prove a thing. Or can he?'

I was astonished to watch Gelding stand, give a thoughtful sigh, and stroll nonchalantly over to the corpse on the carpet. 'I wouldn't say there are no indications,' he said dispassionately, gazing at the disfigured face and then looking up at us with a smile of triumph. If this was Gelding, then the man I had known for so many years must have been acting a part. The chief constable came in at this point and stood in the doorway as Gelding dropped lightly to one knee and pointed at the body. 'You will have noticed that the blood flowed freely and immediately from the wound, congealing in long streaks running down the old gentleman's face. The streaks are virtually parallel and extend to the side of the chin and beyond. You are sure that the body has not been moved?'

'Not at all,' said a startled Fitch. 'Not an inch, right, Jenkins?' An attendant constable confirmed that the body was as discovered, lying on its back in the middle of the rug.

'Then Franklin's story that he heard the murder committed in this room is an absolute nonsense. If that had happened, if the body fell at once to its present position, with, as you will see, the chin jutting slightly but quite unmistakably upwards, then the blood could not possibly have run down the face. The streaks would have run the other way, into the hair.'

'That's very ingenious. And quite irrefutable, I'd say,' said the chief constable, coming forward. 'It seems to be rather a good thing you brought your friend along,' he added to me. 'There's just one thing: isn't it possible that when the blow was struck the old man slumped to a sitting position, then later regained consciousness sufficiently to fall the rest of the way on to his back?'

'Medically almost impossible with that wound,' I said.

Fitch rubbed his chin. 'Still, a good defence counsel might work on that doubt. So far as I'm concerned, Mr Gelding's observation throws a completely fresh light on the case, but I can't see it leading to a conviction. Still, having got so far, let's see if we can't find a clincher.'

Gelding was standing at a side bay window. 'I think,' he murmured, 'that it might be a good idea at this point to take a stroll outside.' The rest of us looked at each other rather sheepishly, but of course no one by now was inclined to disagree. 'If you say so, sir,' said the chief constable in a tone that reminded me slightly of Uriah Heep. With the manner of someone who knows exactly what he is about, Gelding led us in silence out of the front door and round to the vegetable garden, where the crops were neatly labelled and clearly well cared for; Fitch remarked that old Mr Leonard had been an ardent vegetarian who liked to see his food grow before he ate it. The scarecrow, on its high ground, reminded me as we approached of Gelding's 'man on the tor'; and when Gelding came to a halt, it was the scarecrow he was studying.

'Do you ever watch old films on television, Mr Fitch?' he asked crisply.

Fitch, startled, said that he very often did.

'Then I expect you'll remember an item rather irrelevantly called *North by Northwest*. In the middle of the prairies the hero is attacked by a crop dusting plane. The only warning he gets that all is not well is when a passer-by before he gets on a bus remarks that the plane is dusting crops where there ain't no crops to dust. Rather similarly, I am made uneasy by the fact that this scarecrow is scaring crows where there ain't no crows to scare.' He smiled at his own lapse into the American idiom. 'It stands in fallow ground; the nearest crops are at least twenty feet away.'

The chief constable rubbed his face thoughtfully. 'I believe it's been moved,' he said. 'When I was here a month ago, I'll swear it was on the other side of the path.'

'Exactly,' said Gelding. 'It was moved because it was needed as a marker. If I am right, you should find the supposedly stolen silver, stolen as a blind for murder, buried beneath it, in the only loose ground convenient to hand. We can in fact see where the soil around the scarecrow has been recently disturbed, then raked over. I am personally satisfied that Franklin, the nephew, murdered the old man and staged the robbery. I even noticed on the gravel outside the front door faint traces of what seemed to be heelmarks as the already dead body was dragged into the house. I shall be surprised if you do not also find spots of blood on the pebbles, though this morning's light drizzle may have dissipated them. I would add that in my limited experience thieves who have committed one murder do not baulk at another; they would not leave a keen-eyed witness merely locked in a cupboard.'

'Astonishing,' said the chief constable.

'Elementary,' said Gelding with a smile.

'In what limited experience?' I asked Gelding as we drove back towards London that afternoon. The nephew, returning from hospital treatment for supposed shock, had no doubt been dumbfounded to be arrested for murder. We never met him, but Fitch told us later that his demeanour alone amounted to a confession of guilt.

'I don't understand what you mean,' said Gelding mildly, in an approximation of his normal rather strangulated voice. I peered over my glasses at him. His demeanour of the morning was now inconceivable, just as it had been almost unbelievable when it happened. Sitting beside me once more was the myopic bachelor with whom having an intelligent conversation was like drawing teeth.

I shook my head and smiled. 'I gather you don't feel quite so brilliant as you did a few hours ago,' I said. 'It must be the suet pudding we had for lunch.'

'Brilliant? Me? You're joking.'

'No, I rather thought you were. You do realize that by a series of moderately brilliant deductions you were solely responsible for the arrest of an undoubted murderer?'

'Oh, you exaggerate. It might have been anyone. It was just that a few thoughts occurred to me and it seemed that I might as well put them forward.'

'I don't exaggerate at all. It was just as though Sherlock Holmes had come alive.'

Gelding smiled with quiet satisfaction. 'Can fictional detectives have ghosts, then? Was I taken over, so to speak?'

I sounded the horn at a stray sheep and tried to collect my thoughts. 'It would be nice to think so, to believe that the man you saw on the cliff really was Holmes. But in my view, if this morning you were lent somebody else's ghostly brain, your benefactor was rather more likely to be Arthur Conan Doyle. It was Doyle after all who worked out all Holmes' deductions and set him to retire on the cliffs of East Dean. He also interested himself in solving a number of real-life crimes before he retired to Crowborough, which is just up the road. Very likely he couldn't resist, even though he did die fifty years ago, helping out with a murder committed right on his patch.'

THE MOST CHILLING HORROR STORIES NOW AVAILABLE IN GRANADA PAPERBACKS

Max Ehrlich
The Cult   95p □

Mendal Johnson
Let's Go Play at the Adams'   £1.50 □

David Seltzer
Prophecy   £1.50 □

Charles Veley
Night Whispers   £1.50 □

William K Wells
Effigies   £1.95 □

Alfred Hitchcock (Editor)
Death Bag   40p □

Jan Anson
666   £1.50 □

David Cronenberg's
Scanners   £1.25 □

Suzy McKee Charnas
The Vampire Tapestry   £1.95 □

All these books are available at your local bookshop or newsagent, or can be ordered direct from the publisher.

To order direct from the publisher just tick the titles you want and fill in the form below.

Name _____

Address _____

_____

Send to:
Panther Cash Sales
PO Box 11, Falmouth, Cornwall TR10 9EN.

Please enclose remittance to the value of the cover price plus:

UK 45p for the first book, 20p for the second book plus 14p per copy for each additional book ordered to a maximum charge of £1.63.

BFPO and Eire 45p for the first book, 20p for the second book plus 14p per copy for the next 7 books, thereafter 8p per book.

Overseas 75p for the first book and 21p for each additional book.